Cassettes

Matthew M. Bartlett

DEDICATION

To Jonathan Dennison for the idea.
To my subscribers for saving my life.

Contents

Dead Hands

Why are my hands so cold, but when I put them on my hips so that I may shimmy, they feel hotter than unshod heels on the floor of Hell? Why, when I do handstands, do I freeze the grass, turning soft stalks into frosty knives? Why, oh dark and musty and cruel lord, why, when I grab my wretched tool for fun time, why do I leave finger-shaped furrows and feel this unbearable pain—a living, pulsing thing—that lasts the whole day long and into the night? Why do I dance the pain *in*, not *away*? Why are there no death rattles for me, but instead death maracas? Why does dust dance in my throat, causing me to wheeze and cough? I have…so many questions. I ask them with the help of my dead and blue hands; I wave them in the stagnant air. I ask my questions undaunted, even as my fingers swell. I ask them even over your mocking laughter.

The Skull Thief

The house lay empty. Even the clocks were silent. Though the windows stood open, no sounds from outside came in, aural vampires denied entrance via invitation. There were no living ears to hear them anyway.

The Oriental rug lay clumped in the center of the living room, the yellowed rubber fishnet of the carpet pad bunched near it on the hardwood floor. A table lamp lay against the arm of the yellow couch, its shade askew, its bulb blinking erratically.

On the dining room table sat a cooked turkey, perfectly browned, on a platter with a blue and white floral pattern. A ceramic bowl held an ocean of mashed potatoes, piss-yellow butter like oil slicks on its surface. Stuffing towered in a smaller bowl. Cranberry sauce jiggled residually due to recent commotion.

Glasses of red wine stood full and proud, the rims of the glasses free of smudges, lipstick or otherwise. All of this was lit by the dimmed lights of the chandelier, lending the setting a theatrical aura and spilling shadows hither and yon. The film atop the gravy in its boat was wracked with fissures.

In four high-backed chairs sat the remains of the occupants of the house. The flesh of their heads and faces lay about their chests like scoop-neck sweaters, draped over their newly bared brains, rendering the expressions of their scrunched features grotesquely comical. The fifth high-backed chair was empty, and a generously filled plate sat before it. You eased yourself in, cut some turkey into inch-wide strips, forked one, sent it through the mashed potatoes and gravy, and raised it to your mouth. That's then the skull thief entered the room. He was handsome, if you didn't count the thin, barely-there nose and the tiny mouth and the tangled brows. He was tall, if you didn't count the fact that he stooped. He was merry, unless you saw the irrationality and savagery in his eyes. His fingers looked short until they unfurled. His hair looked sleek, until you saw exactly with what it was greased. His serrated nails. So sharp. So very, very sharp.

It hurt. It hurt a lot. The pain shot from your head to the whole of your flesh and your eyes felt as though they were burning in your sockets. You felt the searing, burning tactile shriek of flesh and muscle pull apart and then something akin to the dull but jarring pain of the dentist's machinations freed from the fetters of Novocain. The room sank slightly and flesh closed around your eyes, your vision fading and blurring in proportion to which the pain intensified. Through the eyelash-filtered slit you saw the blur of the handsome or not so handsome man standing before you with your wet skull in his hand. He did not make a Shakespeare joke. He did not say a word. You regarded the familiar shape of your skull. You would not have expected it to be so recognizable. But you'd seen it all your life, hiding behind your face like a dangerous stranger. In mirrors. In storefront windows. Looming on the screen of your phone. In spoons upside down. There it was. You could almost see your eyes in the sockets, your fleshy nose. You could *actually* see your teeth with their ancient silver fillings, one of the front teeth slightly overlapping the other. Embarrassing for a self-conscious teenager, a hallmark of uniqueness in a more comfortable middle age, now a nightmare to see in front of your emptied, sagging face. You unconsciously push your tongue forward to feel those teeth, but they're not in your mouth anymore, obviously. I mean, duh. These are your thoughts even through the agony.

Tall but hunched, he steals through the suburban streets with his bulging sack dragging behind him, the skulls within clicking and clacking. He was too greedy tonight, he knows. He is very nearly caught. The searchlights sweep in his wake. Police lights make barbershop poles of the bare trees to the east. The rotors of the helicopters angling in from the west slice the wind into thin sheets, fill the night with blade slap. A fat squirrel stands on its hind legs to look. There's always time, reasons the Skull Thief. Plus, it's small. Ish.

Moments later the squirrel zig-zags away, its emptied-out head flapping behind it like the hood of a sweatshirt, its tiny exposed brain swiveling left and right.

The Skull Thief makes it back to the studio with time to spare. It's almost 9. To be late would be unthinkable. The ON AIR sign lights his face redder than it already is. He spills his sack on the vestibule floor and heads to Operations, where he checks in with old Ben, dances down the hall past Studio A to the strains of Burton Stallhearse's Styx Fix (Thursdays from 8 p.m. to 9 p.m., tune in, won't you?), sees Stallhearse through the window, the worms festooning his head and flossing his nostrils, his rot-caked hands spinning dials and gesticulating spasmodically, maggots tumbling like living rice from his cufflinked sleeves. He sings to the magic and mystery. The magic and mystery.

The Skull Thief hurls Stallhearse from the chair. The latter stumbles from the studio to file a complaint, a strew of wreckage trailing him like a radically deconstructed snake. The Skull Thief adjusts the mic stand, toys with the levels. As the harmonizing vocals in The Serpent Is Rising intertwine and climb and reach their peak and fall away, he pulls a skull from each pocket and fits them over his hands. He claps them together, CLONK CLONK, CLONKity CLONK, for this is the introduction to his show, the opening theme, very important in setting the mood, decorating the sound stage (in a manner of speaking), preparing the audience for a tour along the contours, in the cracks, through the nose and eye holes.

Good morning, you sheets of skin, you empty masks hanging on hooks in the Halloween store. Good morning, you hoods and yarmulkes and trilbies and scarves. May you flap eternally in the fragrant breezes from Hell. May you fit yourself over the heads of your comrades to disguise them for their secret campaigns, their shadow-wars. May their hair not make your skin itch. May your eye-holes stretch and shrink until you see their enemies fall before them, spitting geysers of blood from new mouths. May you bathe in the warm, sudsy waters of victory.

Now here's Chet with traffic.

Thank you, Skull Thief. A minor fender-bender is delaying traffic on North King Street. The driver at fault claims to have swerved to avoid hitting a headless squirrel…

Grave Thoughts

A Christ Spider is crucified to an asterisk. In sunnier days He descended on a glistening thread and spake to the populace of vermin. "Messed up are the freaks," he said, "Like Deke and Zeke and the unknown Greek."

Satan rolls in like an unbolted Ferris Wheel, screaming souls falling from his limbs, crashing to the pavement, transforming into gory piles.

The thin red Devil sings ribald carny songs, just as his forebears did as they roasted fat weeping weenies under a pin cushion moon.

Saint Sebastian on weight gain pills from the supplement store. He glows with an inner light but no radiation can burn away that old timey ravenous cancer.

Dead dancers spin on rotisseries in metal rooms with horizontal red window slits, quadruple-vision sunsets flattened at the decree of some meaty god. I sit in the deep cushioned chair popping maraschino cherries like fat red pills, and I doze off as I watch.

A Quarter in the Ear of the Deer

Six days and five nights lost and gone. Six days and five nights in a darkened motel room in a long, low building held in a palm of sylvan green. Outside, unmown grass sways and whispers between a moss-encrusted pool-cover and towering pines. Cars sit blank-eyed and bored in the potholed and weed-strewn lot. A rusted-out three-wheeled shopping cart leans on a crumbling curb, the emblem on the red plastic handle long worn-away.

In the room hangs the smell of an untold number of smoked cigarettes. Thrift store art adorns the wall at uneven intervals: a basket of pears on a green table; a beach scene with an unevenly proportioned, top-heavy little girl flying an afterthought of a kite; a grinning spaniel with a bird in its chops and teardrops of drool dangling down. On the nightstand a diaphanous red skirt hangs unevenly over a lamp with a globular glass base and a dust-fogged bulb. Next to the bed clothing sits folded in two neat piles, a red brassiere and thong like a ribbon and bow atop one of them.

The ceaseless song of the peepers underscores the television's brainless blare. Soap operas, news, vacuous daytime talk. The noise and the theme music and the blather and the blue light washes over the couple as they explore each other's bodies, touch and taste and inhale, slurp and lick and chew, bite and scratch, fists burrowing and unfolding like stop-motion flowers in bloom. The thrill of discovery, of every sense fully engaged, of new landscapes of skin, each pore, each fold, each wrinkle a marvel.

On the second day, a clandestine trip with a handful of coins to the snack machine, conveniently just outside the door. A blast of salt and electrolytes and sugar. Daniel turns on the shower and the two wash the salt and the orange dust from their fingers. They face the faucet as he pushes himself back inside and up. With upturned faces like baby birds they let the water splash on their tongues. They sing a faltering, worshipful duet to the faucet, giver of life, provider of rehydration.

Back to the bed. Grunting and snorting, squealing, speaking in tongues. Flesh bends, bone cracks, hair is pulled free, trailing swaths of red flesh. Engorged and lightheaded, they pummel and slap and snarl, circle one another with teeth bared. Neither reaches climax; they know they mustn't, and they don't know how they know.

On the third day they taste each other's waste and it is not enough. On the fourth night they drink each other's blood, separate and mixed, and it leaves them even thirstier. She bites open his blackheads. He runs his bottom front teeth under her Rorschach-red toenails. And, still, none of it is enough.

On the morning of the fifth day something in the room buzzes and stops and starts up again. Daniel looks over the edge of the bed. His pile of clothes glows with light. He pushes the sheets away and reaches down to pull the phone from the pants pocket. A word he doesn't recognize fills the lit-up screen as the phone spasms in his hand. Squiggling lines. Hieroglyphics. Meaningless. Eventually the vibrations stop and the screen goes dark, the word mercifully disappearing.

He slides the phone between the mattress and the box spring and reclines on his back, arms bent at the elbows, hands intertwined under his head. How had he gotten here? Who was this *Audra*? All he remembers is a shapely silhouette in a convenience store parking lot, swinging a small, red-lit box by its cord, the sound of tinny music spiraling like fireworks into the evening sky. As he approached her, she had wavered, turned into a static-spangled rainbow, a blocked channel on cable, then reformed. Then what? Then here. This strange room—the whole world in its walls.

He falls off to sleep. Audra wakes. She blinks. She cannot call to mind her bedroom, but this is most certainly not it. The décor, the location, it's a mystery to her, as is the man snoring lightly beside her. She searches her memory and all she finds is a glowing sign advertising cigarettes, next to it a man, this man, with his strong forearms and his tousled tower of hair, leaning against a brick wall, a man with red numbers in his mouth, a long, thin, black tongue dangling to the sidewalk. It makes no sense, and it makes all the sense in the world. She lets her mind drift, stares at the grit on the ceiling, an undiscovered universe with constellations of brown stars.

The television makes a dull, flat popping sound and then another, slightly louder. It sends a thin line of smoke up to the ceiling, startling the couple fully awake. The clock radio turns itself on with a shriek of static-choked feedback.

As the screech fades, notes from a flute stretch in the musky air like worms of unnerving length. Faraway voices rise and fall in warped chorus. A voice speaks, booming out in the middle of the room. TO DIE IS TO CONSENT TO EVERYTHING. Its echo takes minutes to finally fade. In its diminishing wake a cello strides mighty and thick from wall to wall to wall to wall, eventually overtaken by the rhythmic stomping of a thousand boots.

Lust grips Audra. She reaches down and touches Daniel gently with her fingertips, watching his eyelids flutter as her fingers wander hither and yon. Then she flicks him underneath with her nail, hard. "Gah," he says, and reaches out for her throat. She grins an evil grin as she pries his hand away.

"I don't even know if I like you," she says, rolling onto her stomach, lifting herself up, climbing onto his chest.

"You don't. We are no good together—a match made in Tartarus."

"You know what? Let's get ourselves a third."

"Turn a straight line into a triangle. Yes."

He flings her to the side and lopes to the door, flings it open. And there is their third, plucked from who knows where and dropped here like a gift, a pale offering, leaning against a telephone pole by the road, smoking, a slender girl in abbreviated shorts and a fast-food top with her name pinned to her breast. Within five minutes they have her in the room; twenty minutes later she's out the door, breathing hard, weeping a little, her shoes in one hand, her sopping underwear in a ball in the other, a cut on her lip, her hair standing up in spikes.

"What an absolute nothing," Audra says, slamming the door.

"She wasn't very cooperative."

"Who could say no to *you*?"

Daniel plucks the name tag from the tangle of sheets. The pin is stained with blood. "'Wren' could, apparently," he said.

"What the hell kind of name is Wren?"

I HAVE JUST THE IDEA, the radio says. The two turn their heads.

Showered, shampooed, clothed, they exit the room. Daniel's hair is oiled back; Audra's, blonde with red highlights, hangs limp. Their skin is blotched red, peeled and torn in places, revealing darker red skin beneath. A curved dotted line of bite marks adorns Audra's armpit. A white blister, red and blue at the outer edge, stands out on her lip. Her pinky finger dangles, the metacarpal bone broken at the base. Daniel's neck bears bruises in psychedelic colors. Something yellowish and cakey gilds his ear. One eye bulges from its socket, wheeling around as though planning its escape. The pair limps and bounces and mutters. In the moonlight they are gaunt, grotesque, a random assemblage of features. They are ugly. They are beautiful. Audra holds the clock radio by the cord, the red lights of the display blinking zeros. The radio hums a giddy extemporaneous tune as though pleased to be out in the world. The night is some giant thing squatting between them and the stars. The motel shrinks more rapidly than seems natural as it fades into the background and is subsumed. They lumber down the forest-lined road.

At a lonely cross-street a silver sedan sits at the light, breathing cobalt blue smoke from its backside. When Audra approaches, grinning a lascivious grin, the bald, plump man at the wheel rolls down the window, an eyebrow arched. Her hand shoots in, grabs him by the collar. With her other hand she grabs his wrist as he goes for the lock, just as Daniel comes out from his crouch behind the car and opens the door. They spin him out onto the road, climb in, and speed away. In the rearview mirror they watch the unfortunate driver clamber to his feet and dig his phone from his side pocket.

Stars creep above the cloud line like glowing insects, pulsating appreciatively as though the darkness had ducked down just a little to let them see.

Leeds Mart occupies the left-hand side of a building shaped like a pair of fat open legs; the other leg is Leeds Package. Audra goes into the packie, the radio hanging at her side, its cord hanging over her shoulder. Daniel enters the shop. The lights buzz, everything over-bright, like a stage set. The smell of curdled milk and burnt hair permeates the place. Display racks lay mostly bare, what little remains clad in long-outdated packaging—snack cakes, scrub pads, donuts powdered with green mold, a dented detergent bottle in a puddle of its own blue blood. Yellow newspapers tied with browned string sit in askew piles in front of the empty freezer cases. Across from the registers on a coffee-spattered island sits a roller grill atop which twelve dead rats slowly spin, buck-toothed, shut-eyed dancers in an obscene horizontal ballet. One of them had at some point burst open, its intestines tangling like wet blue yarn in the rollers, brown blood bubbling on the chrome plating.

Daniel glances up to the ceiling, where a widescreen television hangs adjacent to a fish-eye mirror. On the screen a talk-show host lolls at his desk, his eyes half-lidded as his guest, a starlet in green lingerie, one bulbous bare leg crossed over the other, babbles incoherently and without pause about her latest role, that of a housewife beleaguered by a philandering husband and twin sons with faulty clairvoyance who have fallen under the spell of an evil psychiatrist. "May I ask her a question," bellows the naked, bug-eyed bandleader from behind a kettle drum where he crouches, ignored by the host and starlet alike.

"Just a question," the bandleader cries. "Just one question. One question? One harmless…innocent…"

A cough from behind Daniel. He turns. A baby-faced, red-cheeked clerk in a yellow vest over a metal tee-shirt stands behind the counter, arms at his side, legs tightly together, chin slightly up. Cigarette boxes lay piled at his feet. He resembles a soldier in a casual-dress war. His name tag reads "Wren."

Daniel blinks. He approaches the clerk, who leans forward. He is whispering to himself. Daniel leans in close to hear. "On this site before Leeds Mart was Leeds Gas and Variety, the clerk said. "Before that was King's Market, which for decades previous was known as Kinglet's Variety. Lost to a tragic fire was the building that stood here a century ago, a brothel of some notoriety. That shut down after a controversy involving a hostler and the mayor and a befouled whore. Before that the land was unclaimed, wild, a tangle, with a small clearing where certain powerful men plied an unspeakably unseemly trade."

The clerk looks up at the dented tiles, across the fingerprint-fogged freezer cases, down to the scuffed floor. "How far we have fallen. This place needs a thorough cleaning. Or…not. Deterioration is healthy. Rust and rot. All the fixtures worn or dented or bent, every surface marred, veneers curled back. There's only one way to escape corrosion. You have to let. Let it. Let it do its dance. To die is to consent to everything." His eyes show fear and confusion, as though he doesn't know what he'd just said. He stares at Daniel and smiles shyly. His eyes swim into focus, fix upon Daniel's eyes knowingly.

Daniel says, "Do you know me?"

The clerk's smile blossoms into a toothy grin, teeth overlapping teeth like yellow creatures crowding an exit. "I know your sex," he says in a low voice. "I know your hands. I know your curdled come."

Daniel says, "You don't know shit, son." He looks down at the clerk's feet for his brand of smokes, and steps back with a bark of surprise. A clock radio occupies a low shelf, the same clock radio Audra has with her, the exact same, the one from the motel room, wedged in between two chewing tobacco displays. The red lights, leaning rectangles with x's in them to display numerals, blink rapidly in no discernible pattern. But the radio isn't what had caught his attention. Atop it crouches a fat, ribbed, blue-red bug of some kind, its wings a blur, its many legs bent as though ready to launch. It looks at Daniel with wet, ichthyic eyes. Something akin to recognition blooms in them. Daniel forces his gaze away. He points with a shaking hand. "American Spirits," he says. "The blue pack.

"And I'm gonna need a pack of matches with those."

Daniel is just stepping onto the concrete and lighting a cigarette when Audra exits the package store with a brown bag full of bourbon nips. "Anything?" he says.

"Weirdest thing." Her hair is soaking wet. She opens her mouth to speak, revealing a gap where her left front tooth had been when she'd gone in. Then she shakes her head. She doesn't appear to want to get into it. She looks up and past Daniel and her eyes widen. Daniel turns to follow her gaze. Under the store's sign, between the posts, crouches a man in a pink parka, his pants at his ankles. His hands twist furiously in his crotch like he's wringing out a washcloth. The man moans, and a chorus of moans replies. Across the street in a strip mall parking lot, there are others, huddled between cars, at the base of light poles, all of them tugging at themselves and crying out.

Daniel's phone vibrates in his pocket. He lifts it out. On its face glow the words "Please come home." The clock radio screeches a blast of searing feedback and the words dissolve into a million tiny stars. The phone grows hot in Daniel's hand and he drops it with a wince. "Come on," he says.

The pair get in the car. Audra smells like maraschino cherries. He starts the engine and glances over at her. She has hiked up her skirt. He looks at the outline of her tibia, her bruised knee, the flawless skin of her thighs, a patch of inviting cellulite in the shadows. His hand finds its way over and down. His other hand follows, and he hoists himself from the passenger seat. She fumbles with his buttons. She is new to him again as he is to her, all new, fresh for rediscovery. When they go to change position, they look up to see faces pressed against the windows, staring in, mashing their lips against the glass, fogging it, leering, drooling. The radio sighs. It ticks like a bomb in a movie. Daniel rights himself in his seat, throws the car into drive, and takes off, the car bumping and tilting as it caroms over a tangle of writhing bodies.

They are on the road, on the way to the Final Place, the roofless motel of the dead. The body of the car is now warped and profusely dented, the windshield rattling loosely in its frame. The radio ticks louder now, like a loud clock in a silent room. Audra's hand dives and rises, cresting the waves of the summer wind. She sings along with the ticking in a loud and clear baritone:

There's a quarter in the ear of the deer
There's a quarter in the ear of the deer
There's a quarter in the ear
Of the dead and rotting deer
There's a quarter in the ear of the deer

"Lovely," Daniel says, "but I need you to shut up now." He turns the radio up all the way.

"Left," it commands, and Daniel jerks the wheel, nearly tilting the car over onto its side. "Hit the gas," and the streetlights speed by the car as the ticking gets faster and louder. Fat stripes of light sail across the interior. A march fades in over the ticking, something tinny, with trumpets. A baritone voice babbles, like the nonsense of an infant trying to approximate human speech. "Another left," the radio says over the babbling.

They arrive.

WREN POINT CEMETERY reads a crescent-shaped metal sign affixed to a pair of tall stone stanchions. Lit only by the moon and distant streetlights, the cemetery looks like a ruined city overgrown with drooping trees and limned with moonlit moss. Among the stones and the memorials in the long grass, fog curls like the ghosts of snakes. Fat flies buzz, lighting like birds on the iron fence and the mausoleums. A pile of lidless caskets towers against an ancient oak whose limbs span the entirety of the cemetery.

Audra and Daniel leave the car on the strip of scrub grass outside the gate and pass under the archway, holding hands. With his other hand Daniel holds aloft the clock radio. It spills static like litter. When they reach a fork in the narrow road, Daniel shifts the radio to the left, and the static grows louder, then to the right. It fades. The two turn right. As they walk on, the static lessens further, and a female voice breaks through, singing a high and merry note. The stones are older in this section. Many have fallen on their faces and sunk partway into the ground as though seeking the person they memorialize. The oldest stones are grey-green and profusely chipped, their epitaphs mostly eroded away. They stand crooked as though hobbled, or else lean back in shock. Patches of grass between the stones are upturned, revealing churned, worm-strewn earth.

In the center of the cemetery on a hillock is a mausoleum, an ancient mansion in miniature, partially subsumed by the hill on which it stands. Rusted bars crisscross its mud-smeared windows. Stone bats line its turrets. On each corner of its slightly arched roof perches a stone goat, one hind leg crossed over the other, blowing into a thin stone flute. Adjacent to the padlocked, rusted double doors a metal sign reads:

ABRAHAM ROTTFIELD
BROTHER, SUN, UNCLE
ACCURSED INTERLOCUTOR.

THOUGH I DIE, I HUNGER
THOUGH EATEN, I WISH TO EAT

Cloudy beams of pink light shoot out through the windows, causing the surrounding stones to blush. The padlock explodes in a puff of red-brown dust and the doors swing open with a creaking duet.

The pair enters.

A cobwebbed, stone-walled room. Before them an ancient, sagging, stained mattress, held up by crouching blue bodies with melted faces framing glowing green eyes. Candles melt into grotesque, wart-covered lumps, flames bouncing in them. Curious coins and trinkets and figurines clad in crinoline and wound around with cobwebs. In the corner a casket stands upended. Its door opens, and a man steps out. He is clad in a top hat and a wig of spindly black hair. His face drips with white makeup. Green glowing plastic vampire fangs overcrowd his mouth. He starts to speak, then with some effort spits the fangs onto the floor. "He's been waiting for you," the man says in a thin, tired voice. "He's very excited."

He reaches back into the casket and pulls open its bottom, another door, revealing a curved wall that resembles the inside of a dog's ear, all warty excrescences and dried waxy abrasions. The sound of footsteps, muddy and rasping. A hollow-cheeked dead grey face rises into view, behind it a plump, shining face that strains with effort. The latter face is attached to a heavyset man-child with a bowl haircut and smeared glasses; the former is that of the cadaver he hoists.

"Lay him on the bed, Curtis," the white-faced man says, and Curtis does so with dutiful haste.

"Face up," says the man, now sounding aggravated, impatient, and Curtis flips the body onto its back, groaning and drooling, his shirt untucking, revealing his ass-crack.

The cadaver is grey, its skin hardened. Its desiccated hands lay slack over the hollow of its chest. Its toes are spread akimbo as if he'd died in a state of ecstatic pain.

Daniel is as hard as steel now. Beside him, Audra shifts her weight, rubbing her thighs together. Drops of moisture spatter in the mud at her feet. The man in the tall hat snaps his fingers. "Come and get it," he says, and he and the man named Curtis blows out the candles behind them and backs up into the shadows to watch.

Daniel climbs onto the mattress and then onto the cadaver. He aims himself between two ribs and pushes until a soft wet pop heralds his entrance. Audra nestles her face behind him and she bites and gnashes and chews. The couple writhe up and down on the dead man. The dead man crumples from the pressure. Its eyes open. Daniel shrieks and flees to the far wall as Audra scrambles off of the other side of the bed and crouches on the dirt floor, her breath coming in great screeching rasps. The cadaver sits up. Pink patches grow on its grey skin and clouds disperse from its eyes. In a high, wavering voice, it sings:

There's a penny in the throat of the goat
There's a penny in the throat of the goat
There's a penny in the throat
Of the wicked grinning goat
There's a penny in the throat of the goat

"He's back," yells the fright-wigged man.
"And better than ever," shouts his plump companion.
Moans from under the ground provide a wordless chorus. Aglaonice crushes the moon between her giant black-gloved hands. The stones and trees shake and the great iron gate warps and buckles. Daniel and Audra scream themselves dead.

Cassettes (Part 1)

This is where it happened. Right here. Place used to be a record shop. Records and tapes only. Never sold CDs, on principle. Here, to the left just after you enter, one narrow set of bookshelves stuffed full to bursting, horizontal books stacked upon the tops of vertical books. Rock bios, books cult and occult, some rarities, mostly mass-market stuff, a little overpriced, some in unnecessary protective sheaths, dollar amount penciled in on one of the first three pages, but you could talk the guy down. Past that was a rack of old Rolling Stones and Playboys and Spin Magazines. Further down, showtunes, movie soundtracks. Above them, on the wall, plastic-enclosed valuable stuff, picture discs, rare, out of print. The middle racks were rock, alphabetical. On the right, everything else. Metal, country, spoken word, comedy. Above those were the cassette racks. Far corner was the weird stuff. Consignment, homemade tapes, curiosities, the shopkeeper bought them in bulk, sometimes from shops or flea markets he encountered on his travels, sometimes from internet bazaars. Back wall was where you could try out cassettes. You'd sit at a small round table, fit the headphones over your ears, turn it up as loud as you'd like. Just here, to our right, the counter, a kind of cubby for the owner, a comfortable chair and his favorite records all around him.

The owner of Fuzzbuzz Records & Tapes sat back on his stool, the back of his head resting on the cool brick of the store wall. Two oscillating fans blew stale air around, the only tangible effect the fluttering of thumbtacked posters and the shimmying of the cobwebs that clung to the tiles where the ceiling met the walls. He snored, snorted, and jolted awake from the semi-somnambulant state which had held him in its gauzy grasp for the few post-prandial hours, the dead afternoon, the slow time, a Tuesday. The sound of the fans, of traffic whooshing by (and, notably, not stopping) had not helped. The store sat empty. The cassette in the sound system had stopped; but it was set to reverse sides automatically, so he forced himself to his feet, wiped his glasses on the hem of what used to be a Ramones shirt (the screen-printing had washed away flake by flake after decades of the endless cycle of sweating, laundering, sweating, laundering), and knelt to peer into the cassette window.

All he could see was bunched and tangled brown magnetic tape—it had kinked and jammed in the guide wheel as he dozed, had unspooled until the mechanism jammed. He'd go at the mess with a straightened-out paperclip later, when he had the patience. In the meantime, he slipped a Cambion Brothers record from its sleeve and dropped it on the turntable. He lowered the needle and power chords shook the ceiling tiles. He winced and turned the volume down. Bourbon was the harshest of whores, even after all these years, and he had paid her tolls until his pockets were empty. His head throbbed. His leg had fallen asleep. He hobbled to the center of the store and yawned mightily, thrusting out his chest, making fists, leaning backward like a guitar player performing an impassioned, searing solo.

The door dinged and a kid slouched in, hair hanging in front of his face. Roaring red acne. Denim jacket festooned with buttons and patches over a Bad Religion tee, engineer boots scuffed and scribbled with slogans in Wite-Out. He was gnawing on a piece of chewing gum, scratching his ass with long fingers tipped with unclipped nails.

"'Sup," he said, then brushed his hair back and peered. He dropped his fragile pretense of coolness when he recognized the man yawning in the main aisle of the store—that long, jet black hair tied in a ponytail, the square jaw, the huge, thick glasses—he was iconic in the local garage band scene, a solid guitar player and a notorious smartass. "You were in Tainted Blood! Holy shit, man, I saw you at the Iron Hawk when I was 13. Don't tell me…*Paul!* Paul…"

"Cooperford. Thanks for noticing, man, thanks for noticing." He laughed, scratching at his chin, looking at the ceiling. "Man, no one remembers Tainted Blood. That's a good thing, by the way."

"*I* remember," the kid said, staring worshipfully, not even trying to hide it.

"Those guys were total dicks, though, man. Like, two of them were U2 fans. Jesus. I mean, Jesus *Christ.*"

"What was Mickey Bricklayer like?"

"First of all, his real name was Gregory, which means "watchman," which, if you're referring to watching television, then, yeah. Last name Scanlon, which is Nordic, I think, doesn't mean much more than 'man who is Nordic.' He was okay. Talked in complete, grammatical sentences, not one for eye contact. Probably what you'd call autistic, now.

16

"This place is *awe*some," the kid said. "How's business?"

Paul had sort of hoped the kid would've asked what he was doing now, but it was cool. It might come up later, while the kid was browsing or something. He could show the kid his solo record, maybe get a sale, if the kid had dough. Hard to tell with this type of kid. Could have rich parents, could be a trailer park hero. The kid wandered over to the cassettes, started looking through them, tapping each with his finger as he dismissed it.

"What does this mean?" he asked, pointing at the hand-scrawled sign above a cassette rack nailed to the wall below a shelf teeming with action figures and models. "Tapes of the Weird"?

"Yeah, man, we got a bunch of those in over the last couple of weeks. We got, let's see…okay, we have the tape of Jim Jones's speech—the actual suicide speech, man, from Jonestown? Side one is just the recording, side two has got this wicked accompaniment by Bloodburn—you've heard of him, the anonymous synthesizer dude? No? Accidentally ran over his kid backing out of his driveway? Became a recluse, started putting out these really bizarre recordings of strange tunes? He accompanies the speech with his synth. Really out there, really dark. I'd pay to get my hands on a version without the speech— there's probably an app for that, or, like, a website. Have to look that up later.

"What else? Oh, man, have you heard of Lawrence Bittaker and Roy Norris? No? Okay, they were these terrible killers who taped themselves torturing and murdering their victims, like young girls. Pleading for their lives, sobbing, trying to make deals, that kind of thing, just heart-rending stuff. That's a really rare tape, man, but…you have to have a really strong stomach. A *really* strong stomach. Far as I'm concerned, anyone buys that tape from me is a sick fuck. I'd probably ban them from the store, you know? In fact…"

He strode over to the kid, pulled a tape with a photocopied newsprint cover from the rack. He dug a finger in and tugged out the thin shining brown tape until it dangled in bunches like intestines, walked back over to the counter and threw the mess in the garbage. "You're not FBI, kid, are you?"

"*Me?* Do I look like FBI?"

"You never know, kid." He was breathing heavily now, brushing his hair from his face repeatedly, squeezing his eyes shut and opening them wide. "You never know, man. Friend of mine used to sell bootleg DVDs at the flea market down in Catterton."

"I'm not FBI. I'm in high school."

"All right, kid. I believe you."

"What else you got?"

17

"Check it out, man." He walked back over, pulled another cassette out. This one had a red insert with BUTTON WORM MANEUVER typed on it. The cassette was jet black, otherwise unmarked. "You heard of this? Prank caller, no one's ever figured out who the guy is, right? But this guy's got a dark, dark edge, man. And the people on the other end of the calls, well. Man, if you buy it, I can give you a link to the news stories. This isn't no Jerky Boys or Musacha Tapes, or even Longmont Potion Castle."

"Can I sample it?"

"Sure can, but if you break it, you bought it."

Michael popped the cassette into the player, which sat on an old-style classroom desk, with the chair connected to the desk. He kept one eye on the clearly paranoid Cooperford, in case the guy was planning to sneak up behind him and strangle him with cassette innards or something. But the man was back behind the counter, bobbing his head to the music, flipping through an ancient copy of Fangoria. Michael hit PLAY.

I Do Not Pray in Churches

I do not pray in churches. I pray on access roads and shunpikes. I pray on gently sloped rooftops. I pray in abandoned bassinets. I pray in the torn-open remains of the truck-struck moose, my words rising with the midnight steam from its shit-filled guts. I pray in the curved caves of the retinas of dying children shut in abandoned refrigerators in desolate fields.

I do not pray in churches. I shout my revelations and imprecations from crumpling rooftops in the Holyoke Flats. I whisper them into sewer drains.

Leaves skitter across the roadway from east to west and birds fly above in a great undulating black cloud from west to east and weathermen, their hair mussed and their neckties askew, weep on the floors of blue-lit studios while the anchors kneel to console them, revealing flowered underwear and white curves of flesh to the lust-stricken audience.

That is where I pray.

I pray on computerized maps striated with black veins, counties colored in various violent shades of red; above, in white, impossibly high numbers like alien spacecraft in the sky above. "There's nothing you can do," cries Brad Fieldingly, clicking the controller in his hand, as the map spins off-screen and is replaced with footage of goats streaming through a verdant meadow, their mouths and eyes wide, the toddlers impaled on their horns flopping like dolls. Behind them squadrons of twisters follow, black as vengeance, tall as Satan. Brad is no meteorologist; he barely earned his degree in Communications. The meteorologist who provides him with the forecast isn't speaking to him. His supervisors mock him in conference calls. The anchors avoid him, make plans behind his back. He cannot keep the trembling out of his voice when storms are coming. He was suspended for two months after viewers reported a visible erection in his pants when he was reporting on particularly poor air quality.

This is where I pray. In the pissed pants of failed weatherman Bradley Jeffrey Fieldingly. In the blood-filled bathtub from which his comely daughters pulled his drowned body. In the dark tunnels of their bowels. In their closets that smell of sweat and cinnamon and clover. In their mercifully closed caskets. This is where I pray. This is where I pray.

I do not pray in churches.

You're listening to WXXT, the fear in the face of the pig in the pen of the Pioneer Valley.

Cassettes (Part 2)

Hello?

Better check on the baby!

Very funny. Is this Chris?

Better check on the baby!

Okay, not Chris. There's no baby here, buddy. If you mean Pearl, my cat, she's curled up next to me fast asleep. Maybe you have the wrong number.

Better check on the baby!

You know, normally I'd hang up, but I'm bored. Bored, can you believe it? I have the entirety of the Internet on this phone. I have a wall of DVDs and more books than you could count. No baby name books, you might want to note.

Better check on the baby.

No baby, okay? No little Jacob or Jessica curled up like a bug in a crib. No crib. No bassinet. No mobile with woodland animals spinning around. No stupid colorful toys or cloth books to spit on. No poopy diapers. Maybe you have the wrong number?

Better check on the baby.

Okay, I'm going to humor you. Where's the baby? I need to know, like what room he's in, if I'm going to check on the baby, right?

Better check on the baby.

Is it a he, or a she?

Better check on the baby.

You're right, it's a little early to impose a gender on the little creature.

Third door down the hall.

Whoa! He speaks! I was starting to think this was a recording, like you were just hitting play after I was done talking! I'm actually a little freaked out now. Well done!

Better check on the baby.

Well, here's the problem, Chris. I'll just call you Chris, okay? There is no third door in the hall. There's the door to the bathroom on the left and the door to the bedroom on the right. That's it. No third door. So where's the baby?

Better check on the baby.

Okay, fine. I'm bringing you with me. Hang in there. Don't go anywhere. Don't pick up your call waiting unless your mom calls you, okay?

Better...

Yeah, yeah, I know. Check on the baby. Gimme a sec. I can't just pop up off the couch. I'm not in my twenties anymore, y'know?

Better check on the baby.

Okay. Hold on. Heading to the hall. Bear with me...almost there. Okay, wait. What... What is this? How is this possible?

Better check on the baby.

How is there a third door? Who is this? Am I dreaming?

Better check on the baby.

The doorknob is cold.

Better check on the baby.

I'm hanging up.

Better check on the...(click)

...baby.

No, no, no, I hung up on you. Why is (thumb tapping on phone)…why can I still hear…?

Better check on the baby.

(the sound of a door creaking, the whoosh of the breeze guard against carpet)

So dark…hello? I'm trying to find a light switch…

Where is the baby?

I don't know, okay? I can't see a thing in here!

Who is the baby?

(the sound of a fussing baby, a small cough, rustling, cooing)

I am the baby?

You are the baby.

Who's going to check on me?

I'd better check on the baby.

(an eardrum-shattering scream, the sound of tearing, splashing, then a long, long silence)

Better check on the baby.

Beh. Che. Ooh. Glrk. Beeeee…

Bebberh. Chek. Ah.

Good baby. That's a good baby. That's a succulent, briny, bony, powdery, delicious…

***

Michael hit the EJECT button and looked at Cooperford, who was now dozing behind the counter, his chair tilted back, hands clasped behind his neck. Michael cleared his throat. Cooperford blinked and opened his eyes. "Trippy, kid, right?"

"Yeah, wicked. You got more by him?"

"I do. There's another nine calls on that tape. They're all different. But let's get you something else to sample, yeah?"

He pushed himself up out of the chair and farted. "Hooo," he said. Then he walked over and grabbed another tape from the rack. This one had a photograph bent into the box as a cover. It depicted two men in white underwear, black dress shoes, and tuxedo shirts with brown shopping bags over their heads. They were standing in a wood-paneled living room, a brown and tan pattered couch behind them, an open doorway beyond that.

"This is a tape of a live show in Leeds," he told Michael. "The band had no name. The show was unannounced. Anyone who heard about it would have had to hear about it on the radio. The kid who sold this to me told me to take it to the police. He was afraid to himself. He said there were about fifteen people in the audience at the show. That night and over the next two days, fourteen people were reported missing by their families. He was the last. The next day his house burnt down. He lived there with his parents. Only two bodies were found."

He handed Michael the tape. It was black. The reels inside were red like drops of blood. Michael ejected the other tape, put this one in. He hit Play.

About the DJs

Clarence "The Lich" McMercury

He runs around all higgledy-piggledy, higgledy-piggledy, hither and yon, back and forth, side-to-side, every which way. He dreams of slow-motion waterfalls pouring upward, decayed bodies doing the breaststroke, upward, upward, breaking into gory pieces even as they ascend.

He keeps a penny under his tongue. He keeps a bloody fingernail in the right front pocket of his tailored pants. He keeps a memory in his head, a memory of a screaming moose, belly-burst and sitting like a human in a drained pond, an orgy of squirming fetuses dying before it.

He prefers RC Cola to Pepsi and Coke.

He was born in Scranton but he gave his soul to Leeds in 1913 and his blood runs in the veins of the trees, it colors the rivers, it stains the sinks and bathtubs. When he reads the call letters, dead birds drop to earth. When he talks up a golden oldie, wax boils in the ear. He dies on the air daily for your sins.

He's all about that bass.

He is a disgrace to his family and the scourge of his church. He is a vandal and a scallywag and a tramp of the lowest order. He is a baby-killer, a blasphemer, and a believer in Evil. He works the weekday morning drive time, 6 a.m. to 10 a.m. WXXT, the festering boil in the brandy of the Pioneer Valley.

Death Squad Dreams

Listeners, I ask you now to fulfill the duty implicit in your sobriquet: Listen. Listen to wisdom. Listen to your elders. Listen to the voice of authority. Listen to what the flower people say. Stop, collaborate and listen. Listen to the mandolin rain. Whoa-ooh-oh, listen to the music. You better listen to the radio. The country is in a state of diapause. Disease reigns; it jumps from mouth to mouth, a grim and savage perversion of artificial respiration. The air-kiss of death. You distribute droplets as though you're tossing candy to the captive crowd, their eyes lid-locked open like Malcolm McDowell's, watching their pageantry, their pandemic parade.

Every radio station has their street team, their marketers, their promotional units. WXXT has death squads. The anonymous marauders are here to take down the stupid, the willfully ignorant, to knock down doors, to smash through windows, to dismantle barricades, to pull fools screaming from their fortresses, to lock them in together in hermetically sealed trailers to share air and wheeze their way into eternity. The survivors will be blown apart by anti-aircraft ordnance, North Korea style, their remains scattered across a half mile of scrub and sludge. Glory glory hallelujah, my teacher dropped me in Fallujah. Our bother who farts on Kevin, sallow be thy flame. Hail Mary, full of shit. Hey Judas, don't make it bad. And so forth and multiply and bags to snitches, and blessed pee, and Miss Jackson if you're Namaste, lift up your hearts, we lift them up into lard, it is right to give me thanks and praise and pancakes with syrup artificially flavored like butter, Tommy used to work on the doxologies, deliver us to evil, Priority Mail Overnight, please, and put in on my Master-of—Darkness Card, of whom should you be afraid? Of meem. Of memes, dank or otherwise. Wait on the lord, even if he asks where the goddamned appetizers are; it's been an hour since we ordered and those fuckers in the booth across the aisle came in after us and already got their Devils on Horseback, Horshack, ooh, ooh, whores, smack, boors, crack, hardtack, heart attack, may your name be stankified, stankify yourself by dimpled hinds, Leather from Paul to the Corinthians as he strangled the rosy-cheeked with the rosary, oh Lord chap my lips and wiggle my hips and give me clumps of cucumber dip in which to dip the tip of my disco stick. Torch singer, yogurt flinger, pull my finger, tony danza....

WXXT Sunday Night Programming

7 pm – 8 pm: Douglas Houle's Screaming Hour

9 pm – 10 pm: The Floyd Void with Rexroth Slaughton

10 pm – 10:30 pm: Acid Polka with Piotr Gajus and his dead son

10:30 pm – 11:00 pm: Disquieting Silence

11:00 pm – 12 midnight: Bauble Swap with Crazy Michael and Dean

12 midnight - 1 a.m.: There Shall Be Meat: Hecklers try stand-up

1 a.m. – 2 a.m.: The Shriek of the Impaled Martinet – Supervisors Apologize Under Extreme Duress, #39842 – Don Vorcella, 41, Assistant Manager at Burlington Coat Factory, East Hartford, CT

2 a.m. – 2:30 a.m.: musikalische phänomene – a trampled trumpet briefly speaks perfect German, foreseeing the death of one lucky listener

2:30 a.m. – 6:00 a.m.: Czech Occult Hip-Hop with DJ Jakub

Legal Steroid Turning Men into Beasts – without Exercise!

At the Sick Rooms

Marceline was in my dormitory room, which was forbidden. But I had been seven months in The Sick Rooms, Marceline just shy of six, and by this stage we had the run of the place. We were inmates in name only.

Eric came barging in. He hadn't even fully used up his outside ten. His face was as red as his hair.

"What's the matter?" I said.

"Michael," he said, "was talking to a dog."

"And?"

"And I heard laughter from your window. Mad laughter."

"Nothing funny in here. Besides, Michael always talks to animals."

"Not to dogs," Eric said, crouching and fanning the fingers of both hands, and he stormed out. The access door slammed and the alarm began its exasperated bleating as the lights blinked red.

"'Hello, Pup,'" said Marceline.

"Likely just that or something similar," said I.

***

At the Plaza Stralenkrans

Two hours later Marceline and I walked briskly up the fan of stairs to the double oak doors of the Mob Rule. *Loi de la Populace*, Marci said under her breath. I had donned my tux, she a black shift with a plunging neckline and

29

shoes that exaggerated her already high height. ENTREZ NOUS SOMMES OURVERTS, read the sign, and so we entrezed.

We stood before the hostess's podium, waiting to be noticed. On the television a devil danced on an orange-lit stage, a troupe of angels in black with smoke-smudged faces twirling behind him. "I'm terrified of the Devil," Marceline shouted above the clinking and chattering din.

"There is no Devil."

She whirled to face me, grabbed my shoulder. The movement adjusted her dress, and I could see the faint upper curved line of her areole. Someone behind us cursed and swept by, brushing against my coat. I made a note of his face.

Marceline pulled down her glasses and looked at me over the frame. "What?"

"There is no God, and I certainly don't believe in any Devil. The only thing worth fearing is being in the company of a bad man."

She shook her head sadly. "He's right there," she said. "On the television. Besides, in your paintings…"

The hostess appeared with two absurdly large menus in her small hands. She led us to a large table where Kurzon and his *kuklala* had already been seated and the former was sipping at a goblet of something bluish.

On our way to the table Migridichian, the owner, blocked our path. The hostess rolled her eyes. "I'm afraid I must ask you to leave," the former said, with a frost in her voice.

"Don't be afraid," I replied. "But I must refuse."

On that I proffered her three folded bills from my breast pocket, but she slapped them from my hands.

"Those have no value here."

"They do in the Sick Rooms."

She was shaking, I noticed, trembling like a branch from which a bird has just taken flight. "And I do not want a waiter," I added. "You shall serve us."

Migridichian waved away the hostess and brought us to the table. Kurzon barely looked away from the menu he was holding up to show his unseeing *kuklala*. He grunted acknowledgement.

***

"I shall have the steak au poivre, rarer than a virgin in the Sick Rooms," said Kurzon, "and Griffith shall have the same."

"Snails," said I. "With beet root."

Marceline requested a water with milk and a side of julienned serpent.

"It is a fine thing to be happy after having made a wrong choice," said

Migridichian, and she turned on her heel to walk our orders to the kitchen.

I placed my hand on the cold thigh of the kuklala. "Come now, Keiger," said Kurzon, his mustaches twitching, the disco lights playing bumper-cars on his bald pate. "Mara's body isn't even cold."

"Surely it is by now," I said, and took a long draught of my sangria.

Michael came in, his black hair plastered to his forehead, his tunic soaked. It hadn't looked like rain.

His eyes found us and his body followed, leaving muddy footprints on the parquet floor. He stood at the foot of our table and lifted his phone from his pocket. He clicked on the Facebook icon, then swung the phone slowly from west to east so we all could see it, scrolling with one long-nailed index finger as he went.

"I do not know," he said. "*Any* of these people."

***

"Sit here by me," I said to Michael, pulling the chair out from under a thin man at an adjacent table. The man hit the floor like spilled toothpicks and his full-to-the-brim whisky sour followed, splashing everything sticky. Impressively, the glass stayed intact. As the toothpick man tried to arrange himself into human form again, his companion, a capybara-faced bodybuilder with a nose like an eight-iron and a large brown wart fighting with his head for dominance on his neck, stood and pulled a small red pistol from his coat. He shot, and the bullet went past me and hit Griffith, the kuklala, shattering his arm. Satisfied, the man sat down and ordered another drink for his still-struggling companion.

Kurzon knelt to pick up the fragments as Michael sat. "Let me see your phone," I said.

He handed it over. I scrolled past news stories with names and places I did not recognize; personal pictures of ugly little families situated around swimming pools; eight-paragraph anti-tree screeds; a short gif on a loop of a mafioso slapping the thorny crown off of Jesus's head and then sucking his punctured hand; declarations of impending suicide from chipper looking blondes; quotes that looked like they were from movies but that I, a noted cinephile, did not recognize; advertisements for deliquescing cadavers with inexpensive shipping costs; pictures of blood-spattered toast lit luridly; children's heads protruding from large uncooked meatballs; cobweb-strewn marmot carcasses formed into a roller coaster with maggot-filled skulls for carts; toddlers providing PayPal addresses and begging for cocaine money. There was no one I recognized, nothing that looked like it was even from this country. Road signs were black with red lettering, stoplights arranged in a crude triangle rather than the usual totem pole formation. The interiors of apartments and houses showed walls standing at untenable or even dangerous angles, the artwork decorating those walls beyond my comprehension; even light sources seemed unattached to fixtures and faces seemed somehow artificial. I, myself, had posted thirty-two extraordinarily handsome (unfiltered) selfies prior to our arrival at The Mob Rule, and those were nowhere to be found, not even after I changed his setting to "Most Recent." I looked at his friends list and recognized no one—no Kurzon, no Griffith, no me—even though I knew our lists were for all intents and purposes identical. I fumbled for my own phone but couldn't find it. Meanwhile, toothpick man had apparently used *his* phone to summon backup, which had arrived in the form of triplets with red hair and white wife-beaters and sunglasses with round blue lenses. Migridichian led them in; grinning savagely, she pointed to our table. The ginger squad pulled fat little knives from their belts. The blades barely protruded from their white, pimpled fists. Marceline yelled her war cry. Kurzon shielded Griffith, whose pieces still littered the floor, now in a pool of whisky sour.

I felt my collar tighten and knew that toothpick man had risen and now had the back of my shirt crumpled in his tight fist. With the other he grabbed my hair. This was beginning to be a terrible night out and I longed for the knowable, homey, pedestrian dangers of the Sick Rooms. All I was going to do now would be in the service of getting us all back there alive and intact, and finding out what the fuck was wrong with Michael's Facebook feed. At best, it seemed like a massive privacy breach.

***

We easily dispatched The Ginger Squad. Two of them lay on the ground, clutching their groins and howling in agony, the third quite dead and being zipped into a body bag by Mob Rule security staff. The toothpick man, a coward, had fled, Marci, my folding girl, following with her folding knife (and with all my folding money, so I dearly hoped she'd return). This whole time, the bodybuilder who'd shot Griffith sat and fussily picked at his meal, some kind of curious raw chicken twisted into an uncomfortable looking shape and balanced atop a rhombus of clear gelatin, ignoring the melee.

Him I'd leave to Kurzon, who likes to take his time with revenge.

Michael retrieved his phone from the broken glass on the floor and wiped it down. Our entrees and drinks came, delivered by a clearly vexed Migridichian, who practically slammed everything down on the table and turned on her heel.

We'd better tip well, I thought.

After we ate, I requested that Michael show me the phone again. This time I found my name in the "People You May Know" notifications. The picture looked like me, but in it I wore a beard, which I never have done, and I was grinning a grin that definitely is not my grin and was missing a front tooth. I clicked on the profile and the posts appeared to have been locked down. I could still access the list of friends, however, and so I clicked there to see the sort of person with whom my apparent doppelganger associated.

The first profile was a man with the name of John Policetripper. In his picture he appeared to be in some sort of sporting arena, and he was wearing a red turtleneck shirt and square-framed glasses. His head was shaped like a rounded pyramid and he was affecting a teeth-together grimace over a triple-chin.

The next, someone named Qrs Tuv, appeared in his profile picture to be upside down and moving very quickly. This I could surmise despite the picture showing only his blurred bald head (which was right-side up) and the grassy, hilly landscape (upside down). Judging from the visual trail left by the blur, a pair of spectacles in the bottom left corner of the picture were tumbling away from the man's head.

The third's face—nothing there indicated a name—was a pair of sad blue eyes peering out from a mass of pustules and burns and scars and pimples and actinic keratosis and seborrheic eczema and melanomata. Jutting from his profusely blistered mouth was an orange-colored cassette, and a line of thin magnetic tape dangled from one of his curiously small ears.

The next was a woman apparently named Lofty McSofty in a pose and with an expression so comely as to be parodic. She was false-blonde and salon-tanned and had full, heavy legs and very red lips. Scrolling down, her other profile pictures showed the same woman in various outfits and similarly absurd, exaggerated poses, then the few after that were of a man very white and of medium build, with eyes entirely black and red nostril hairs sticking out like dustmops from his nostrils. In his pictures he held aloft a complex looking gun of some kind with several barrels and a variety of triggers.

Reader, I did not immediately recognize these people, but something in me was moved. Jarred, even. Maybe I had known them from dreams.

"...and maybe they are inside you," said Michael, as though he had heard my thoughts.

I looked at my watch. If we were not back at the Sick Rooms within the hour, we might be missed during rounds. And Marceline had not yet returned. "We should eat," I said to Michael, handing him back his phone.

Kurzon had re-seated himself and put back into the chair adjacent to his that which remained of Griffith in the meantime, and they were halfway through their own meals. Michael and I dug in too. I repeatedly checked the lobby for Marci, but it remained empty save a haggard skeleton reading a paperback romance and a toddler fashioning a castle and a moat out of his own excreta.

But the fifth time I checked, who should burst through the doors but Eric. He was soaking wet, though it was not raining outside. He wore a tall hat and a monocle I'd not known he had in his wardrobe. He took me by my shoulders, gripping them, causing me some pain, and said, "Don't trust Michael," he said.

"And why not?"

"Because he was…"

"…talking to a dog, yes, yes, we know. So?"

"Do you trust me? Look, there's no time to answer. Go outside. There's a stagecoach. Get in it. I will grab Marci and bring her out."

"I'll get her! She's my girl!"

"If you go back in there, Michael will kill you. And her."

Though conflicted, I did as Eric said and I went to the door. As Eric had indicated, a heart-shaped coach waited just beyond the walk, topped with luggage. Two black horses stood in front, looking all around with haunted expressions, as though they heard voices speaking all around them, voices warning of impending calamity. I opened the door and climbed in. Moments later, Eric and Marci and a third woman who I did not know, a beehive-topped blonde in a frock and pearls, exited the Mob Rule at a full gallop. I blinked. It looked like both Michael and this third woman had the nubs of horns growing from their heads just below their hairlines. As well, something about their eyes was off, wrong; I could not focus well enough to see exactly what it was. Behind the glass doors came the star-shaped lights of high-powered weaponry, followed by the concomitant rat-tat-tat-tat. The doors exploded outward. I could not see who was shooting through the smoke and the spraying glass. Marci climbed in the back with me, her breaths coming in short, high-pitched bursts, and the other two without a word clambered up into the driver's box.

"To Leeds," Michael cried. The horses galloped off, the coach jerking hard and then bouncing along. Behind us, shadowy figures climbed upon the backs of their own horses to give chase.

Marci looked at me, her face streaked with tears. "The Sick Rooms' staff will be looking for us as well," she said. "What is to become of us?"

Another Mary, Fleeing

I was there at your arraignment. You
didn't see me in the back, sitting low
like a shamed widow in a tarnished pew

No one but I saw the smirk when your hand
hit the Bible. The judge was playing with his phone;
the bailiff stood, arms crossed,

trying to look tough. Your eyes were klieg lights. Your voice was hoarse. I felt
the loose lozenges in my pocket, opaque nuns in wax
paper habits. No one made you peel your

sleeves. Your wounds were hidden. Mine
leaked wine into the aisles. I saw your sons,
their Adam's Apples bobbing light streetlights in a hurricane. I missed what was said

but the court led you away, your leg-chains playing a jangling tune.
A cab took me home,
a lynched Virgin Mary twirling under the rear-view

I cleaned out my closet, my best dresses, your grim cache of Polaroids. I woke
on a bouncing train trailing a necktie of smoke. Rain battered the roof. The
conductor took my ticket.

Outside the tinted window, unreadable signs flew by, like planted skillets with
burnt strands of pulled meat. At a 4 a.m. station I lit a cigarette and bellowed
smoke into the sky.

Witch Wolf in the Grove of Eglantine

I am a working-class mystic. I am lignite under pressure. Bituminous, I crack, a victim of frost heave and heartless women. Wanna split? Let's split.

I am a cell, not a terrorist cell, not a cell in a deadly-dull spreadsheet, not a cubicle. Like a toddler surrounded by werewolves I am devoured by my own enzymes; fickle friends, fair-weather fouls, autolysis is my fate and my end. Deprived of oxygen, I rupture like a boil, my tissues separating and floating away on formaldehyde-scented air. God grabs a stray tissue, blows his bourbon-swollen nose into it. I rub the snot under my armpits and it sticks in the hair, lubricates the skin tags.

It's nice out, I say. You say *then leave it out.*

Do you know Satan? Every house is incomplete without Him. Every meal lays uneaten until the flies arrive. Every maggot is a man-in-waiting.

I prowl the suburban neighborhood at night. I peer in windows. I plunder a crib in an unlocked bungalow. I peel the chain-link skin off the wooden bones of a rabbit enclosure. I strew and swaddle. I deck the parapets with dreck. I bring my prizes to the grove and devour them. I howl not at the moon, but at a quiet black star that sits unobserved in the cosmic miasma and watches. Waiting. I pray to it, and it prays back. It puts motes in my eye and I blink them back into my brain.

Cast an eye my way. I do the sordid things. My tongue dabs at your pores like a flat rock skimmed across a pond. Its reach is otherworldly. I can send it to your deepest depths, swab your innermost floor until you submit. I sing to you through the radio. My voice is velvet draped over steel. My words are your most terrible thoughts and your hidden musings. My lunch pail is full of your giblets. My raucous laughter shakes the girders.

It's nice out, you say. I say *then leave it out.*

I'm your overnight man, your witch-wolf, your grotesque lover in the grove that is WXXT – The Lurker in the Loins of the Pioneer Valley.

Meet the DJs

Guy Ronstadt

He is selfish. He is capriciously cruel. He is ugly, but the odd woman finds him beautiful. The odd woman's name is Marcia Bell and the less said about her the better. The rumor regarding his incomprehensibility is that whilst eating ill-gotten fox grapes he accidentally bit his tongue and liked the taste of it so much that he finished it. Undaunted, he hosts "The Ronstadt Chadt" every odd Tuesday from 9:17 a.m. to 10:05 a.m. His guests, unable to comprehend his questions, answer whatever they guess each question may have been for the length of the show, and after, many must be reassured that they have not been the victims of a prank. They are then disemboweled, violated most egregiously, and then rëemboweled and sent on their way. For this is the m.o. of Guy Rondstadt.

Guy likes daffodils and dancing on his flesh-shorn legs. Top-heavy he is and also dead these many years. He likes the taste of living tongue and dead offal. He can read a person's future in his or her vomit, and often carries an emetic secreted on his person for just that purpose. For music, he prefers Church Organ hip-hop. He'll steal your wife.

The Card Sharp's Ploy

He carried himself with a pharaonic air, but he was lower than a mudsill, wickeder than a witch, uglier than a mongoloid – his rancid mouth harbored Hutchinson incisors and Mulberry molars; his malformed neck held up a pimpled, misshapen pale dome ringed by tangled hair, a nose like a stepped-on plum, and one eye swollen, with a curious horizontal oval pupil, and his eyebrows? Forget it.

His askew visage lent him an advantage: his expression was perpetually inscrutable. Happy or sad, conniving or genuine, terrified or resolute, his face always looked like he was watching a particularly poorly acted stage play and wanted a refund but was loath to ask. When he sat at the table one of the other men rose to his feet and stumbled away, gagging. The rest stayed. They did not smile. One put his hand over his mouth, and then brought it down when he saw that no one who remained was reacting.

The dealer pulled his weathered deck from a small brown satchel. He shuffled the cards assiduously and with an almost absurd complexity as all the men watched with rapt attention. They had imbibed little, contrary to their usual heroic intake. Money was at stake. Livelihoods were at risk, as were marriages, families, real estate, other investments.

The dealer was a curious looking fellow himself. He was entirely bald, possessed of wickedly arched brows and two thin mustaches as black as burnt matches. His teeth gleamed white when he grinned, and his pupils were almost the red of a ripe apple, but somehow also not at all red. It depended, perhaps, on the angle from which they were viewed. His clothing was pressed and fit him perfectly: a purple shirt enclosed in a black vest, a sharp thin tie of curious Asian design, cuffed black pants, and shoes shined to the point that they reflected the soft lights of the candles that hung on sconces on every vertical surface, from beam to bar-side to wall.

The card sharp had cards tucked away in his pocket. The dealer's deck was standard issue. Without moving his eyes, under the table the former moved from his right pocket to his left the non-matching cards. That was another advantage he held; others kept their eyes off of him, even when it might be to their benefit to watch.

Then the bald man dealt the cards, tossing them so that they landed in a fan pattern. The precision was impressive. The card sharp picked up his hand. He coughed as he made the switch, and then looked down to behold the cards he'd swapped in, the ones that had been in his right pocket. For the first time in his life, his expression changed. He looked frightened.

A brief aside, if you'll indulge me, regarding the card sharp's father. Picture an outhouse, the classic kind, with a small half-moon cut out of the door at head-level, while standing, that is. Picture the outhouse as somewhat ramshackle, shelf-cocked like a book, standing on the edge of a great wood. Picture it as evening falls, the rich blue grey of just past dusk. Picture this all taking place in late November, the trees bare, the wind whistling, the aroma of encroaching winter in the air. Picture the old man sitting down with the Sears Roebuck catalog in his hands. Got it? Good. The old man's nuts hit the cold toilet water when he sat. His first reaction was a jolt, naturally, and a yelp. His second was graver: he reckoned he'd got too old to live anymore. So that very hour, back in the cabin (picture the cabin) he blowed half his head away with his trusty shotgun. It was the card-sharp-to-be who found him, too, drawn by the muted blast. The ceiling still rained plaster, wood shards, and gore—a splintery mix, if you will, but I don't see why you should.

In the days following this, he feared he'd be haunted by his father's body. In his mind he could just see the old man doing a ghastly jig out among the dead and snapped-in-two cornstalks, gore spilling out the broken basin of his lower head like stew from a bowl in an earthquake. But instead, it was the pieces of the head that haunted him. A big old shard of bone would rise up from the dirty bathwater, an ear stuck to it. He'd take a pull from his beer and look back down on his chicken soup to find veiny lumps of brain matter floating on the surface like an archipelago of grotesque islands. After a time, this stopped. For that the card sharp was most thankful indeed.

Back to the game. The card sharp was frightened because the cards he had swapped into the game were not the cards he had brought. Instead the King he held bore the face of his own father, for a crown the old man wore tentacles of gore. The Queens were his mother and Aunt. His own face was on the Jack, and the Joker was—no, oh, no—it was the jolly face of Uncle Don, he of the sweaty hands and the fat exploring tongue and the jutting prick, which he would wield as one does a bludgeon, capering Don, randy Don, Don with the threats of reprisal should the card sharp-to-be dare to tattle.

The men put down their hands. The card sharp held onto his so hard his fingers went blue.

"Well?" said the dealer. "Let's see your hand."

"What is this?"

"Show your hand, pal, or I'll show it for ya."

"Up your ass," said the card sharp. "Up your ass and around the corner."

The dealer stood and snatched the cards away. He lay them on the table. "What the unholy fuck is this?" said Clem.

Clem was another one of the card players. Don't worry if you didn't know that. I hadn't introduced him yet. He had a large mustache and small eyes, and was a very violent man, even compared to the other roughnecks at the table. His vulgarity was due to the fact that the face of each card depicted not a number nor a member of royalty, no club, no spade, no heart. Instead each bore a picture of the card-sharp rogering his, that is, Clem's wife. On one card he had her so that her shoulders and head were on the bed, the rest the card sharp was holding in the air, her feet at his ears. He was in the middle of a lascivious wink. On another she sat astride him, her breasts held up by dirt-stained hands. The others I cannot in good conscience describe. I can say that each of the other men at the table saw on the cards his own wife with the card-sharp.

Oh, they beat him without mercy. They beat him til the inside of his left ear bumped up against the inside of his right ear. They beat him til his brains spilled out of his neck. They beat him til his ribs were shards and his pelvis was powder, til his blood painted the floor, walls, and ceiling.

And yet still he lives. He's our Wednesday morning man. He's your wife's Wednesday morning man. See him wait until you leave. See him slithering under your bed. See him dangling from your ceiling like a thousand red dripping fingers. See him rogering your wife like a pile of gore fell onto her from a plane. See her wicked, lustful smile, the one you haven't seen since you were teenagers.

The card-sharp, our overnight guy, he plays the hits and he's a hit with the ladies too. No amount of damage can undo that.

You're listening to WXXT, the gore under the floor of the Pioneer Valley.

Cassettes (Part 3)

Artie didn't want to go. He'd given Jay a six-pack and half the cash for the tickets back in March. What was it called…the sunken cost fallacy? The money was already gone, long gone. Didn't matter if he went or not. He had a tickle in his tonsil, maybe due to blossom into a scorching sore throat. Or he was tired. Whatever. "I don't think I'm gonna go."

Jay was having none of it. "This is going to be *awesome*," he said. A band without a name playing in the woods? The first date of a world tour? I betcha it's a big name, wants to play to a small crowd in secret."

The two sat on a bench in Child's Park, a person's width between them lest anyone get the wrong idea. Artie pulled a chunk of bread from the loaf in the bag in his lap, rolled it into a ball, and tossed it toward a nearby duck, which sailed away, webbed feet pedaling rapidly just below the surface of the murky water, beak in the air.

"Yeah, but why haven't I heard anything about it? Except from you."

"It was on the radio, middle of the night. A gathering in the woods, they said. There'll be girls."

"Yeah, like you said in March."

"Did I tell you how I bought the tickets?"

"Yeah, online?"

"Nope. Check it out. I had to leave money in the front pocket of this moss-covered suitcase leaned up against a light pole in the school playground, then look for the tickets three days later in a pile of tires at the landfill."

"Don't talk shit."

"No, seriously, though. That's how the radio said to get the tickets." He pulled them from his pocket. They were two strips of thick paper, yellowed with age, the approximate size of arcade tickets. The printing on them was smudged to the point of incomprehensibility.

"The whole thing sounds sketchy to me. They'll probably rob us and leave us for dead."

"Where's your sense of adventure?"

"It's cold."

"Your sense of adventure is cold?"

"Ha, ha. You're a natural. You should do Open Mic night at The Perch."

"Listen, it's not that cold. It's New England, you should be used to it by now. Wear a jacket. Wear a hat."

"I look stupid in hats."

"You look stupid anyway. Come on."

They set out. Artie pulled his hat down over his ears and shoved his hands into the pockets of his peacoat. "I'm gonna get frostbite."

"Uh huh," said Jay. He had grown taciturn, introspective. They headed down the dead-end road behind the hotel and Jay held aside the brambles and thicket. They passed through a mostly overgrown path until they reached the disused train tracks, and headed north. The trees whispered secrets to one another. The moon went behind a cloud. Jay flicked on the flashlight he'd kept in his pocket. It made a conical shape on the ground, barely illuminated anything.

The half-shell loomed, a large bluish moon rising improbably in a clearing like a planet breaching a grassy horizon. Opposite the half-shell a curved row of loudspeakers on tall poles marked the outer edge of the lawn. A few kids lurked around; a small circle of four or five stood shivering, passing around a tiny orange light that glowed fiercer under each face, lighting it up, rendering it sinister, with arched brows, hollows for eyes.

Artie couldn't feel his fingers. "What time is this thing starting?

Jay lit a cigarette. He looked at his watch. "Fifteen minutes ago."

"Punk rock time," Artie said.

"Punk rock time."

Light spread across the field like an expanding pool of blood played in fast-motion. Artie and Dan looked up. A hooded figure had lit a candle at the easternmost corner of the stage by the back wall and was scuttling forward to light another, and another. The candlelight shot great trembling fingers up the curve of the half-shell. Revealed on the stage was a set of bongos, dilapidated and punched-in drums impaled on bent branches, and upturned trash cans. In front of that on a stand leaned a makeshift guitar built from the ribcage and spinal column of some unidentifiable animal. It was strung with long blonde hairs. The hair formed a tangled knot at the tuning pegs, which protruded from a mummified hand. A microphone stand stood at center stage. A tapestry hung on the back wall, a strange symbol something like a cross between a capital A and the number 4.

Jay and Artie went up to the stage for a better vantage point.

Off to the right a kid in a hoodie and low-slung baggy jeans put his pinky fingers in his mouth and whistled shrill and long. Then he started clapping a slow beat. The others in the audience joined in. Jay glanced at Artie and the two started clapping along. Somehow it sounded like more than just fifteen or so pairs of hands. The claps echoed in staggered time, like a hundred pairs of hands slapping together in rounds, seeming to come from the trees, the sky, the dirt below. A gust of wind spun through the treetops. Artie glanced up and around. The other audience members were facing away from the stage. Their clapping was perfectly in time, as though all their hands were connected by a hidden mechanism. He nudged Jay. "We should turn around," he whispered, jutting his chin towards the others. The two turned away from the stage, still clapping, looking at the backs of the others' heads. Then the others spun in time to face the stage, to face Artie and Jay.

Artie spun back around, but not before he detected something wrong with the crowd's faces. He said to Jay, "Did you see that?" but his friend was staring enraptured at the stage. Artie looked up.

Something had come out from behind a false wall, waving a flag with the same symbol as the tapestry. Artie couldn't figure out what the hell he was looking at. It appeared to be a six-legged thing, covered in burlap with toadstools growing from the top. Its shoes, brand new striped sneakers with Z's on them, were fastened to the legs with brown packing tape. In its side was sewn the blank white face of a Halloween mask. Next to that was a malleable clear plastic window of sorts, divided into quarters by dark strips of tape. Behind it a giant red eye blurred by cataracts rolled wildly. A yellowish sludge dripped down from the thing's undercarriage onto the stage. A long, thin, many jointed arm jutted from its side, holding the knotted flagpole. The creature moved with surprising agility back and forth along the lip of the stage, surveying the small crowd.

Artie glanced at Jay, who was still staring at the stage, unblinking. He, Artie, slipped his hand inside his coat pocket and hit record on the microcassette player he'd borrowed from the desk of his father—a journalist at the Gazette.

A hail of trumpets sounded from the loudspeakers. Cellos plodded, a dark march, a lurching dirge. Something gloppy and bulbous roughly the size of a cantaloupe dropped onto the stage from under the six-legged creature and slither-rolled over to the drum set. It oozed up onto the stool and expanded into a great, veiny, purple lump. Bare human arms, muscular and veiny, mallets gripped in its slimy fingers, burst through its sides. It pounded out a slow beat on the drums, throwing glop from its shoulders into the air with every movement.

The six-legged creature approached the mic stand and raised the mouth of its mask to the microphone's wire-mesh glans. In an elegant accent Artie couldn't quite place, something between Eastern Massachusetts and London, it spoke clearly and with fastidious enunciation. "With gratitude to the city of Leeds and the largesse of its leaders. With a great debt owed to Anne Gare and her exquisite collection of antiquities and ancient tomes. With much else intangible owed to the community leaders who own and operate Annelid Industries Incorporated and its diabolical subsidiaries, we come to claim what is ours. We are," the voice proclaimed, "so very hungry." From either side of the stage strode two headless guitarists in black jumpsuits and high boots. Pitchforks jutted tines-up from their tattered necks. Their left hands moved in unison up and down the guitars' fretboards, the right hands churning out a barrage of shattering power chords. The six-legged creature picked up its strange instrument, squeezed two strings against a length of bone, and played a piercing, shrieking, soaring note.

***

Artie ran through the woods. He didn't know what he was running from nor what he was running toward. One second that dissonant sound was savaging his eardrums, the next he was crashing through underbrush, ears still ringing, headlong into who knows what. Something flapped on his head. He reached up and grabbed what he at first took to be a hat, or a tangle of leaves. He looked at his hand to find he was holding part of his own scalp, the size of a pancake, bloody and covered in hair. He flung it aside, ran faster, as if he expected a hospital to rise from the twig-strewn forest floor somewhere up ahead. Then the pain came, spreading through his cranium, burning in his forehead and crown, causing his tongue and eyes and teeth to ache.

He hit a down-slope and held out his arms to keep from tumbling. Then he crested a hillock to find wedged between two trees a table covered with folded t-shirts and stickers behind which a figure in a robe swayed slightly and trembled. Some of the shirts displayed the symbol from the tapestry and the flag; others depicted eyeless cartoon faces that he recognized as crude caricatures of some of the people in the small crowd at the show. He spotted his own face, all buck teeth and stringy hair and pointed nose. The figure manning the table made a gurgling sound from its stomach. Artie looked up.

The man who stood there among moldering boxes piled with what looked like hundreds of shirts...it was *Jay*. Artie recognized him despite the fact that his eyes were now gory black holes and something was wrong with his mouth and chin. They were all bunched up just under his nose; it reminded Artie of a documentary he'd seen about crystal meth addicts—and then his friend grinned. Of course. His teeth were gone. Jay's horrid, bloody mouth emitted a high-pitched wheeze and then something beige and oblong and striated rose up from his throat and angled like a Pez onto his tongue. He started to gag, claw at his throat. The thing jutted forward and tumbled down the front of his shirt, trailing a mucousy string. The piercing stench of excrement hit Artie full force.

Artie bolted, screeching and crying. In his periphery he saw tables bearing pastries smothered in plastic wrap, bins of featureless rag dolls, wigs, and animal skulls. In a shady hollow robed figures worked a long, rusted-out grill, flipping smoking beige patties and sausages the color of human skin while toasted rolls shot out of a tall toaster onto a tray and something yellow-green burbled in a carafe with a spigot and all the workers started to hum and the tape recorder rolled in Artie's pocket as it had since he'd hit record and the reels rolled and recorded the rest too, the laughter, the screaming, the squelching, the weeping, and then, finally, the encore, which was cut off because the tape had reached its end, but which undeniably and indisputably and most definitely fucking *rocked*.

WXXT March Events

March 11 – Elagabalus Day – Join local actors Reggie Liveright and Marceline Vurzon as they are beheaded and thrown into the Connecticut River. 8 p.m. at the Coolidge Bridge. Festivities begin with a parade at City Hall at 7 p.m. Stop by the WXXT booth for the Testicle Raffle. Masks encouraged!

March 14 – The anniversary of the birth of Johann Georg Gichtel – Readings from the Theosophia Practica and more at the Forbes Library. Heckle Lutherans. Quaff bitter libations. Tasteful, non-stimulating attire please. Yes, even if the weather is warm.

March 17 – Roxycodone and French Fry eating contest, bottom level, E. J. Gare (no relation) Parking Garage – hosted by Indolent Mike

March 20 – anti-Ostara day. The light will never defeat the dark. All throughout Leeds. Wear black. Bring a purse with stones for admittance to the Feast at the Strike Zone Bowling Emporium, Rumpus Room, sub-basement.

March 21- Human Sacrifice Night begins at 8. This year it's a free-for-all: victims can be any age. Animals OK, except for cats. Guns prohibited. Knives encouraged. Safety First.

March 28 – End of the World (or not) orgy – Banquet Room, Bluebonnet Diner. Devils on Horseback & Bacon-Wrapped Scallops 10 pm - ?

WXXT Monday Night Programming

7 pm – 8 pm: Handle With Scare – Occult Messages in Appliance Instruction Manuals 1978-2003

9 pm – 10 pm: The death throes of Sammy Davis Jr. and the stomping to powder of his glass eye, with commentary. Approved by Davis and paid for by the IRS

10 pm – 10:30 pm: Leo Buscaglia having a difficult shit, recorded in secret, 1992

10:30 pm – 11:00 pm: The Innermost Thoughts of Randall W. Buckleknuckle, Sex Pervert and Squash Court Pest

11:00 pm – 1 a.m.: Newly unearthed exclusive audio of The 1981 Hostile Takeover of St. Hans Schmidt Church by the Light-Bringers Unitarian Society, in which the Unspeakable happened to Four Congregants, and a reenactment of the subsequent trial by the Pioneer Valley Players (having inhaled helium)

1 a.m. – 2 a.m. Confessions of a Compulsive Coroner – Stark Bonniton Tells All, Yes, Even What Happened to Ms. Minorkay and her Unborn Childe

2 a.m. – 2:30 a.m.: Beheadings in B-Minor, a dirge

2:30 a.m. – 4:00 a.m.: Ruminative Sighs and Skulls Being Crushed, with violin

4:00 a.m. – 6:00 p.m. Botched Castrations and Polka Mega- Mix

You Ess Bee

As Jeskin droned on and on at the head of the crowded conference table, Turcotte felt a dot of warmth against his upper leg. He tucked his hand into the pocket of his Dockers and touched his fingertip to the small severed paw. It was hot, almost feverish. Its tiny fingers curled around his index finger in what felt like an affectionate embrace.

"What are you smiling about, Turkey," stage whispered Furdd, next to him on the left, "Fourth quarter projections turn you on?"

Turcotte forced a chuckle.

Jeskin must have heard; he practically whirled to look at Turcotte, his expression sour. "So," he said from the head of the table, pointing his finger like an accusation, mockery dancing in his voice. "As you can see, your figures were off the mark. *Far* off the mark. How do you explain that?"

Turcotte felt his face and the tops of his ears grow warm and knew they had turned bright red. It was a different kind of warmth than the paw's embrace of his finger, which tightened slightly at the sound of Jeskin's voice. The others at the table pretended to doodle or take down notes, or else just stared down at their notepads as though scrutinizing them with great interest. Turcotte looked over at Houck, but there was no relief there—his friend's face was tilted toward the ceiling, his eyes closed, hands clenching his notepad. He looked as though he might be deep in meditation or prayer. He had probably willed himself out of his body. Turcotte wished he could do the same.

"Well?"

It's called an error. Maybe you've made them too. Maybe you weren't called out for it in front of the whole staff.

He stammered, and instantly hated himself for it. He was finally able to mutter a too-sullen sounding "I don't know."

A dramatic sigh. "You don't *know*. Well, it was you who came up with the figures, right? You reviewed them? You ran them against last year's projections?"

Turcotte sat silent. His mind ran. *Let this be over, let this end, let this be over, let this end.*

"At some point 'I don't know' isn't going to cut it any longer, you hear me?"

Turcotte's ran through a number of potential replies, but nothing seemed quite right; in fact, anything he said, he surmised could easily be fodder for further abuse. Finally, Jeskin shook his head in exaggerated disgust and continued with his presentation.

In Turcotte's pocket the paw dug tiny claws into his finger, and he winced, prying the thing away with his thumb. He withdrew his hand and held it against his hip. Furdd was looking at him with a quizzical expression on his face, his brows lowered. Turcotte turned his head to stare at Jeskin for a few beats, feigning interest, let his gaze sweep over the box of donuts on the table, then placed his hand on his notepad and peeked at it. The tip of his finger was bright red. He could still feel the paw moving restlessly in his pocket.

Jeskin droned on. Furdd was texting now. Houck had fallen asleep. The others might as well have been carved out of wax.

After, in his grey-walled cubicle with its letter-box Plexiglas window, he sat stewing. *Is it time?* he thought. *Have I had enough?* He stood and looked around the warren of cubicles. He couldn't see anyone. All he could hear was typing, the occasional throat-clearing or sigh.

Is it time? It was time. He'd had enough. Enough humiliation, enough people talking to him as though he was a kid rather than a 55-year-old man. Enough evaluations with *needs improvement* on them. Every day before work and, horribly, all day every Sunday, he'd sit and fret, unable to do much of anything. Every weekday morning he'd choke down a single hard-boiled egg and half a cup of coffee. His shoulders were perpetually stuck in a hunched position, anticipating the next humiliation.

Recently he'd looked around his house on a worry-fraught Sunday evening, and considered how illusory it all was, how all of it—his life, his existence in this space, everything from his rent to his car payments—depended not only on the caprice of that dense bully at the conference table, but ultimately on some men he'd never met, nor would he ever meet, men in some distant high rise, men who were set for life, men who never had to worry that their walls would dissolve, that their marble floors would drop out from under them, that they'd have to wear out their welcome on some relative's couch and use their computer to navigate the dark, deep waters of job search sites and agencies that wasted your time with an interview and filed your carefully filled-in paperwork in a drawer where it would rot for as long as the agency lasted, unconsulted, forgotten.

Now, at his desk, his temporary, rented desk, as impersonal as a hotel room, he pulled the paw from his pocket and glanced down at the USB port on the tower of his computer. A curious greenish light emanated from the port…and from the stump of the thing's wrist.

Then came the sound of Houck clearing his throat, like jagged rocks scraped against a brick wall. Turcotte shoved the paw back into his pocket and turned around. Houck was standing in the doorway, arms crossed, a parody of a grin splitting his face, flakes of dried skin bracketing his mouth.

"Well, *that* was fun," he said.

"Yeah, a hoot and a half."

"Here's my problem with all this," Houck said, his eyes twinkling with merriment without losing his characteristic look of deep, abiding sadness. "Mount Everest and a pile of dog shit both come to a point at the top. But the dog shit is still dog shit."

"What is that supposed to mean?"

Houck shrugged, tightened his tie. "I have no idea," he said. "Something I heard somewhere. It felt somehow appropriate."

Then he shrugged and said, "So, lunch?"

***

Turcotte had bought the paw at an outdoor flea market. His 17-year-old son David dragged him there to accompany him on his weekly search for vinyl rarities and curious décor. David was a sensitive kid, a reader, bright but self-conscious. He messed around with illustrating, seemed to have a knack for drawing unique cartoon characters with angular jaws and scrunched-up eyes, and Turcotte wished his son would pursue art as a career; maybe the kid could avoid cubicles, office politics, punishing lighting, office gossips and snitches. On the other hand, Turcotte wanted David to have the stability and safety afforded by a 9-to-5 job. The two thoughts often arm-wrestled in Turcotte's tired head.

The flea market was hemmed in on three sides by sagging, disused barns and trisected by dirt paths worn in from five decades of foot traffic. At both sides of every path, crowded tables chock full of this-and-that sat under canopies, manned mostly by older men in too-small t-shirts with facial hair in every conceivable formation, wives and children with them, either lounging in lawn chairs or playing in the dirt. Turcotte had on his grey sweats and red Crocs over tube socks, his typical weekend and day-off attire. As the cold of the October morning burned off, the sun beat down and the temperature rose gradually. By noon it was 85 degrees and cloudless. Turcotte's back was soaked and he kept having to wipe the sweat from his brow with the back of his hand. David, by contrast, had worn cargo shorts and a white tee. The denim jacket he'd worn on the ride in he threw in one of his canvas shopping bags as the shadows retreated.

Limping along behind David, whose bags now bulged with merchandise, he almost passed by the pickup truck whose presumed owner sat like a proud king in a frayed and rusted lawn chair up by the cab. The man wore navy blue coveralls, dirt-crusted black boots, and an ancient ball cap whose faded logo barely stained an oval white patch on its front. His glasses were huge on his square Yankee face and the wiry hair that sprouted from under the cap like grass shone blindingly white. His eyes were squeezed shut, one leg bent under the chair, the other stretched out. An open can of mixed nuts sat between his legs.

The bed was otherwise full of junk from cab to lowered tailgate: a cluster of dolls, all in various stages of deterioration and decay; pristine antique beer cans in a plastic tub; movie monster action figures with loose limbs and flaked colors; black plastic flies with translucent wings; milk crates full of tattered copies of Penthouse, Playboy, and Taboo; an umbrella stand stuffed with gnarled walking sticks, bayonets, samurai swords, crossbows, and battle knives.

The paw lay in a velvet-lined ring box at the outer edge of the tailgate at the corner where Turcotte stood. It was curled loosely into a fist. The light-brown fur stood in clumps.

"What kind of animal is this from?" Turcotte asked the dozing man, whose eyes and mouth sprang open. Both his eyes and, curiously, his tongue and teeth, were blue, the latter just slightly lighter in color than that of Bullet, his childhood pet, an agreeable and playful Chow Chow.

"Ah," the old man said, proceeding with what seemed to Turcotte like a memorized spiel in a purposefully exaggerated New England accent. "It's neither monkey nor ape, Kobold nor Clurichaun, not trowe, not faery. No sir, this was as New England a creature as you'd know. Straight from the forests of Leeds and Huntington. Don't got a name that I know of. Don't need one. That's how rare this little fella is."

"No, but really," said Turcotte.

The man put a pink hand white with dead skin up to his chest. "Hand to God," he said."

"How did you get it?"

"Pappy was a trance medium out to Montgomery. Born in Hubbardston, worked the market there as a boy. Moved out this way at twenty to join the spiritualists in Leeds. One November in his later years, he found the little beastie in his skunk trap. Surprised the hell out the old man. He freed the little fella and told him to scoot, but he stuck around, he did. Slept on a blanket by the wood stove. Ate people food, not much of it either, so there were not much at all in the way of cost. Drank water. Pissed outside, never in. Never got sick, never saw a veterinarian. Did some trickery and some *diablerie*." He wiped his hand across his brow. "Changed the history of a few towns," he added somewhat ominously, squinting up into the haze-blurred sun.

Turcotte knelt, his knees popping, and peered in at the thing. The six miniscule paw pads were rose-colored, the fur a darker brown at the roots, the claws tiny off-white needles. At its wrist a triad of wire-thin bones protruded from the red-brown muscle, which looked as though at had been cauterized long ago. The odor of burnt bologna wafted up. It seemed to vibrate in its case. He reached out to touch it.

"No touchy," snapped the old man.

No touchy?

"How much, then?"

"He...or she...passed on three years after Pappy passed on to the other realms. Was in my care since then. Got into some astringent and died ugly. Who knows how long it'd of lived? Who knows? t's hard to let any part of it go." Incredibly, the man's voice had started to hitch and eyes filled with tears.

What do you want for it? A hundred?

The man looked aghast. "This is a flea market, sir. Anyone charging exorbitant rates for so-called antiques is a huckster and a fraud. Me, I'd rather take something in trade."

This puzzled Turcotte. *Changed the history of a few towns.* "In...trade? What does it...does it...do anything?"

"Come closer," the man said.

"Dad, what happened to your finger?"

The car felt small under the tall trees of the road back to town. Turcotte had hoped David wouldn't notice the bit of gauze taped around the tip of his ring finger, the little spot of brown blood on it. "Just cut myself on the edge of at that last vendor's tailgate."

"You need to get some Bactracin on that—the filth of those places. Jesus, Dad. That's the last thing I need...to lose you to a goddamned staph infection!"

"So, what are you going to do?" Houck said through a mouthful of pastrami and brown mustard.

Turcotte shrugged. The plate before him was empty but for a splotch of hamburger grease, a couple of thin, not-worth-it fries, and a sprig of parsley curled up like a corpse. He barely remembered eating. "I should quit before they fire me," he said. "They're going to fire me. I know they're going to fire me. Oh, Christ."

His voice broke. The paw flexed slowly in his pocket.

"How do you know, though?" said Houck. "They're kind of shitty to everyone. It's like they never heard of positive reinforcement. They try to use intimidation as a motivator. Not smart. And they put *way* too much emotion into all this. It really is their lives. Like, the *whole* of their lives. You'd think a mistake or a misjudgment on your part is somehow an assault on their identity, that's how much ego they have tied up in this shit."

"I don't know," Turcotte said. "I think Jeskin is a bully. He's *proud* of it. Of his bullying. It's disgusting."

He shook his head. A pall of silence fell over the table. Houck filled it by sipping the dregs of his Pepsi noisily through his straw.

"You know," Turcotte said, "it'd almost be worse if they *didn't* fire me. If they fired me, I could collect unemployment for a while, consider my options. But…if they do fire me, I have to endure the whole shitty process. Humiliating meetings that go on and on. And if they aren't going to fire me, they're probably trying to make things so unbearably shitty that I quit. And no unemployment then. Oh, god, I'm babbling. Tell me to stop babbling."

Houck chuckled. "You're fine," he said, but he wasn't very convincing. Turcotte could tell he'd gotten bored with the conversation.

***

When Turcotte got home from the flea market, he sat the boxed paw on the kitchen table next to his plate to keep him company while he ate. He kept it next to him on the couch while he watched television and later brought it to his nightstand so he could continue to be near it. He couldn't get to sleep. Restless, unable to decelerate his racing thoughts, he stared up into darkness.

Finally, he turned on the light and opened the box. The paw sat palm-up, fingers slightly bent. It trembled slightly. A sound emanated from it, soft and comforting, like a cat's purring. Turcotte held the box on his lap until his eyelids felt heavy. He placed the box next to his alarm clock and fell away to sleep.

In the morning he pushed himself up into a seated position and looked at the box. It was empty. A few brown hairs rested on the velvet. *Where...?* He went through the bedspread and covers, increasingly frantic, flinging the comforter off the bed and shaking out the sheet. *Not there. Not there!* He looked in the open nightstand drawer. Nothing. Gone! As he headed in a near-jog down the hall, vertigo hit him like a massive fist, accompanied by dull nausea and a throbbing behind his eyes; ahead, the light in the doorway strobed slowly, getting faster, faster, still faster. The computer, which he'd shut down, was now on. The widescreen monitor was blinking grey, black, white. Red symbols appeared at the top left corner of the screen and spilled across and down, filling the monitor, scrolling like the red-lit words on the marquee on the front of Radio City Music Hall. They looked like a cross between the letters of the alphabet and strangely limbed alien bugs. *Space Invaders*, Turcotte thought. *But smaller.* In the lower corner of his vision, he sensed movement. He looked down. The paw's wrist jutted from the USB port, the tiny fingers wriggling in a mad blur.

He looked back at the screen. It hit him that this was a *language*. The arrangements of the characters had now separated into clusters, some long, some short, punctuated by strange almost-asterisks and small, curious shapes. But what did it mean? The nausea faded and a strange elation set in. Absently he pulled back the chair and sat. He watched. The characters slowed, changed shape. They scrolled, stopped, scrolled again. A strange hum filled Turcotte's ears. The hum slowed, separated into curious sounds. Then into words that aligned with the clusters on the screen, words that started out unintelligible, but gradually started to align with ideas.

The monitor's frame creaked and buckled, forming a strange, cloud-like shape. The tower crumpled like rotten fruit. The white-lit letters on the keyboard transformed into the strange symbols from the screen. He touched them and they made his fingers tingle. Slowly at first, then faster, he let his fingers move across the keyboard like agile dancers. He was learning to write all over again, and the excitement of learning gripped him in a way it had not done since college. Sometimes he typed; sometimes his fingers moved of their own volition. Typing out revelations, ideas. Each was like a small explosion in his brain, forging new neural pathways, sparking previously unthinkable connections. The world split into oblong cells, gelatinous and pulsing, the strange letters of that impossible alphabet jumping from each to each and in all directions like crazed cats. Was this all coming from the paw? From God? From Turcotte himself? These questions swept into his mind and then dissolved. It didn't matter. Faces rolled in a swirling red mist before him. Revelations, ideas...plans. Sounds popped in the air; fluttering exclamations, half-heard voices shouting out strange syllables. The sound of squelching electricity, of exploding flesh, of bones twisting like earphone cords. Drool formed at the corners of his mouth, then dangled and swayed. His fingers tingled. His eyes swam in their sockets.

***

Tuesday morning. Tuesday was always the worst day. It didn't have the cultural anti-cachet of the dreaded *Monday*, and it didn't have the midweek, halfway-there feeling of a Wednesday. Dizziness. Vertigo. He hadn't showered. He could smell himself. Houck was out for the day. That was best. The paw thrummed in his pocket. The USB port glowed red. He felt heat coming from it, heat coming from his pocket. A buzz sounded in his head.

Now, he yanked the paw from his pocket and went to jam it into the USB port. It wouldn't go. He pushed and twisted, gently, wary of the delicate bones. Then he flipped the paw to palm-side up. It slid in like it was designed to do so.

The screen blinked. The strange alphabet blossomed on the screen. The monitor and the tower changed, then the keys, just like at home. *Just like in rehearsal.* He began to type, hesitantly at first, then with confidence, then bravura, like a manic piano player, his hands jumping and landing, jumping and landing, fingers moving like piano hammers. The fluorescent lights flickered. From somewhere down the hall the fire alarm bleated once, then emitted a strange, wavering electronic groan.

Down the hall Jeskin rose from his desk—the fire alarm!—then paused. Silence. *Okay, must have been a glitch.* The wind kicked up outside. An errant leaf rolled along the window like a kid tumbling down a hill. A car alarm sounded, then another. *Hm. Storm.*

Jeskin sat back down and resumed typing. Then the tip of his middle finger stuck to the K. *Hm.* He tried to pull it free, and the skin stretched. *Itchy.* The itch morphed into pain, then into agony. Below the knuckle his finger swelled into a purple globe. Then it burst, muscle and bone transformed in an instant to scraps and shards.

Jeskin stood, but something was wrong, a heaviness, a drag –the chair had fused to his pants. He stared down stupidly at the severed tip of his finger, still stuck to the keyboard, a shorn bone sticking out like a smaller finger pointing back at him.

He put his hands on the arms of the chair to prise the chair away, but it was stuck fast. He strained, pushed hard, grimacing … and something in his gut burst. It felt like the hernia he'd suffered while moving house a few years ago, but this time the pull was followed by what felt like a great complex movement all through his body, a chaotic migration of liquids and solids pushing their way in all directions around and amongst his organs and muscles, shoving them aside as though impatient. There was a crack like a tree breaking in a storm, a jolt of agony, and Jeskin stared stupidly down as a rib sprung from his body, having sliced through flesh and fabric, knocking his tie askew. Black liquid spurted out from the wound. It hit the wall in a concentrated stream, boring a hole right through. Through the widening hole Jeskin spied Barker sitting at his desk in his adjacent office, head turned in Jeskin's direction, staring in horror. The hole widened, the paint reverting to liquid form, the wall crumbling to dust, girders twisting like rope and falling from view. Fat blisters formed on Jeskin's skin, translucent bubbles that distended as blood and fatty fluids squelched out into them from his body. He screamed and blood filled his throat.

Festooned with those sloshing, gory balloons, he pushed his way through the door and into the hall, where people started and stopped and turned to flee at the sight of him.

***

Down the hall, Furdd stared at the spreadsheet splashed across his screen. He thought he'd been spared this task when the fire alarm had blurted, but nope. No fire. Just this stupid, all-encompassing grid. The numbers had lost all meaning, the formulas turned to alphanumeric gibberish. A wave of exhaustion washed over him. More coffee. Yes. That's what he needed. He rarely had a second cup, but if there ever was a day to do so, it was today. Looking stormy out. A cold front. Even the bulk so-called coffee the office bought would suffice at this point. It wasn't his beloved Dunkin', but there was no time to run out and buy a cup.

He turned back to see the spreadsheet trembling as though caught in some kind of electronic earthquake. The borders bent and jerked and wavered like EKGs, the data trembled in their cells. Cells bulged at random. The numbers that populated the cells sank below their lower borders, leaving them empty. Now, this was a glitch he'd never heard of...or some bizarre virus? He hadn't even saved the damned thing in how long? At least two, three ... he glanced at the clock in the bottom right corner, but it had disappeared. There was just blank space there—a void.

Into each cell of the spreadsheet a digital, animated animal face rose, replacing all the numbers, all the meticulously entered data. Little yellow pixel-teeth, flaring nostrils, strobing red eyes, fur whose yellow lines twitched back and forth as though in a high wind. Furdd rolled the chair away until its back touched the window.

Throughout the office, the ceiling-speakers squealed and shrieked through a miasma of static. Then came the frantic voice of Pearl, the receptionist, distorted by feedback and squelching sounds: *Everyone* please *shut down your computers immediately! Right now! Right now! We have a virus…situation! Unplug them! Quickly! Qui-"* and her voice was cut off by a roar of static. Her voice continued behind it, the words lost in the cacophony.

The little creatures were more than just faces now. Their little bodies hoisted themselves up into the spreadsheet cells and they poked tiny fingers out at the screen until its surface blistered.

The blisters popped, emitting the acrid odor of frying circuits and melting plastic, and the creatures pushed their way out through the smoking apertures, falling onto the desk blotter, tiny and grotesque, pale, covered in spiky fur. The first one out skittered across the desk and up into the framed picture of Furdd's wife and son smiling with their white colonial house in the background. More piled in, scattering across the lawn as the picture came to life. Clouds jerked free from their stasis and sailed eastward. Chad's arm tightened around Marilyn's shoulders. The pair looked down in horror as three of the creatures climbed up Chad's leg. His image put up its hands, mouth and eyes growing wide with terror as the things burrowed into his body. Marilyn started batting at her legs and her right femur snapped like a toothpick, her knee buckling, spilling her out of frame. Blood welled up at the bottom of the picture frame and poured out onto the desk as all the lights in the office sputtered and sparked and strobed.

Screaming sounded in the hall and Jeskin stumbled in, clothing in tatters, strange red-purple bags swaying from his flesh. Blue light blinked in his mouth.

Furdd screamed as the lights in the office went out, turning everything blue grey. Rain lashed the windows. Jeskin's bulging blisters burst, spilling gore onto the carpet. He bellowed wetly. Furdd shrieked. It was almost harmonious. Sirens matched Furdd's pitch. Oh, the demoniac chorus. Oh, the sweet, sweet sounds of pandemonium.

The fire alarm joined the chorus. Screams like emotive wordless solos bounced around the building. The floors trembled and cracked. At his desk, Turcotte sat dead, his hair standing up, his head jouncing as the floor rippled, bouncing and jouncing his chair. The paw had caught fire and burnt; now it was just a blasted, blackened twig dangling from the USB port.

Outside, the tinted windows revealed nothing more than a slight flicker. Business continued as usual at the other offices in the business park. Keyboards clacked. Copiers hummed. Coffee dripped into carafes. Cars rushed by.

Somewhere in the woods, small creatures unknown to most of mankind chittered and shook and gestured obscurely with red-glowing hands at the stained, splotched moon.

Help Me Please I'm Scared

I was in the grip of a terrible mortal panic when I left the meeting. I had to squeeze past the client, duck my aghast supervisor as he began to rise. I at first tried to push, rather than pull, the door, cursing and making a racket. I don't care how it looked now, but at the time, even in my wretched state, I knew I had just thrown my job away like so much refuse and I was in a frenzy of despair and upset.

The office had two kinds of restrooms, the kind with three stalls and urinals and sinks, and the kind which are small private rooms with one toilet and one sink. The latter were farther away from the conference room, and more likely to be occupied, but if anything called for privacy, it was this.

The pain in my navel had begun as a small uncomfortable feeling, a pinch too deep to reach. I'd stuck in the tip of my pinky finger and drew it back to find a red bubble of blood on the nail. Then I dabbed at it with a cotton swab. This time the blood dot was miniscule. The uncomfortable pinching feeling subsided. It was over, I figured.

That night, pain gripped my midsection, like a knitting needle had been stabbed into my navel. The green glow of the alarm clock read 2 a.m. Groaning, I slipped from bed, careful not to wake Emily, and walked, hunched over, to the bathroom. My navel had swollen – a thick bulb of purple flesh protruded, about an inch long. It was covered in fine, downy white fur. I touched it and it retracted as if stung. It was gone. Everything looked normal again. My heart hammering, I retreated to bed. I mentioned nothing to Emily, but I remained awake for the remainder of the morning, alert for any odd sensation or discomfort.

The pain bounced around my midsection. A dull ache was punctuated by jolts of stabbing, bright white flashes. In the privacy of the small restroom, I lifted my shirt. The fat of my belly had gone purple-black. The flesh looked like off-brand cellophane - fragile and thin, like a touch of a fingernail might cause it to burst or deflate or…God help me…*leak*. I let my shirt drop gently. I took a deep breath. And I exited. I hurried down the hall, head down, avoiding conversation with any coworkers whose paths I crossed.

Now I'm sitting in my car. My belly is swollen up so bad I can't get out… It's wedged under the steering wheel, spilling over so that it's pressed up against the door handle and lock. My shirt is torn. I must look like a thin man wedged into the hole of a giant powdered donut. People are walking by, leaving work for the day. They glance into my car and look away quickly.

I've managed to grab my phone from my pocket. I'm about to dial 911 when a piercing pain jolts my midsection and a fat hand shoots out from my navel with a horrific squelching sound, spilling wetness that I hope isn't blood into my groin and down my legs. It grabs my phone away. The small finger taps on the screen, opening the notes app. I try to reach down and wrestle it away, but my arms are paralyzed at my sides. The little hand pushes itself further away until it's by the windshield, out of my reach. It types out

The Blood-Gargling Mimes of Hatchet Pass

The Leeds Sidewalk Sale is in full flourish, the broad walk jammed with shoppers toting bags by the hand-and-armful. Along the curb stand kiosks of pottery and trinkets, clothing, shoes, and restaurant setups with trays of steaming soups and pizza slices and fried rice. Racks of dresses undulate in the breeze like a colorfully attired line of dancers. Shoppers flip through racks of DVDs and CDs, pulling out the slim packages and piling them up to purchase. Slim, limber theater actors in leotards weave throughout the crowd, mugging and prancing and reacting with exaggerated gasps to the kids and the moms and the dads and the breezes and the little white dogs on long brown leashes. The lights change. The walk signal bleats. People fill the crosswalks, drinking from coffee cups, eating food from cardboard containers.

The killing doesn't register with the crowd at first. One of the actors, a man with a greasepaint-white face, crouches in the street over what at first appears to be a large doll in a blue dress. It appears as though the man, clad in a black leotard, is pulling a series of knife blades from the doll, some kind of curious magic act akin to pulling quarters from behind a child's ear. An arc of blood shoots up, a living candy cane without the white parts. The crowd parts to accommodate the bit of theater, streaming around, conversing excitedly, red-cheeked and merry.

Finally, a blonde in a puffy vest over a grey top glances down and stops cold. She shrieks. The crowd goes silent, the quiet spreading from the scene outward, ripples in a pond, layers of an onion, silence supplanting sound. Mirroring that silence, a puddle spreads from under the doll. Ripple, ripple, run, run.

The little lit-up green Walking Man has disappeared. Under where he stood is a red Standing Man. The streetlights turn green in the eastbound and westbound lanes. But the cars don't go. The drivers sit, their faces frozen agape behind their windshields. Behind them, other drivers test their car horns.

Over the din sounds a keening, like that of a hysterical cicada, thrumming, shaking the street. Doors tremble in their casements. Glass shimmers. Ice cream melts, painting hands and wrists in sugary stickiness. Ripple run, ripple run, what fun, what fun until we're done. The mime lifts the girl up, she's dripping, spilling, pouring now. He clamps his mouth over her throat. The sound of chewing is loud and fervent. It goes on for a long time, his adam's apple bouncing like a ball, then he drops her, the body splitting nearly in two, the white-faced man opening his mouth wide to reveal a line of white fangs. Rivulets of blood pour down his chin, then turn his neck into a thick red and white peppermint. It separates into discs. You can almost taste them, taste them waste them all on the street and at the mall a placid pall a magic thrall.

The mime's head spins counterclockwise atop the pile of clockwise-spinning peppermint discs. He gargles, a septic sounding burble. The crowd, held rapt, applauds. Someone whistles shrilly. A young woman whoops. Shoppers resume shopping. Pedestrians resume pedestrianing.

The crowd moves on, except for the dead girl and a man and woman we presume are the parents. The woman is wearing an elegant brown coat over a grey wool dress, the man a suit and tie. But who cares? Cars start moving again, swerving to avoid the mournful tableau. The noise of a busy afternoon resumes.

The police ride in on bicycles. Some shoo away the remaining looky-loos. Others lead away the parents. Still others erect orange DETOUR signs. Coroners in dead-coyote masks scoop up the remains with a large, curved snow shovel as DOT workers in googly-eye goggles use translucent orange squirt guns to wash the blood into the sewer grates. They whistle as they work. All of their faces are very white.

Hatcher Street is the official name of the street, but we call it Hatchet Pass. Pass the hatchet, pack of matches, pile of ashes. Merry be, minuets and masques, bask, bask, bask. Ripple ripple run-dee-run-dee-run-what-fun-what-fun. But that's not what happened, at least not in my slinky, stinky dreams. We killed them all and crouched among their remains, our heads upturned, the chorus of ululations pleased the black-clad, white-faced God, and he shone his sunshine upon us until our faces leaked white and mixed with the x of bloody rivers that once was a paved intersection.

And I read what he wrote, trapped, as I am, under my steering wheel, and I wonder from whence it all came. My belly continues to swell, as does my chest, almost subsuming the arm. My hand drops my phone down on the dash. The car starts rolling. I can't control it. It exits the lot, cresting a curb, then runs over a patch of lawn and continues down Long Hill Road. I still can't control it. I can't even enjoy it. For the pain is overwhelming. The hand lunges, its arm feeling like a distended intestine shooting from my midsection, and it turns on the radio and I hear a pleasant, paternal voice saying

Uncle Red Reads To-Day's News

A spokesman for King Street Market reports that Henry Wafflesworth, assistant manager of the popular locally owned grocery store, attempted, against store policy, which he had read and in fact signed his name to, to grab the neck of a shoplifter who had secreted two issues of the Oprah magazine under his shirt. Mr. Wafflesworth, disputing management, claims to have grabbed at the hood of the alleged thief's sweatshirt, which, he claims, turns out to have been a loose swatch of flesh attached to his absconding body. Both the spokesman and the assistant manager agree that the young man's neck sprung from his body in a long coiling rope and that the would-be shoplifter grinned wickedly as his head lashed this way and that, and that it leveled at them scurrilous and untrue allegations that could be classified as slanderous and that believed or not by bystanders cast a stain upon the reputations and standing in the community of the aforementioned spokesman and assistant manager. The hoodlum could not be reached for comment, as he is reported to have secreted a noxious chemical that rendered him slippery and ungraspable, and then escaped into the night, his head trailing him, facing rearwards, mocking and taunting his deeply alarmed pursuers.

The Tele-Health Call

Dennis sat at the computer staring at his own image in miniature, trapped in a letterbox-shaped window in the center of his monitor, slouched, his bookshelves filling the space behind him, providing him an intellectual-looking backdrop that he liked, but the face, one he barely acknowledged as his own, stared slightly off-screen looking drawn, tired. Grey bags under the eyes, two chins, a pink rubber tire of a neck on which his head sat uncomfortably. A red spot next to his mouth where he'd popped a whitehead. Red splotches on his cheeks. The background behind the telehealth window was his carefully selected wallpaper – the outer curve of an island lousy with palm trees, adjacent to an ocean the color of lapis, all of it under a bellflower-blue sky with trenches of white clouds diminishing in the distance.

An electronic *blorp* sounded and his image mercifully shrank and flew down to the bottom left, replaced by the reassuring image of Doctor Timothy Paul, a dark-haired man with a full face and a kindly expression. The doctor appeared to be standing awkwardly in the center of a sparsely decorated but professional looking office, next to a few leaves from an off-camera fern; a few yards behind him a grey wall bare except for a framed certificate of some kind and a standard wall clock.

Mike from work had recommended Dr. Paul, even though the doctor was in North Carolina, where Mark had lived until he was fifteen, almost 800 miles away from Leeds. That distance was a good thing. Dennis didn't trust a soul within transmitting distance of WXXT. Not since Dr. Alespiller had scared him half to death.

And the additional miles were a comforting buffer.

"Good morning, Mr. Fearn," the doctor said in a gruff voice, mitigated by a warm smile.

"Good morning, Doctor."

The doctor's smile tightened. He scratched his scalp. "I have to confess," he said. "I don't have any particular issue with why you've chosen to contact me, but surely there are doctors in your area who…"

Dennis' mind bounced like a grey pinball around the walls of his skull. The black flower of nausea bloomed in his gut. This doctor was going to reject him, was going to refuse to see him. Oh, this was a mistake. Maybe … maybe this guy knew Dr. Alespiller. Met him at some godforsaken witch doctor conference in some creepy hotel. He was doomed. "Nope. No. just no. No way. I'm not going to any doctors here. I'm sorry to have wasted your time."

"No, no, that's fine, Mr. Fearn, I didn't mean to upset you. Your insurance will cover this visit, and I am clear of other appointments for the rest of the afternoon. I have the time. I was just curious. Of course I'm happy to talk with you."

Dennis wiped his brow with his sleeve. It was going to be okay. It might be okay. Just maybe. "Good," he said. "That's…that's good."

"Why don't you tell me what the issue is and I'll do my best to help?"

"I have these aches in my arms, doctor. Sometimes my left arm feels tight, like someone's squeezing it. I know I'm going to have a heart attack. I know it."

"Is there any history of heart disease in your family?"

"Well, there's not, but I heard that when your arm hurts…"

"Well, I mean, that *could* be strain, something musculoskeletal…I can suggest some exercises you can do at home, but…I'm guessing there are other things bothering you as well?"

"I get this rash," Dennis said quickly, as though fearing the doctor would interrupt him. "I used to get it when I was a kid, and now I'm getting it again. It's in my armpits and they get all bright red and nothing helps…"

"Mr. Fearn, I'm going to interrupt you for just a moment. Are you under stress at work?"

"Well, I mean, yeah, there's this new boss, and she doesn't like the way I do things, and she has this German accent and she's very tall and a micromanager and I've tried to explain to her that I inherited this stuff, these procedures, I didn't, like, *make them up*, but still she treats me like I'm some kind of…"

The doctor let him run on for a while, nodding politely, then he broke in. "All of this sounds like physical manifestations of stress to me, Mr. Fearn. Pretty basic stuff. I can recommend a therapist to discuss strategies for dealing with your supervisor, someone local to me. In the meantime, did your doctor suggest any breathing techniques? I've found these can really…"

As the doctor went on, Dennis sank in his chair. Dr. Alespiller hadn't said anything about breathing At least not that he remembered. He let Dr. Paul finish talking, which seemed to take hours. When the doctor finally trailed off, clearly aware that Dennis hadn't been listening, the latter began to speak, just letting it all come out, the parts he was clear on, anyway.

***

The doctor's new receptionist – she'd introduced herself as something like "Sniffle"—had called to inform Dennis that his regular doctor had broken his leg in a skiing accident and, being already within half a year of retirement, had canceled all further appointments. She said that instead Dennis would be seeing this "Alespiller" instead, and at that doctor's home office rather than the Medical Center.

The office was out on a long desolate road that eventually led, if drivers had the fortitude and the patience, to Westhampton, where people went from, not to. Houses were fewer and farther apart and were set farther back from the road the closer Dennis got to his destination, and the forest crowded in on both sides; untrimmed, the foliage covered about half the width of each lane and blotted out the sun above until it seemed like dusk.

A medium-sized rabbit's hop from the Westhampton town line stood what Dennis took to be the doctor's home, a two-story mustard yellow affair with three dormers and a dark green door. On one of two stone stanchions on either side of an open iron gate a sign directed visitors to park behind the house. Dennis pulled around to find a small, weedy, shrub-lined lot adjacent to a two-car garage that matched the house in color.

The doctor waved with alacrity to Dennis from a small deck at the top of a set of exterior stairs that led to the structure's second floor. His hair hung long and stringy and white, framing a gaunt, unshaven face. He wore a tweed coat over a blue shirt and grey wrinkled Chinos. He was, Dennis noted with some alarm, barefoot. A stethoscope that looked fake, plastic, overly large, rested around his neck. The only reason Dennis didn't immediately turn around and leave was an accursed congenital politeness that made "no" the most unthinkable curse word imaginable.

Dennis climbed the stairs, huffing and puffing, his arm aching, his pits itching. The doctor held the door open for him and he walked into a small office with a braided rug upon which sat an examination table, a small desk with a laptop and a printer and multi-line phone in the far corner adjacent to a small, squat door.

The doctor closed the outside door, turned the deadbolt, then pulled and fashioned the brass chain lock. He hit a wall switch and the lights turned from white to green. What happened next in Dennis's memory comes in flashes, darkness washing like ink over one scene as it ends and blowing away like dust at the start of each new one.

The doctor blowing up and twisting some kind of bizarre balloon animal, his cheeks grotesque furrowed blue bladders inflating and deflating, as a saxophone rasped and emoted and wheedled from the speaker of a small radio.

Framed black & white photographs on the wall of elderly men, bent over, their buttocks being spread apart by their own heavily-veined, liver-spotted hands, revealing bulging pustules and inflamed spinnakers and curlicues and boils and curious hard-to-identify protuberances of varying lengths, shapes, and sizes.

The doctor, naked save his toy stethoscope, thin and moon-white, his clothing puddled at his feet, the base of his long, thin red schlong held in a tight fist, the rest of the hideous thing swinging in circles, making a fleshy whooshing sound, a demented Daltrey bereft of his bandmates.

A buzzing microphone descending from the ceiling like a fat black bug with dangling legs and translucent wings and wriggling antennae, and the doctor speaking into its puckered meatus, begging Dennis to interview him about his "fall from grace with Ben and the boys" so that he could "elucidate his vast and succulent listening audience."

The microphone shooting into Dennis's own mouth, stretching his lips, the taste of char and pungent cuticle assaulting his senses, breathing wildly through his nose as he involuntary performed something of Irish step dance across the floor, batting at his face.

The radio melting onto its shelf, a slew of pale white crabs spilling from a widening hole in its crumpled speaker.

***

The next thing he knew, he was stumbling down the stairs. The temperature had dropped. His legs were freezing. His pants flew out the side window like a great chaotic bird, pocket change raining down on the parking lot. His underwear followed, a white billowing flag with a shameful yellow emblem.

His car was gone. He stumbled out on the road. A red convertible full of teenage girls screeched to a halt; they were pointing at him and laughing. One of them, a redhead with pigtails, winked and beckoned him with a long, pretty finger. He stumbled forward, then saw his reflection in the driver's side back window. A crab had been crudely painted onto his pelvis, his genitalia in the center of its body like a grotesque nose.

The girls winked and flirted and teased and snickered. One lifted her shirt and bounced up and down in her seat. Somewhere behind Dennis, the doctor laughed and cackled and sang. Dennis felt his gorge rise. He knew he should turn away, fall to the ground, at least cover his mouth, but he was frozen in humiliation and shame. The girls snapped pictures with their phones and drove off. Dennis stumbled after them, weeping and gibbering.

He woke sprawled in his backyard, naked, his extremities numb. He was so sore. He dragged himself into the house and took a three-hour long shower.

Later, when he looked out his front window, he saw his car parked at a frantic angle in the driveway. He heard music playing faintly from the car stereo. It was Brahms.

**

Doctor Paul sat in silence. His mouth moved around, but no sound came out. Dennis slumped further into his chair, drained.

Finally, the doctor said in a small voice, "That must have been hard for you."

Dennis gulped a few times, and then let out a loud sob.

"That...that is unfortunate."

Dennis wailed.

The doctor raised his voice to be heard: "*I'm sorry that you had that EXPERIENCE.*"

Something in his voice sounded facile, sing-songy, almost cruel.

"What?"

"With the cra-a-a-a-abs...with the CRABS."

"Doctor?"

"WITH THE CRABS! WITH THE CRABS! CRABS! CRABS! CRABS? CRABS! CRABS! CRAAAAAAAAAAA..."

Dennis wiped his eyes. His mouth fell open. His heart rolled like drums. *THE CRABS!* Along one of the fern leaves, on the screen, a white crab ambled in sideways, black eyes on stalks, serrated claws open wide. *THE CRABS!* A few more sidled in after it. *THE CRABS!!!!* A crab the size of a housefly tumbled out of the doctor's ear and danced along his shoulder toward his arm.

"Of course," Doctor Paul said, as a small crowd of crabs descended from his nostrils and began to spread like a living beard across the lower half of his face, "Dr. Alespiller and I are colleagues. We met at a conference at the Supra-Seven motel in Holyoke. By then I guess he had already begun to lose his mind...to lose his *faculties*." As the doctor spoke, the skin on his forehead began to break out in small whiteheads. "That will happen when you break ranks, when you hijack the airwaves for your own agenda." The whiteheads grew legs and claws and detached themselves as they grew in size. A clump of the doctor's hair with his ear attached tumbled down his shoulder. Spiders poured from the side of his head like a casino jackpot.

"You don't just strike out on your own," the doctor said. "He's been sending me these cassettes…" A naked woman with long black hair strode by in the background, her arms full of cassette tapes in plastic cases. A few of them eluded her grasp and landed on the floor, clattering. The doctor's nose fell off and slid down his tie, leaving a triangular red hole out of which a rain of crabs poured—"…you really should give them a listen. They have…breathing…crabs…exercises…crab breathing. Cassettes…"

Dennis rolled back his chair in horror. His face itched. As he reached up to scratch his cheek the computer shut itself down with a low-pitched moan. Dennis just caught sight of his crab-covered reflection in the monitor's dark screen. Then the lights and the sun went out too, and all there was left was to feel.

Meet The DJs

Gus Funk II

Who's got the funk? The funk of forty-thousand beers? Why, Gus does. Gus the Bus with the hernia truss and the blood-struck blunderbuss. Gus the third with his sword and his bird.

Gus has been in trouble for showing the ladies his disco equipment, if you catch our funkified drift, but you can't—no you can*not*, mama--keep a funky man down. Besides, they signed releases in blood, the ladies did. They're in our files, the releases, not the ladies, probably under R. Our clerk can find them for you…or he can once he finds his skull. Someone stole it. We have our suspicions as to who the culprit is. We sent around a memo: stealing is wrong. If the thief returns the clerk's skull more or less as it was, he may not press charges.

But we digress.

Gus has a laffro and is stuck in a seven-decade slap-bass phase. He'll slap ya mama, he'll slap you silly, and he'll slap a flapjack onto your plate and a second one on top of the first if you want it. It's just the kind of guy he is. His soul is as black as the inside of a shut Bible. He has blood euphoria and pus-lust, and he gets into fistfights at the Fixin's Bar.

He used to be loved and now he loves to be used. Tuesdays at 8. WXXT: the home of the funk, the stank from the flank of the Pioneer Valley.

Don't Let the Fires of Redemption Burn Off all your Happy Memories

The Gazette's front page, above the fold, was largely taken up by the full color picture of the child choir's footprints in the snowy field, the one set of adult footprints alongside them.

The choir had been led at gunpoint to the barn, where they were forced to harmonize, to chant, to sing unfamiliar syllables as tribute to the thrashing, mewling, drooling thing lashed to the ceiling. The Sennheiser MKE 600 microphone dangled like a suicide by a rope tied to a derelict tractor's steering column and thrown over a splintery rafter, spinning slowly, capturing it all; after, the culprit or culprits had burned down the barn with the choir inside. The kids were full-throated then, if not before, this I can tell you. This I can tell you.

This I can tell you because I was there, standing in the field outside the barn, watching the smoke surge like a black bouquet of fists into the sky. I smelled the kerosene and the burning wood and fabric, and I smelled the roasting flesh. I inhaled it. It filled my lungs like smoky wine.

I was proud of my kids. They'd trained all year, thinking they were preparing for the end-of-year school recital. They were little angels now, goes one way of thinking. Not my way of thinking. My way of thinking says they were charred cadavers in pugilistic rigor, with calcined bones and withered organs. Sentient? *Conscious?* Fuck, I hope not.

***

In the summer of 1999, I began to experience auditory hallucinations. It might be a bellowing voice or a jarring chord struck on a pipe organ or a blurted one-syllable curse word. It always hurtled me back up into consciousness, my heart beating rapidly, interrogating the night as to the source of the sound.

This stopped with the onset of adolescence; it faded out as the pubes grew in.

Until the lockdown summer of 2020. I was still conducting choir practice via Zoom, while my wife, on furlough, was collecting unemployment and spending a lot of time in the garden.

One night after being demolished by an ill-advised series of shots of tequila and by "Scarf-Knitter Karl", a Words With Friends bot, I swore I heard my wife call me a "loser" as I was drifting off to sleep. Another time I heard a shriek of feedback along with one drum beat which echoed even as I came awake and tried to process what I'd heard. Another night it was a two-second chorus of car horns and goat yells.

Then it was just a voice saying *Exaltation and smoke*. Night after night, those three words, spoken just once in an insistent sibilant whisper. Finally, after a week of this, I woke up one winter night to find my wife sitting astride me, naked except for a large pair of mirrored glasses I'd never seen before on her, nor even in the house. I was as hard as a railroad tie, but she wasn't there for that.

Green light splashed across her bare chest just as a terrible agonizing pain seared through mine. In the reflection of the shades I saw that my chest had become a greenlit radio band, my nipples fat black dials bracketing it. She twisted one of the dials to the right, her eyebrow arching, and I shrieked in pain. She turned it back and forth in miniscule increments until music filled the bedroom.

It taught me a song, a terrible song, an obscene song. And it showed me the red cheeks of the faces of the Choir of Innocents, and their virgin eyes. It showed me their breath like white plumes from ordnance in the night, a 21-voice salute to a long-dead mystic. I pushed my wife off me and ran to the bathroom. A bent antenna was sticking out of the top of my head, whirling around like a finger testing the air. My navel opened its mouth to speak. The teeth. The tongue. Oh, the lips. It said three words. Its breath was pungent. I gagged, gulped, and passed out.

I began training the choir the very next day. The auditory hallucinations stopped. My wife remembered nothing. I fell into bed like a corpse every night and did not wake 'til the sun lit the curtains. I never saw the mirrored glasses again until they were fastened onto my head as I drove the school bus full of kids to the edge of the field that deadly flaming night.

Ecstasy. Exaltation. Transformation.

And smoke.

...And I'm Starting to Smell

It's the body odor, of course, from being trapped in one's car with one's swollen self. Also...have you ever extracted a bit of belly button lint and, before discarding it, given it a sniff? Now is the not the time to be shy, nor to pretend you're somehow something more than human.

You are base. When you are alone. You know it.

Okay, deny it all you want. If you really, truly haven't, then you may not know the smell that filled my car. If you have, well, you know.

I dry-heaved a few times. I really, really didn't want to vomit down my swollen front. Picturing the most disgusting waterfall imaginable didn't help, so I tried to turn my mind elsewhere.

Pain was happy to oblige. This was a new pain, throwing bolts through my midsection and chest, down into my legs and up into my arms, then concentrating back at my belly. I heard and felt my skin ripping. Agony and release. A second hand pushed its way out—I could just see it over the horizon of my gut, and it was followed by something I couldn't identify.

It was squared off, black, dripping with blood and other fluids. It was only when the brim appeared that I recognized what it was. I heard expectoration, then spitting. And then I heard singing. The words sounded vaguely Germanic, and the song had the pitch and tone and cadence of a lullaby. My consciousness fell down a dark well, but the voice stayed. It sang to me in blackness. The pinprick of consciousness that remained felt not scared but soothed. Loved. Cared for. And brothers and sisters and radio listeners, I loved it right back.

I woke up into a nightmare.

Cassettes (Part 4)

Michael took off the headphones. "That fuckin' *rocked*," he said.

"Did it?" said Cooperford.

"You haven't heard it?"

"Whaddaya think, I listen to everything that comes in here?"

"Well, this one you should."

"Did you listen to the end?"

Michael didn't know how to answer. "I…think so? I listened until the music ended."

"Then you didn't listen to the end."

"I thought you said you haven't heard it."

"Don't try to 'gotcha' me, kid. I know because the kid who sold it to me told me. But that's enough of a sample for you."

Michael put the cassette in his "to buy" pile, which now included each tape he'd listened to so far. "What else ya got?" he said.

Cooperford shrugged. Michael glanced at the door sign. "Oh shit, you were supposed to close, like, ten minutes ago. I'll pay for these and get out of your hair.

"Nah, man. Stay."

"But you're closed."

Again, Cooperford shrugged. "I got nowhere to be. I got a little microwave back here, and leftover ziti in the mini-fridge."

"Okay, but honestly, if you need to leave, let me know."

"Oh, I totally will."

The darkness took over. No lights shone outside the record shop, only blackness, as if someone had covered the glass door with black paint. No sounds of traffic could be heard. No car horns. Not even the sound of wind. The shop might as well have been floating somewhere in outer space.

Cooperford walked over to the wall of cassettes and pretended to scan them, to seek out the next tape to play for Michael. Of course, he already had the lineup solidified in his head. His plan was going quite well indeed. The only possible hiccup would come when Michael finally insisted on leaving. Then things would get hairy.

But the kid was in deep now; nothing could save him. Not his parents, not God, not a thousand horsemen wielding whips and swords, not a troupe of winged angels with AMP-69s and fragmentation grenades.

The kid already had the headphones on his ears, his finger on the Play button.

Cooperford grabbed the next cassette and closed it in. He winked at the kid and went to heat up his dinner. The kid hit Play.

WXXT April Events Calendar

April 1 – Outdoor Flea Market, featuring local vendors and farms: Dale's Trinkets and Baubles, Slaughton Farms and Forests, Stonearm's Powders and Pills, Jaundiced Jane's Curiously Shaped Stones. Antiques, curiosities, and more. From hands of glory to feet of derangement, from dumb waiters to ventriloquist dummies to mummified waitstaff. King and Bright Streets, before sunrise

April 9 – Botanical Gardens Midnight Tour – Family Night - Explore our magical gardens, meet nocturnal species. Arum lilies, blackthorn, lungwort stained with virgin tears, and many more plants that burn, sting, and stab. Pull Bryony from the ground and hear its screams.

April 15 – Tax Day

April 20 – Some sort of joke about marihuana

April 21 – Distinguished Speaker Series at Leeds High School: Crazy Michael, who went door-to-door selling twigs as a child and who had his later murder convictions overturned due to several technicalities after Anne Gare cast a Spell of Injustice and Fog.

April 31 – The day we keep in the large trunk of the Paddingcake Tree by Murder Pond in Look Park. No exit, no readmittance, no complaints.

Declan

Good morning, Leedsians. It's ten minutes past the top of the hour. The First Leeds Bank for the Insane has changed its hours today, but for the moment they refuse to release the specific opening and closing times to our reporters. More on this as the day wears on. We'll be looking at overcast skies for most of your Monday, but the sun should start peeking through in the mid-to-late afternoon.

What else is happening around Leeds, Declan?

Well, I don't want to step on Uncle Red's toes, in part because of the havoc his ragged, rough toenails would wreak on the soles of my brand-new shoes, but I can tell you a little bit about Colin Carver of Whickasaw Street, who was holding a book upright in his hand while his Cream of Wheat cooked. Well, the book slid, giving old Carver a papercut in his palm, and some words slid off the page and into his system.

What was the subject of the book?

It was a book about parasite-chology called *Not Much to Do After Dinner*. No, wait, it was a book entitled *Taxonomists of Obscenity* about prognatheism, the elaborate belief system held by a cult that worshipped two twin brothers with malformed jaws and a penchant for infanticide. Or else it was *The Twelve Red Men* about a shadow government run by sentient tachyons. Perhaps it was Pottle R. Snivelfoot's *Do Turtles Dream of Galloping*, a puerile fuckbook set in the wire skeleton of a greenhouse under a cat-claw moon.

What happened to the man?

He slept in spiderweb cellars and under the beds of the elderly and the infirm. He danced nude in the kitchens of spinsters. He drew elaborately obscene fantastical murals on the white boards of elementary school classrooms, causing homicidal madness in one kindergarten teacher and four students. Two policemen were killed trying to subdue them. One of the policemen was partially eaten by two of the students. He concocted a manifesto in which he insisted that medical school cadavers were engaged in psychic espionage. He stole two of them and stored them in a locked freezer. Not trusting the strength of the lock, and suspicious of the cadavers' ability to project their essences though the freezer walls at night, he put them in his queen-size bed and slept between them. He placed them face-down but always awoke to find them on their sides, staring at him. One day all three disappeared, though they are from time to time seen briefly in the hallways of houses when residents waken between two and three in the morning to use the bathroom.

And now Uncle Red has arrived. He looks peaked, perturbed, paternal, and, of course, avuncular. He appears to be ready to read to-day's news.

Uncle Red Reads To-Day's News

The winged things in the Saw Mill Hills frolic and depredate streets of Florence. Reports from residents of that quaint village indicate that the creatures are staining and smearing foul fluids on windows and causing deterioration of joists and frames, swarming around the apertures of chimneys whilst singing curious songs in upsetting harmonies and cadences, defecating surprisingly voluminous thin black faeces onto rooftops, felling horses, enveloping stray dogs, and riding the backs of goats like children on horses. Police are of little avail, their bullets as useless as wadded balls of bread, their nightsticks no stronger than drought-dried twigs. Those not assailed by the creatures are stricken by the strong odours of the latter's secretions.

Recently published and for sale at the bookstore of Anne Gare, a sermon, delivered at Leeds before the Hampshire Council of Cowls at their most recent monthly meeting, by Kline Peckstaine, Minister of the Church of One Thousand Eyes in Haydenville. Price, single, eleven and a half cents.

The removal of passengers and the concomitant delay of the train was made necessary on the Holyoke trolley line this evening when the unearthed and putrefying body of three-year-old Bruno Banks, four days missing from his newly dug grave, wandered onto the tracks, holding aloft by the tail a wriggling and twisting and screaming black squirrel. The deliquescing boy was subdued, immobilized, dismembered, and consumed by the conductor and the ticket-taker before the horrified eyes of passengers, who were subsequently whisked away by four black jitneys with dark windows to parts unknown. The squirrel is said to have escaped physically unharmed.

A newly formed hobby club in the area is the Bratton Court Sorcery Society which meets Tuesday nights at The Eleven House, formerly abandoned and condemned since immediately after the disturbance of 1931, the ghastly details of which need not be recounted here. Soundproofing and black window-shades will be installed at the insistence of many vexed and scandalized neighbors, though the police have ignored or deflected requests for more decisive measures such as the seizing of the property and dispersal of the unruly club-goers.

You might experience corrupted, inaccessible, or missing family members. You might not be able to annex your thoughts. You have suddenly become detached from your memories. You have lost control of your consciousness. The monkey cannot hear the organ grinder. The pus-clotted tide is loosed.

Died at Leeds, May 3, Mr. Isaac Ashman, aged 43 years, after an illness of about four weeks terminating in incessant agonies and difficulty in the acquisition of air, which he bore with (in the approximate order) strength of spirit, perverse merriment, Christian stoicism, gratitude to a merciful God, bafflement, pleas to the Devil for deliverance, uncommon composure, screeching, wheezing, blaspheming, gulping, farting, priapism, writhing, bellowing, frantic onanism, humming an indiscernible tune, scratching at the skin, and, finally, resignation to the Heavenly Will.

Boswell Strandier of Black Birch Lane was the winner of a life-size wooden demon given away at Aubrey's Toys & Distractions on May 1st. Several hundred tickets were handed out to shoppers and a crowd clamored around the store on Friday night. The winner is 33 years of age and a wheelwright of local renown. The demon, a hunched and winged figure, gives the appearance of lifelikeness in its adjustable joints and pulsing musculature, and whose, due to its intricate interior mechanisms, appears to raise and fall as though breathing air. The creature was designed by Robert Ross Lucas, who is a town recluse whose house stirs amongst the townsfolk unfortunate but surely baseless rumours.

The Leeds Detective Part 1: The Tears of Raindrops

Officers Miller, Mankowski, Billson, and Fearn milled about at the western end of the muddy hollow as squad cars, their blue lights flashing, pulled off the highway into the Scenic View lot above.

"Evidence," said Fearn, picking up a rain-soaked handkerchief and placing it in a plastic evidence pouch.

"Blood," said Billson, using his pinky finger to lift a delicate branch from which hung a red-stained leaf.

"Gonna start raining again." This was Mankowski, who caressed the rouged cheek of the dead girl as he stared up at the leaden sky.

Miller crouched by the girl's side, holding her cold hands in his warm ones. "Nothing under the nails," he said.

A few uniformed state cops came slowly and haltingly down the incline, arms out stiff. They looked like a formation of mustachioed airplanes taxiing down a dirt runway. Behind them ambled Detective Specter, one hand in the pocket of his double-breasted black peacoat, the other holding the handle of a sticker-spangled guitar case.

Under the peacoat Specter wore a white shirt greyed from overuse and suspenders holding up knit pants fresh from hamper of to-be-washed apparel. On his feet were a brand-new pair of light-brown Balenciaga hiking sneakers. His long black hair flew about his head, revealing a very pale bald spot. His eyes were inscrutable behind red-framed dark wayfarer sunglasses, but his unruly brows peeked over like nosey animals wakened from a deep sleep.

He departed the incline three-quarters of the way down and made his way over to the base of a massive tree. He sat on a varicose root and undid the rusted clasps of the guitar case as he surveyed the scene.

The guitar now in his lap, he plucked at the strings, his hand sliding along the fretboard, playing melancholy music, notes like the tears of raindrops if raindrops could cry. All around, water provided percussion as it dripped from leaves into puddles. A jet above aped a violin's mournful accompaniment. The deep-buried heart of the earth joined in on bass.

In an untrained but passionate voice, high and light, the detective sang:

How does a sapling grow
Through the belly of a murdered girl?
How does the sun bear such a sight
As it spins around the world

Why doesn't it just shut itself off
With a sigh of despair and…a…
ragged…cough…

Unhappy with his extemporaneous tune, he lowered the guitar. "Gloves!" he shouted, and everyone paused and looked up at him.

"Stop contaminating my motherfucking crime scene with your bare goddamned hands, you lamentable cretins!"

The men shrugged and pulled plastic gloves from their pockets. In near unison and with similar grimaces they pushed their fingers in and wriggled them. Fearn, bearded, gangly, still holding the not-yet-sealed evidence bag, split from the group and hitched his way up to stand at the detective's side.

"What do you think?" said Fearn.

Specter scratched his head. "I don't think. I know. it's the same perpetrator as last week's. It's the same M.O."

"How on earth is this the same M.O.?" Fearn had been the first officer to answer the call to the horror-show crime scene on Fennell Street. Seventeen middle-school-aged children bound hand-to-hand and lashed to the circumference of the above-ground swimming pool at the abandoned Crabman house, their heads bent over the top ledge, throats cut, the pool filled with their blood—too much blood, it was agreed—and poor drowned Ms. Langdon from Leeds Elementary not found until the police had drained the pool in the early hours of the following morning.

"The inexplicable" was Specter's reply. "Both times a puzzle. The extra blood, all, apparently, from the victims, but that wouldn't have been enough to fill the pool. That child down there, a tree grown up through her body, but newly dead and only having been reported missing the day before."

"Couldn't they have lowered her down the tree?"

Specter looked down at the sapling's wide spray of branches, then back up at Fearn. He raised an eyebrow. Fearn's face and ears went red.

Down in the gulley, Miller swung a hatchet to topple the small tree so that the young woman's body could be removed. The chk sound reverberated. Blood spurted from the tree. Miller shouted fuck, what the fuck and dropped the vibrating hatchet, shaking his hands wildly in front of him. He stalked off, hands still fluttering, looking like an orchestra conductor gone hopelessly mad.

"I can't feel my hands," he shouted. "I can't feel my hands!"

Specter and Fearn hurried down. Blood poured from the tree. The girl's eyes, which had been exactly where they should be when the police arrived, now stared at them from the bleeding cleft in the bark. The eyes looked down at the body. Specter followed their gaze. On the cadaver's now-sunken eyelids were drawn two red arrows pointing down at her mouth.

He knelt and parted the girl's pale lips with the fingers of his left hand.

"Gloves?" said Mankowski, the implication thick in his voice.

Specter glared at him. "You wear gloves. I have to feel. Besides…" he said, and he held up his right hand. Instead of whorls on the tips of his fingers were interlocking inverted pentagrams. With his other hand he reached deep into the girl's mouth. He pulled out a black cassette, the words on its label too smeared to read. The other officers gasped.

"What store around here carries cassette players?" the detective asked.

Sonic Raindrops

Ahead of Jo's Tercel, which she was driving down East Street out of Leeds to do some lazy, discursive shopping in Hadley, the red convertible in front of her finally pulled over under the bridge. Great, she wouldn't have to be behind this maniac all the way to Route 9. Above, highway traffic hurried by, a chorus of groans and whispers. hurtled across, glinting mirrors, the tops of eighteen-wheelers. The sun went behind a cloud.

He looked ridiculous, the driver, too tall for his low-to-the-road car, sticking up out of it like a ridiculous flower-stalk, a zucchini-shaped head with whitish hair flying all around atop a curiously long neck atop a not much thicker torso. His arms were jointed chopsticks bent at acute angles. She could see the sides of his aviator sunglasses jutting like blue-black ears from either side of his head. His radio was blasting…the news? It seemed like the typical stilted, affected news-type cadence that drifted back to her ears.

He'd been going no faster than 30 in a 45, and she'd finally dropped back and stopped cold. She kept her foot on the brake. The convertible driver had been going no faster than 30 in a 45, and she'd finally dropped back and stopped cold. She sat until he turned a corner up ahead, and then she gave it a few beats and accelerated to around just under 20, flipping through pictures on her phone, glancing up frequently, keeping her distance, occasionally glancing up making certain she was still in her lane and to make sure the rearview was clear of traffic.

The driver stuck up from the low, flat car like a ridiculous flower-stalk, a zucchini-shaped head with whitish hair flying all around atop a curiously long

86

neck atop a not much thicker torso. His arms were jointed chopsticks bent at acute angles. She crested a hill, and there he still was, braking, drifting rightward, coming to rest with the two passenger-side wheels up on the angled concrete between the abutments. As her car neared his aviator sunglasses jutting like blue-black ears from either side of his head. His radio was blasting...the news? It seemed like a news-type cadence that drifted back to her ears.

As she approached, still going slowly, the man unfolded himself out of the car and scurried underneath it. What the...?

Everything turned dark, just-past-dusk dark. It was only just after 10 a.m. Had she missed something about an eclipse? No, she remembered having checked the weather and seen nothing but partly sunny days for the forecastable future. A faraway roar rose above the highway noise, increasing in volume and intensity.

Brakes emitted a raspy screech on the highway above and the nose of a hatchback jumped up onto the guardrail above with a percussive crunch, headlight glass raining down onto the road. More crashes followed, echoing far and wide. Fireworks of glass filled the sky above the highway, followed by a burgeoning clouds of black smoke.

Something landed hard on the road in front of the car, as if hurled there with great force, Plastic shards sprayed outward. She sat up and leaned forward. The only identifiable item among the mess was a bent metallic antenna like a slender severed arm. Another hit about a yard away from the first, this one an older stereo receiver, followed by two tall speakers with brown casings and black netting, their cords whipsailing above them. She leaned forward and looked up - the sky was dotted with debris, getting larger. A large black boombox exploded just under the bridge, pimpling the driver's side of the convertible with shrapnel. A bird-like formation of handheld radios sailed over the windshield in a suicide dive, the resulting cacophony like machine gun fire.

Frantically Jo undid her seatbelt as something thudded on the roof, caving it in almost all the way down to the headrest of the passenger seat, the plastic of the dome light shattering, the fabric tearing. She snaked into the backseat, twisting her body through the gap between the front seats, then scrambling to the floor of the car and pulling a blanket from the back seat down over her as the deluge hit all around like bombs and giant fists pummeled her car from all directions. She opened her eyes and through her tears she saw old paper packets from fast food fries, the lids of long-gone ballpoint pens, half a dark-rimmed potato chip, a empty iced tea bottle. She closed them again.

The thuds of houses' rooftops exploding inward, the crunches of garages and carports succumbing under the ceaseless barrage. Jo covered her head with her arms and screamed in animal panic. Glass exploded inward. It hit the blanket like hailstones. Pinpricks of pain spread across her arms and sides. Under the car a series of explosions sounded, the car sinking in increments as its frame buckled and hitched. The projectiles whistled as they hurled themselves to the earth. It sounded like a war with a cacophony of drums as a soundtrack.

Then all was quiet except the echo in her ears. That faded. Other sounds crept in. The occasional clink and clattering of debris settling. Then plaintive voices from the highway, calls and cries and howls of pain. The thrumming rotors of a helicopter. She pulled the blanket from her face. The road was gone, covered in radios ancient and modern, shattered plastic and metal and wood and particle board and cords as far as the eye could see, veined with fallen trees. Headphones and speakers and receivers and springs and screws and green circuit boards and red and black wires and dials and capacitors and knobs and windowed cassette-doors.

A crash and a bang and the man from the convertible appeared atop a hillock of destroyed radios, crawling down on all fours, clawing with his hands and hitching his legs. A triangle of plastic jutted from his bleeding forearm and another from the side of his neck - the top of his head was gone, the brain sloshing about within like a patty of meat in a red-blue stew. Little bursts of blue electricity popped and frizzled in the bowl of his hacked-off skull. He was talking through shattered teeth, babbling, really, a long and wild monologue. In the Bronx in 1953 a small dog wandered through an alley, broadcasting sports statistics from small speakers in its nostrils, its tail replaced with an antenna, a small boy scooped up the animal and made off with him, and within two weeks the boy had aged unnaturally, his height remained the same but wrinkles and liver spots and skin tags and fleshy band-aids crowded his body and face and his hair went silver, arthritis claimed his hands, he died barking static-spangled barks, and snarling and foaming, the dog never found; in 1989 in East Berlin radios broadcasting news of the wall coming down sprouted legs and spread throughout the crowd, playing a backwards march and whipping the legs of the gathered crowd with their antennas until the radios were subdued and beaten to powder by a group of drunken revelers; in 2004 in Holyoke, Massachusetts, a man heard muffled voices emanating from his closed refrigerator; the culprit being two jumbo eggs which upon being cracked revealed small speakers bobbing in red-veined yolks and clear gelatin, they were arguing about whether soup and stew were the same thing and whether sports ought to take up so much of the evening news broadcast and whether cicadas felt emotions such as love and if oysters were disgusting and if Satan lived in bubbles of saliva and God under the toenails of soldiers and whether gangrene was good with paprika and who's that under your bed with the long, long fingers like the legs of daddy-long-legs spiders, the ones that tickle your eyelids until you wipe at them and mutter and if your senseless words are recorded and used in grimoires and for the prayers of rib-sprung monks corrupted by gore-lust and the man's wife found him singing along to obscenely explicit songs then right before her eyes he swallowed his tongue and it popped out through his throat and licked the bottom of his chin and the collar of his shirt before shooting out and encircling her neck and strangling her and him at the same time and the radio switched over to an over-emotive but undeniably affecting flute solo, then he began declaiming in French, cackling through and around his words and his brain rose from his head on a warty stalk and sprouted more brains on smaller stalks, all of it surrounded by a living web of crackling veins of blue lightning and a feedback shriek seared through Jo's eardrums until they popped and all she could hear was the blood in her head and everything went a strange orange color and she figured she'd probably never see inside of a store or her car or her dog or her husband or her kids or anything again ever and just for this moment she figured that would be just fine, fine as wine, disinclined, brains in brine, what's yours is mine, the devil take the hind most of the time and

I Must Not Rock

Dean Roueche had acted in three horror movies by his count, both quite early in his career: Skull Eaters 2, Skull Eaters 3, and Marietta & the Hell-Hog. He played the villain, the chief consumer of skulls, in the sequels, both by Van Martin, Roscoe's less talented older brother, and starring Cecila B. J. Sayers in her first non-porn role. In the latter he played a corrupted religious leader who was banging the titular character, (Marietta, not the Hell-Hog, though that wouldn't have surprised him). For a long time, his resume comprised just those low-budget trash-films and innumerable commercials for medications with laundry lists of side-effects or VD creams of dubious efficacy or galling spots touting questionable cures for erectile dysfunction.

He'd gone on, thank the Gods, to relative success with bit parts in larger productions, studio films, and television series that aired on HBO and Hulu. He was not quite a character actor, a hey-that-guy, not yet, but that's what he was gunning for, and the work was steady.

It paid the bills, but only just. Dean wanted a little more. Don't we all? A little vacation every so often, some nice meals out, the occasional frivolous purchase you can make without worrying about fucking up the budget, not holding off on car repairs until the situation was dire.

The conventions, then, were a godsend. He'd done his first one in 2010 in Worcester, Massachusetts, spurred on by his agent, Corsello Blankenfeld. He'd resisted until he finally heard Corsello out. All he'd need to bring was himself (rarely a problem), some head shots, promo pictures, and posters; a couple sharpies; a card reader hooked up to an iPad; and a good-sized pile of fives and singles. He'd clean up.

And did he ever. A seemingly endless parade of black-clad goofballs with unkempt beards and thick-framed glasses, and pale leggy girls in dark eye makeup, stood in long lines to buy his 8x10s for forty bucks a pop or snap a smartphone selfie with him for $20 ("make a horror face and I will too, it'll be awesome!"). All he had to do was refrain from getting annoyed and snappy, which was helped immeasurably by a few hits of Blue Venusian (a good indica all-over high with a buzzy, simmering cerebral calmness) in the hotel room before breakfast.

The con in Leeds was his thirty-first. He did not have high hopes. It was in a hotel just off the highway north of Springfield, cleverly named The Inn at Leeds. The bar and restaurant were set up to look sort of like an old western saloon/bordello, with a fake balcony above bordering doors with buxom silhouettes in frilly hats painted in black on their fake windows. Still, they didn't go to great lengths to be realistic. The waitresses wore black leggings with white blouses and aprons; the hostesses wore all black. They were diffident and careless, but he still tipped well despite that, and despite the watered-down drinks and overcooked steaks.

After his dinner, over-full and distracted and restless, Dean Roueche walked the halls of the sprawling hotel. Doors after doors, all closed, silent, not another wanderer nor guest in sight, soda and snack machines humming to themselves in needlessly romantically lit alcoves, green carpets with gold diamonds, little oases of fake palm trees and blue-painted canals running with water pungent with the odor of chlorine, and rustic benches with tables topped with current magazines, Road & Track and Sports Illustrated for the men, Gardening Quarterly and Marie Claire for the ladies, Word Search books and Highlights for Children for, well, obviously.

If this were a horror flick, he thought, the kind the convention attendees liked, he'd turn a corner and see some slavering maniac with a butcher's knife. Or a shambling corpse with rotting skin and a smile full of maggots. Or a three-headed dog. But, thankfully, each turn revealed just another empty hallway stretching into dimness.

He didn't even *like* horror flicks. These images were far from pleasant to him. All the fans who approached him at these conventions were full of questions he didn't know the answers to, nor did he care. *How did the skull eater break down the skulls so that they were edible? Will there be a Skull Eaters 4? What did you think of Roscoe Martin's "The Monster Test"? Was it just a rip-off of Blade Runner?* And questions about movies he hadn't seen, hadn't even heard of.

He pretended to care, tossed of pseudo-thoughtful answers. Otherwise, word would get around that he was grumpy. Difficult. Fewer fans, less money. The whole affair was tiring. It reminded him of his cashier days when he was a teenager. Customer Service all over again. Remember the money, Dean. Remember: vacations. Remember: high end steak houses. Remember: the massage parlor by the airport.

It was worth it, he told himself. Sure it was.

Eventually he ended up back by front desk, across from the now-closed bar. Catty-corner to the entrance was the set of double doors that led to the convention space. He tried the door and was somewhat surprised to find it unlocked. In the auditorium-like room under sparse lighting and unlit chandeliers, forty or so tables had been set up with white tablecloths and black runners. They lined the borders of the large room. Two rows of back-to-back tables ran down the middle. The tables had folding chairs set up behind them. After a bit of a wander, he found the actors' signing section behind a wall of black curtain, and located his booth in the far corner, between the guy from Machete and some name he didn't recognize, likely just another bit part player in some other low budget crapola. His display table was notably smaller than theirs. A placard with his name on it was affixed to the top of the backdrop. He wondered, not for the first time, if taking a more people-friendly stage name wouldn't have accelerated his career.

Sufficiently tired now, he retreated to his room. Alongside his travel bag, his merch case and cart rested by the small desk. He stripped down, put on his pajamas, and switched on the local news. He slid into the bed and propped his head up on the pillow, eventually drifting off to the sound of unfamiliar newscasters brainlessly bantering.

A sudden, jarring noise woke him up some time later, but before he could identify it, it was gone, just an echo he wasn't sure if he was imagining. The red numbers of the clock radio switched from 2:59 to 3:00. He waited for his heartbeat to slow, and was just shutting his eyes when the sound came again. One beat of a drum, loud. He lay there a while, feeling the pointed discomfort of the need to urinate, offset by the comfort of being under warm covers. Finally, he rose and shuffled to the bathroom. Just as he flushed, it sounded again. *Thud.*

He grabbed his bathrobe from the hook and went to the door. He looked out through the peephole. The hall was a grey ribbon topped by a line of dim lights, fat in the middle from the fisheye effect, thin ribbons dwindling away on either side. At the far left of the ribbon, a light flickered. He undid the swing-bar lock and stepped out into the hall.

At the far end stood a gaunt faced, frightfully thin child. He was pale, stood with his feet together in an almost military stance, a narrow hourglass-shaped drum strung around his neck. He appeared to be otherwise unclothed. His features crowded together in the center of his face, his nose and pursed mouth very small. His dark hair stood up on one side. In his hands were…white chair legs? No…bones. Clavicles, in point of fact. Unconsciously Dean raised his hand and touched his own clavicle with the tips of his fingers. The boy seemed to respond, nodding with solemnity. Dean saw with alarm that blood was seeping from the boy's ears. His feet, narrow and long of toe, were dry and yellowed and peeling. The boy raised one of the clavicles high, and then slammed it down on the drum with an aggressive sneer. *Thud.*

Then the boy grinned. His teeth were a stained, overlapping jumble. He tilted the drum so that the skin stretched across the top was visible to Dean. The skin was a human face, the eyes, nostrils, and mouth sewn tightly shut. Scraggly brows. Red cheeks. An upside-down ripple of wrinkles under the stitched lips. Bruises and abrasions and bloodless cuts from the impacts of the bones.

And now a bone was pinwheeling through the air right at Dean's face. It whistled through the air. The boy's arm was outstretched, his face rapt with anticipation. Dean ducked, shielding his head with his right arm. He was not hit. He heard the bone bounce along the carpet behind him. When he looked up, the child was sliding backward into the darkness of the corner at the end of the hall. He looked down, looked behind him. There was no clavicle bone on the carpet. There was nothing. He shivered. The hair on his arms bristled and rose, pulling at his skin, as though for a show about to begin. The air had grown frigid.

Dean stepped out of the shower. After the adrenaline rush of the strange 3 a.m. corridor encounter with the strange figure with the drum and the bones, he'd put on the 24-hour-news with the volume turned up almost all the way, and started up the Keurig. And in a blink, he'd woken to the grey dawn light. The coffee sat cold in the cup. At some point he must have gotten into bed. He had no memory of the transition, nor of undressing.

It was still early, but he felt oddly refreshed despite having been awakened and up in the very early hours.

It'll catch up with me early afternoon, he figured. *Or it won't.*

He toweled himself dry, dressed, and brushed his teeth—a dull pain in the upper right gum line suggested that putting off a dental visit had been a very bad idea indeed. Wincing, swearing to himself that he'd make that appointment on Monday, he popped a couple Ibuprofen Liqui-Gels. He walked to the window, opened the curtains, and looked down at the parking lot, which was already filling up with cars, some being unloaded by vendors.

Movement toward the near end of the lot caught his eye. A man in a skull mask and gas-station coveralls stood at a small silver Honda Accord between a conversion van and a Toyota Sequoia, and appeared to be trying, with some success, to manually force down the window. Dean peered as the man reached into the front pocket of his coveralls and began to unstring some kind of wet, blue-purple kinked ropes and feed them into the car. The man stopped short and started to turn Dean's way just as an eighteen-wheeler pulled up, blocking Dean's view. Well, whatever the guy was doing, it didn't look like he was robbing the car. A prank, probably. He closed the curtains, grabbed his duffel full of merch and stuff, and headed downstairs.

In the vendor room, people were hauling in plastic boxes on hand-trucks, hanging B-movie t-shirts (*Cannibal Buffet*, *Wereworms of New London*, *Fangs but No Fangs*) on display walls, lining up books with lurid covers on wire racks, standing up walls of posters. A couple teenagers on folding chairs raised a banner reading CADAVERS-ON-DEMAND. In the next stall over, a stunningly beautiful woman in ripped-up fishnet stockings and a short black dress applied black lipstick, staring at herself in a coffin-shaped mirror, then blinking one eye, then the other, faster and faster in turn. Her jet-black hair was in pigtails and on the back of her slender neck was tattooed a stylized 666, the circles of the sixes clustered together, and the upper curves forming an off-kilter circumference. Across from her stall, which appeared to be set up to apply monster makeup to guests, a thin bald man in a Halloween III t-shirt and a pin-striped vest set up hybrid action figures on a broad shelving unit. One of them appeared to be Star Wars action figures of R2D2 and C3PO, but with the heads of Columbine shooters Eric Harris and Dylan Klebold. Another was Jason from the Friday the 13th movies on a gurney in a hospital gown, giving flesh-ripping birth (in incredibly graphic and anatomically accurate detail) to a curled-up, heavyset fetus with the scowling, grotesque head and hideous coiffure of Donald Trump. Wincing, Dean maneuvered through the crowd, jealous of their white, pink, and orange Dunkin bags and their coffee cups in corrugated cardboard sleeves.

As quickly as he could, he laid out his 8x10s on his table, set up everything for his Point of Sale except for the cash drawer, which he kept locked in the duffel, and used the provided large binder clips to affix to the wall behind the table a vinyl poster with his name in a splattery font and several pictures of him from his horror roles. Then he went back through the crowd of vendors, bustling bees in a lurid, garish hive, in search of a snack.

Outside, the sky was still slate grey. The top of the tree line flickered with an echo of far-off lightning. The trees that lined the highway exit genuflected with theatrical reverence. Dean wound his way through the parking lot. The car he'd seen earlier between the conversion van and the SUV was gone, a red slick of liquid with an archipelago of spilled meat of some kind filled the empty spot.

Across the state highway sat a moribund two-pump gas station and food market, and he jogged over when a break in the traffic allowed.

In front of the market on an old wooden bench sat a grey-suited, haggard man. Beside him was an orange striped packet spilling crumbled crackers. Pigeons sat all around him on the bench and on the ground before him, milling about and cooing and flapping their wings. One stood on each shoulder and three vied for space on the liver-spotted dome of the man's head. His arm, lain across the top of his belly, formed a ledge populated by a crowd of the filthy things. One pecked at the man's hip. The man nodded his head at Dean, causing the birds to have to regain their footing. Dean hurried past.

Just inside, he stopped cold. This store must have been connected somehow to the convention. The entryway was lined on both sides with racks of cleavers hanging on hooks, some brand new, with logos in various languages etched into their blades, some old and dotted or stained with rust, a few whose edges were stained with blood; some had clumps of hair and flesh stuck there as well.

To his left, adjacent to the registers, stood a display rack that held an array of newspapers, all of whose above-the-fold pictures showed in lurid colors bodies strewn across parks and city streets, piled on fast food restaurant floors, hanging like bloody suits on the racks of some backdated, orange-tinted JC Penney or Macy's, crowding the bottom of a still-moving mall escalator in bent, broken profusion.

He rushed past the rows of snacks—in one aisle, an emaciated, red-eyed raccoon stood on its hind legs, a cloud of bubbling foam at its mouth—looking for the glass-door cases of beverages that typically border the backs of such stores. But here behind glass were hunks of raw meat speared with black iron hooks, hideously realistic shrunken heads wrapped tightly in cellophane. He peered into one narrow door and immediately became dizzy with nauseous vertigo—though he was looking straight ahead, the view was from the top of a multi-floor staircase, looking down, a shadow of a man carrying a long, sharp knife ascending it. He pulled the door shut. To his right were the drinks. But all the bottles seemed to be gimmicks, boasting flavors like Bassist Sweat, Whore-Spit, and Octogenarian Blood. He opened the door and examined that last one. The label was a grainy black & white photograph of an old man face-down on the grounds of some factory. His white hair ringed the back of his head. He wore a light blue vest over a white shirt, suspenders, and khaki slacks. There was no ingredient list, no bottling company named, no recycling information nor any other symbols nor markings. The liquid inside was clear, with globules of red and clouds of some tiny insects or…he peered more closely…fish?

He put back the bottle and turned to get the hell out of there. Just turning away from the counter, holding a cup of coffee, was a poster for a forthcoming action movie in which the hero, a muscular man in a black sleeveless t-shirt and black pants hung suspended, spreadeagle, between two passenger train cars in the process of violently separating. The night-blue background was splattered with an array of city lights. Fire was bursting from the train compartment on his left; from the one on his right jutted a profusion of hands firing shining guns. The star was Roland Simon, Dean's former friend and acting partner. Dean had studiously avoided seeing him, turning off the television during commercials, arriving to movie theaters after the half-hour of cloying trailers had run. In a land where pop-culture is shoved into your eyes and ears as often as possible, he'd been surprisingly successful at keeping away from any mention of Simon. And now here he was, faced wrenched into a sneer, eyes looking out of the poster and into Dean's disappointed heart. *Really?* those eyes said. *A horror convention? You had such promise. I'll think of you when I look out over Hollywood.*

Well, Simon wasn't exactly doing Oscar-worthy work. But still, it hurt. If he really examined it, his career may indeed have dried up. Was he really getting decent roles? How long had it been? Maybe he'd call his agent. His shitty, stupid agent who seemed annoyed, preoccupied, every time Dean called. In a hurry to get off the phone.

Nothing like feeling like a nuisance. He put his hand on his belly flab. Then he turned his face away from the poster and headed for the doors.

The entire body of the man on the wooden bench was now completely obscured by a twitching and flapping mass of grey birds. The percussive cooing was almost deafening. Dean hesitated. Was the man alive under there? But the people gassing up their cars paid the man no heed, and Dean could just make out that one of the man's pigeon-covered legs was crossed casually over the other.

When he got back to his table, it was empty; standing behind it was a slender redheaded woman in tan slacks and a black polo with the venue's logo on the breast. Her hair was pulled back in a tight ponytail. She had a face like that of an apologetic sparrow. Don raised an eyebrow.

"Sorry, Mr. Rouche, we've had to relocate you," she said, her nasal voice full of cheerily false sympathy. "If you don't mind, will you follow me?"

In point of fact, Dean *did* mind, and it was probably a battle worth choosing. But as his mind grasped at something to say in the way of protest, his shoulders betrayed him with an obsequious shrug. So back through the vendor hall he went, silently cursing himself, until they reached a table half the size his had been, situated in a weird little dead end. His 8x10s sat in a haphazard stack, and his poster had been hanged crookedly. Next to his table was a muscular, completely bald guy stocking a plastic rack with pornographic parodies of horror books. Dean saw *All Heads Turn When the C*nt Goes By* (the asterisk presumably supplied by the publisher) and *The Long Shadow Over Lynn's Mouth*, and *Dork Entries* by a Roberta Ache-man, most of the cover of which was obscured by plain brown paper.

"Thanks," I said. "People are going to have to look really hard to find this."

"Ha ha," she said, in place of actually laughing. Then her face softened. "I'll be handling the crowd..."

"The trickle, more like," Dean said, hoping to forestall any deprecating addendum she might have been considering.

"...such as it is. You need anything, food, something to drink, more pens to sign with, coins, whatever, let me know. Otherwise, I'll just sit and play word games on my phone. I won't be a bother, and I won't bother *you* with needless chit-chat unless you want me to, in which case I can expound on any number of topics really, uh, easily! Or...*readily*! Oh! My name is Emily. Emily Spire." She finished with a deep breath and a self-effacing "Whew!"

"That's fine," Dean said. "I appreciate it."

Without prompting, she began laying out the 8x10s, and he straightened the poster. When that was done, the static-filled 15-minutes-to-showtime announcement sounded over the ceiling speaker's. "Coffee?" Dean said, feeing like a heel, like some kind of seventies businessman asking a secretary for something he could just as easily done for himself.

"Of course," she said. "How do you take it?"

"One cream, one sugar," he said.

"Gross," she said, and headed off.

At first the crowd was small, a smattering of people in horror flick t-shirts, a lot of acne, a lot of splotched skin and bellies obscuring belt buckles. Dean was overcome with sudden exhaustion. Ten more hours of this? He didn't know how he was going to do it. Couldn't figure out how he'd ever done it before. Time to call the doctor and up the goddamned Fluoxetine. Again.

A shadow fell across the table. Dean looked up. This one was a corker. Tall, almost freakishly so, but with a face that looked like that of an eleven-year-old, his hair stringy and fake-looking under a sweatshirt hood that was either officially yellow, or formerly white. Cargo shorts clearly slept in. His teeth, which he revealed in a hideously wide smile, were worthy of their own horror booth, or maybe a thing at the state fair where you pay a buck to go into a dark trailer and look upon an abomination. One of his hands was rubber, more likely a gag item from a novelty shop than a professionally made prosthesis. The other was swollen and bruised all over. The smell of body odor, underarms and crotch, wafted off the kid, almost visible as ripples in the recycled air.

Dean waited for the man-child to say something, but he just stared. Starstruck? Dean doubted that very much. "Jeremy," he said, finally, in a puberty-cracked voice.

"Dean."

"What do you say to a famous person?"

"Whatever you like?"

"D'ya think the rain'll hurt the rhubarb?"

Jesus Christ. "What?"

"Nothing. Just a canned joke. So, you're in movies?"

"Evidently."

"Ever think of doing radio?"

Alright, enough of this freak. "Look…" he said, and suddenly Emily was there next to him.

"Excuse me? Jeremy? Sweetie? Mr. Rouche has some business to attend to, so I'm going to have to steal him from you," she said, with a blatantly sarcastic sweet lilt to her voice, "if you don't mind moving along. Or would you like to buy a signed picture?"

The kid reached into his sweatshirt pocket. Dean instinctively held up his hand to block his face as he felt Emily stiffen next to him.

But it wasn't a weapon. It was a small, rectangular plastic object. Dean exhaled. Jeremy slid it onto the table, winked luridly, and strode off in a herky-jerky swagger, hip-checking a kid in a clown mask into a spin-rack of bootleg DVDs, causing a few moments of clatter and calamity.

Dean picked up the thing Jeremy had left. It was a black cassette tape with a light blue and white label. Something was scribbled on it in smeared marker.

"What does this say?" Dean said, lifting the tape between two fingers like it was a dried turd.

Emily lowered her glasses. "It says *Michael Death Incantations.*"

"How the hell were you able to decipher that?"

Emily shrugged. "I'm into puzzles."

A shriek rang out over the chatter of the crowd.

Listen

Spring thaw. We've been here before, haven't we, you and me? The suburbs of Leeds? 2004 or so? Not much has changed in the intervening years, at least not here. The bright mornings. The exquisite evenings, warm and lit as though by a profusion of bonfires. This morning, as then, the suburbanites' doors are open, the windows too. Some houses are accompanied by adjacent dumpsters, like cats sleeping alongside their owners, and the residents, parasites in the house-body, fling the built-up detritus in from the porch with clangs and clatters. Houses fart clothes-dryer steam into the morning air, chemicals aping the odor of cleanliness itself.

People emerge blinking into natural light. What will they get up to this summer? I see a pool party. In the pool a cadaver floats among scraps of clothing and flesh. The chlorine odor is overwhelming. Over by the fence, as far from the pool he can get and still be on the property, the homeowner wields tongs, flipping four sausages and one severed finger. The finger keeps curling up like a caterpillar, and the homeowner uses tongs and a spatula to straighten it back out. It is thinner than the sausages, and he notes it's been charred on one side. Under the scorched, blistered fingernail the flesh should be delicious. He is wary of cancer, though—cells splitting like atoms, damaged and proliferating like black foam, insurgent bubbles of corruption and toxicity— and has certainly considered flinging the finger over the fence into the Goodrich's yard. Fuck it—let their dog eat it.

At the back of the house at a large table, umbrella-lidded, on the deck (many spiders underneath, weaving worlds), Grandmama pounds a beer and belches. She is resplendent in massive Terminator sunglasses, a too-black wig, a sunny yellow tube-top under an unbuttoned white linen blouse. That's the totality of her wardrobe this day, in point of fact. Her eyes are defiant. *Mention it, I dare you,* they say. A singular, instantly identifiable couplet of stenches wafts upward. She lifts and separates her painted toes, revealing clusters of black lint, lets them rest in the air, then brings them down, relaxes them, returns them to rest. *Fuuuuck,* she says.

Stay bent.

In a basement room of a white raised ranch (landscaping by Murragh & Sons LLC, impeccable work: a wavy-edged flower bed, color wheels carefully consulted, lots of yellows and purples; a vine-limned pergola shielding Adirondack chairs, a glass table, a brass ashtray, and a rabbit cage; a play area for the kids replete with a quicksand pit, swing set, monkey bars, sandbox, trampoline, and a ladder-and-slide; Ray Murragh arrested last February for hosting underage parties in the camps in the meadows, cocaine packaged for sale in the pockets of his sequined Jordache jeans, an unregistered pistol with a sanded-off serial number, forbidden juices drying on designer underpants, anyway, anyway), I see a killer sitting astride his victim. He has all the time in the world, and all the privacy. The room is soundproofed; the victim's son, now away at school, had used it to practice with his band (the Geneva Whoresons) whose guitarist, incidentally, is the second cousin of Ray Murragh, and who, or, rather, which, or is it in fact who, I don't care to look up the particulars of grammar, English is such a maze of rules anyway, who fucking cares, also, incidentally, had a minor local hit with their raucous rendition of Please Don't Close the Casket Lid (Down); three guitars will do that, won't they, dissonant and brash, defiant like the bottomless grandmother in the previous long paragraph...

Stay bent. Land on the meat.

...on the radio, I hear a rhumba of fingers using friction to snap out an irresistible beat. *I'm gonna gut you like a trout,* the killer mutters in time with that beat, *dress you like a deer, undo your black strings like a corset, bend your boneses like rubber hoses,* he is affecting the deepest, darkest, most evil tone of which he's capable. But he cannot do any of the tasks he promises to. He is impotent, not in that way, all that works just as it should, no, in the more important, deep-down way. He is a failure. She is so pale, so naked, so perfectly proportioned, so smooth of skin, sweet wrinkles at her hips, her lips slightly parted, her hair gorgeously, mathematically disarrayed, her eyes squinting with smoky seduction. He cannot keep his promises. He is a failure. A failure.

A thin, cheap, tall mirror backed with brown paper and a twisted set of wires like arms with clasped hands leans against the wall. By chance, the killer spots himself. He's shocked at the image he sees. He's *handsome*. Trim. Louche. Slick. Skinny as fish shit, his belly flap vanished. His bald spot, that cold, pimpled planet, is replaced by a luxurious, generous coiffure. That wasn't 40 cent ramen he slurped last night; it was Buddha Jumps Over the Wall, it was Talon Club with exquisite cordyceps, it was pho with blue lobster noodles. He is a jester on fire, the ass's ears, the cockscomb's crest, scorched bells trumpet his arrival with weak and muted clinks; she is a blunt force mama, a wintry minx, obscene in the context of impending summer. They are two performers in a one-act play, and he's the only one with lines to speak: after all, he's classically trained, a keen adherent to the teachings of Father Stan, with the discipline of a marine, the stoicism of a sage, the resolve of a castrato. She, however, is by far the better actor. Critics might opine that playing dead is easy when one is actually dead, but how on earth would they know? What conception of its difficulty could they possibly have? How much discipline it takes? The study that goes into it, a lifetime's worth, and the infinity of nonexistence that precedes that lifetime.

The killer is tethered to each of his victims by an intertwined vein of fluids. How do they say it on the news? Muriel's killer. Harriet's killer. That connection is stronger than that of blood family, the tether unbreakable. And the serial killer is nothing more than a polygamist with a slew of wives. And he is owned by them, not the other way around. Heather's killer. Muriel's killer. Cathy's killer. The harem builds the man, not the other way around, and they share him, they surround him. The media, that many-headed god with necks of coaxial cable, draws up the marriage licenses.

…and with the abrupt illogic of a dream you're sitting on a plastic seat on the red line from Park Street to Alewife and the sun is glinting through dark grey clouds and across from you sits a man in a houndstooth suit with a thin black tie and hair like a rising column of brown smoke. *Why*, the graffiti behind him scrawled into the wall reads, *are the police so goddamned interested in looking at my hands?* All around you are Asian teenagers in school uniforms reading Kindles and Nooks and actual books, tired-looking women in blue scrubs with multicolored pants, an older black guy deeply absorbed in the Globe, a white-haired man in tweeds and full clown makeup. The speaker crackles to introduce the electronic voice announcing the next stop in an uninflected monotone, and the voice skips like a record, falters, then there's a high, lovely note as from a flute and all the people around you raise their voices to match the note, and it's kind of beautiful, and you feel self-conscious because you cannot sing, not even in the shower, and you look up and instead of the dingy curved white metal of the ceiling there's a vaunted wooden roof with piloerection crossbeams and mote-crowded rays of light and the man in the houndstooth suit with the thin black tie and hair like a rising column of brown smoke stands and with his right hand he takes a handful of his coiffure and pulls up, stretching his neck, the flesh pulling taut, and an Asian student pulls a hunting knife from her blue backpack and the man takes it and nods an unspoken thank you and he's looking you directly in the eyes as he saws into the side of his neck, his expression unchanging, a gout of blood and it's pouring and now it's splashing his neighbors and the crossbeams and the seats and the handhold bars and everyone still harmonizing and he's hitting bone now, the sound is like grinding wood and there's a *snap* and his head tilts unnaturally to the right and he lifts and the last tendril of skin stretches and snaps and he hands the knife back to the student who returns it to her backpack and the man tucks his head under his arm and the lips are moving and the eyes looking left and right as the light disappears and darkness claims the train at an acute angle and you're underground now and the voices are separating into words and the music is now an orchestra and the man walks down the aisle and the standing commuters crumple and four students stand and saw off their own heads in ff motion and hand them to the man who juggles them, tossing his own into the mix, all the eyes looking left and right and the mouths speaking silent words in unison and the rest of the seated commuters slide to the floor as he passes, heads switching places in the oil-stained air, the spilling blood forming a circle in front of the man, and the headless four dance in herky-jerky movements, swinging their hips from side to side, and now the windows are stained glass and this is your church and you are the priest and it's time for the homily and you don't have anything prepared to deliver to the congregation of the stricken and the dead and the only living man is leaving with the heads circling the air in front of him and the train slides into the station and all the people waiting are in clown suits and makeup and there are lions and an elephant with his head ducked down tramples some of the clows (*kee-runch, toot toot!*) as he lumbers toward the yellow line that separates the platform from the track and as the brakes squeal the clowns pull assault rifles from their suits ... and we're back in the suburbs. The killer stands slowly, groaning, his legs hurt, the hamstrings. A feeling hits his ear, like something's being vomited up from inside his head and has jumped the stirrup, slouched under the drum and is pushing its way down the canal. He digs in a pinky. A stinky pinky. The thingy sticks to it and he pulls it into his range of vision. It's a tiny head, eyes and mouth squeezed shut, dots of dried snot at the nostrils, a small tower of hair. The killer squeezes it between his thumb and his pinky and the tiny eyes open and are pushed out and brains like oatmeal ooze from the ears. He pops the tiny head into his mouth and he chews. It's tangy. Dried sweat provides a natural saltiness and the tiny teeth provide texture. Kee-runch, toot toot!

Stay bent. Land on the meat.

New ways won't open old doors.

Across the street in a well-appointed living room a wall-mounted widescreen television, muted, shows a well-known Peruvian pianist on a parquet stage flanked by gold-gilded violet drapery, caterpillar-fingers bouncing off the keys, white-haired head tilted upward, the butt of a pistol sticking out from his mouth. He plays in a frenzy, his one-size-too-large tuxedo shifting on his body, in a trance, tears welling his eyes, the hammers in the piano hitting the strings as his feet jounce the pedals and the bench bows slightly under his prodigious weight, an oaken smile. Drool pools at the corners of his mouth and spills down. Periodically he gags, the pistol shifting in his mouth.

Oblivious to this, two small boys play with rubber dinosaurs on the carpet, bashing the little heads together, each growling in a different pitch to differentiate Triceratops from Stegosaurus. The couch behind them explodes like a building being detonated. The resulting smoke cloud consumes them. It consumes the television. It climbs the stairs. It buzzes with insect life, but we, the audience, can't see wings, carapaces, dangling legs. Just the cloud. Watching from outside, a newspaper delivery boy, who runs increasingly late each day, watches the windows. At first, he sees only the across-the-street houses in the reflections, then one by one each window turns grey. He shrugs and flings a newspaper into the middle of a large shrub and pedals away.

New ways won't open old doors.

And redemption is for coupons.

Land on the meat.

Kee-runch, toot toot!

Two houses down, Dan pushes his arms through the sleeves of the yellow cardigan. He pours himself a cocktail, glug, glug, glug into the glass, amber minus its prehistoric insect. He sits in the slate-colored loveseat across from the matching couch. A tri-folded newspaper slaps the picture window and falls between the bushes and the house. Zayra stalks in wearing a short black dress, holding a gold necklace in front of her. "Get this for me?" she says, and she turns away. Dan stands with a middle-aged grunt, puts his glass on the mantel, and he takes the ends of the necklace from her, fastens the clasps, admiring her long neck, the freckled symmetry of her back, her buttocks pushing against the fabric of the dress just right. He looks back up and thinks about the fact that long necks are irresistible advertisements for decapitation. He thrusts his hips forward, pushing against her, opens his mouth against the back of her neck below her towering bouffant. The contact, top and bottom, is dizzying. For him, anyway.

"No time for tha-*aaat*," says Zayra in a taunting sing-song voice, and the doorbell chimes in harmony. It's Patrick and Patricia. Pat & Pat. Pats pending. Patrick is the new administrative assistant who shares an office with Dan. They both like situation comedies with boisterous laugh tracks that signal the desired response to insults and unimaginative, obvious quips. They both golf, Dan badly, Pat so-so. Big U2 fans, though Dan has seen them live and Pat has not. They have matching New England Patriots flags flying from their houses. High fucking five. Zayra goes to the door, barefoot, opens it. *Oh*, she yells, and the pair yells back. *Oh, oh—ooh-ooh-ooh! It smells so good in here.* Patrick is clad in a grey suit and a purple tie, Patricia a purple dress that matches her husband's tie, white pearl earrings, an end-to-end-S-shaped caterpillar pin at her breast. Patrick grabs a handful of peanut M&M's from a bowl and fills his cheeks like a squirrel and Dan says *What's your poison*, and it's gin, of course, it's always gin, easily identifiable as a word even through candy-coated milk chocolate and peanuts and Zayra pours some liquor store bargain bin Cab into goblets for the ladies.

Pat and Pat take in the surroundings, impressed. The art matches the furniture. The curtains match the art. There is much beige, tasteful maroons, some blue. There's not an iota of dust. The mirrors are placed in such a way as to make the room seem expansive. Decorative old books line rustic shelves, lending a visual cacophony of colors that offsets the rest of the space. Patricia notes that though Zayra's Facebook profile picture is that of her two boys in shirts and vests and gap-toothed grins, pictures of them are nowhere to be seen in the room in which they plan to entertain; in fact, there's no evidence of them to be seen. This strikes her as particularly odd, as her own boys are everywhere, visible, detectable; they're a presence in the house even when they aren't at home, like visible poltergeists with endless energy. Odors, howls, dents, stains, broken CD cases, echoes, impending puberty.

Fifteen minutes later Dan pulls the roast from the oven. He bends, revealing two inches of hairy ass crack, pinkish, a whitehead like an eye without its pupil under the hitched-up hood of cardigan and polo shirt. His oven mitts are black with red pentagrams. The oblong roast has a face, popped-out eyes; a nub of a nose; small, jutting ears; agape mouth, chipped, burnt teeth; a withered black stub of a tongue. The scorched, truncated hands at its sides grab weakly at the rack for purchase. Some combination of a moan and a whistle accompanies the smoke that pours from it. Dan places the roasting pan on the oven burners. The roast, suspended above its own oily juices, sighs and clucks. Patricia walks in and screams, her hands flying up to her face. Zayra strides in quickly behind her, grabs her around the stomach in a bear-hug and lifts. Patricia kicks at the air and tries to reach back to claw out Zayra's eyes, but Zayra leans back, turns her face toward the ceiling. Patrick runs in. Dan hurls the roast at him and it beans him square on the forehead, burning, leaving a grease mark and red skin, *hey, is it Ash Wednesday?* He pinwheels his arms as he stumbles backward, and Zayra turns, still holding the kicking Patricia, whose feet inadvertently kick Patrick down the cellar stairs. Dan and Zayra join forces to subdue Patricia, who passes out. They haul her chaotically downstairs. Patrick lies sprawled on the landing. His chest is still moving, albeit unevenly, and his eyes are unfocused and he's bleeding from the back of the head. His fingers jump and twitch. His left leg is bent the wrong way, twisted, too; if his vision isn't completely compromised, he sees the bottom of his own foot.

The basement is all red velvet curtains over black walls. Sigils of dazzling complexity and suggestiveness decorate the curtains. The ceiling is pimpled with green, glowing stars purchased in bulk from Amazon. Strings of red Christmas lights line the ceiling, blinking in time with U2's "I Still Haven't Found What I'm Looking For." A giant black pentagram decorates the red floor. Atop it stands a white goat in a black cape. It watches the proceedings with what appears to be interest. He's studying. Learning. As Dan and Zayra undress Pat and Pat and lay them across from each other just outside the circle, the goat rears up, its front legs leaving the ground. Its pink pecker juts upward. It releases a stream of urine that splashes its beard, browning it, pouring back down his chest, piddling on the floor. It appears to be appalled by its own obscene display.

Or maybe it just fucking hates U2. Zayra does. So do I. She disappears behind a gap in the curtain and changes the music to something more fitting. Drone-and-distant-drums and ardent melismatic vocalizing. The goat bellows along, its voice lilting on the off-beat. Dan fits plastic vampire fangs over Patricia's teeth as Zayra pulls Patrick's two front teeth with pliers – byoink, byoink, blood— and places them in a 69 formation at the bottom-most point of the inverted pentagram. Redemption is for coupons. The goat and the couple harmonize. Dan tosses the roast one-handed into the pentagram. It lands dead center. Bob celebrates like a bowler who just rolled the Big Four, hand in a fist, pulls it down. *Yes.* Patricia and Patrick vibrate and levitate. They rise to the ceiling and hover there, spinning slowly. Their blood showers into the pentagram, splashing the goat's horns and head. Dan and Zayra are now allowed to enter the pentagram. They doff their robes and couple. The goat joins in. They all eat the roast under the rain of blood. It came out pretty good, Zayra admits. For dessert there will be apple lattice pie, served with ice cream. The coffee will be so, so strong.

Outside a mail truck with a bumper sticker reading 999 hitches up onto the curb to the left of the driveway, digging a muddy rut into the grass. The mailman exits with a scuffed plastic bin full of letters and small packages. He spills out everything on top of the storm drain grate and then with both hands pushes it all through the gap down into the water. He's humming happily to himself. Your copy of the July 2021 WXXT Program Guide is in there, in a manila envelope. So are cable bills; love letters; last-notice we're-going-to-send-this-to-collection medical bills; urgent credit card come-ons; Bic pen death threats; collage-font ransom notes; moon-tune-June poetry chapbooks; powder that could be anthrax or could be baking soda, mailed to a local politician along with a rather unlettered but passionate missive; a perfumed snapshot of a spectacularly furry vagina under punishing light, making it look like a dessert in a sixties cookbook; a child's letter to Santa with list of kinds of desired ammunition along with the question IS IT COLD IN SPACE?; a postcard reminding you that your cat is overdue for his examination and rabies shot; a personal letter whose text appears at the end of this issue; Dear John letters; obsequious pleas for clemency; letters of resignation; of marque; of intent; of credence; of feral obscenity; carefully worded recommendation letters; a booklet of coupons, for which redemption is; crossed letters; and a letter complaining to a casket company about a defective product which lists in detail what the consumer saw as flaws: the lack of a lock on the outside, a rusty swing bar, a misspelling on the personalized head panel, a coffee-colored stain on the pillow, a valance made of material to which he was allergic, an unaesthetic ogee ratio, a misleading color swatch that disguised the ugly color of the actual product, and the omission of a radio, which was a violation of the initial arrangement, as unorthodox as that may seem to the uninitiated. There is also in a Hallmark card shaped rose-colored envelope a Polaroid picture of a man with a bullet hole in the center of his forehead. One eye is half shut, the other bulges. Brain matter protrudes like shrink-wrapped oatmeal from both nostrils. Parallel lines of blood, bracketing the philtrum, lead down to his mouth, which is frozen in a snarl, blood filling the gaps between his teeth. The floor underneath the man is consistent with that of a public-school gymnasium. Written in slightly smeared marker across the white bottom border of the Polaroid is the name CARL. All of this, into the water, headed for a catch basin, breaking down as it goes, all becoming unreadable, unseeable, some of the data rendered irrelevant, other exacerbating a variety of issues.

The postman stands up and, arm swinging, walks toward the truck with the now-empty bin. His plan is to apply moisturizer to his hands, the tips of whose fingers now feel unpleasant when he rubs them together.

Land on the meat.

Casing, projectile, propellant, and primer.

A 1970 Chevrolet C/K pickup, red with a wood-grain strip, rumbles around the corner, spewing black smoke, engine grumbling grievances in monotone. For just an instant, the sun splashes glowing gold paint across the windshield, then it's washed away. Gripping the wheel with oil-stained hands is a thin man with a prodigiously bruised face, swollen eyelids, a fat lip, and comical buck teeth. He is wearing a tuxedo shirt unbuttoned to just below the nipples and pink boxer shorts (resting upon two phonebooks because he is quite short) with a red cartoon heart on each buttock. His gnarled bare foot mashes the brake pedal hard and the vehicle comes to a jolting halt, throwing three men from the truck bed into the slider windows and one right over the truck cab; that one hit the curb forehead first, opening a new mouth above his eyes, a mouth that speaks in grey comic book thought-bubbles and sings a cantata of spreading blood. The three other men clamber from the truck. The slider windows are cracked, the cracks retaining clumps of their hair except that of the bald one.

The men swagger toward the mailman, aggression in their arm-swings and their boot-falls. They intercept the mailman, each grabbing an arm above the elbow. Two lift him off the ground, their hands sliding up to his armpits, the mailman screaming, his shirt hiked up, showing vulnerable pale flesh, and the third man opens his grey camouflage shoulder bag and pulls out a large rivet gun that resembles a black and red automatic weapon. They flip the mailman head-down and the man rivets him to the side of his truck below the knees and at the wrists, spreadeagle, to avoid any resemblance to an inverted crucifix (too gauche). The driver stays seated. The men ignore their deceased comrade, not even glancing his way, and pile back into the pickup, which takes off with a roar and a final retort of black smoke, the radio playing a Laura Branigan backwards, which, if one listens carefully, sounds like *vestibule of hell's nose, finger-fuck a garrulous gendarme in November's aloof philosophies, Satan moisturize my heel, love you we do, taste you we do even despite your having washed in the cool milk of mid-morning. Fatal event, fatal event, fatal event, fungal infections, congestive heart success.* It must be noted that in order to interpret it that way, one must struggle with the perverse bending of vowels and the occasional inapt consonant; anyway, these are truly words around which one might form a postage-cult were one so inclined.

Around the corner in the dining room of a well-appointed French Victorian, known among the high school kids as the House of the Rising Stepson for reasons I need not go into here, Wiegel adjusts his Buddy Holly glasses.

"Security guards are often the most reliable soothsayers," he says. Wiegel is a rag doll come to life, clad in a motley jacket and torn jeans, dry skin knees peeking out, hair like yellow pipe cleaners, chaotic teeth, gravestone eyelids, acne scars like moonscapes at his temples. He is a disgraced schoolteacher, an alco-demic, a libertine, an anglophile with a cockney accent that's a half-note off, bastard inflection. His income now comes from selling sanguinary pornography online. His audience today is a defrocked priest deep in the gonzo study of barbiturates, his favorite being phenobarbital, which he calls phenobarbiedoll. The priest has a brutalist head, an asymmetrical cloud of brown hair, misaligned eyes. He is stout, wears a discordant 15-UV lamp tan, small, delicate hands.

"They are my only source of predictions now," he replies. "God is a liar, it is His heaven in which souls are scorched, He who falls and penetrates the earth and gives it syphilis."

They fall into a fraught furrow of silence. The priest studies the painting hung over the couch. Houses like lanterns on a tumble-down Asian mountain, a river of red fish, trees exploding green heads atop striated necks. To crack the silence open he says, "I can taste your cologne when I lick your shadow."

"I was thrown out of church for taking notes," Wiegel replies. "I prayed harder than my neighbor. I broke a man's Hook of Hamate and two of his metacarpal shafts during the sign of peace. I throat-sang the hymns and stained the hymnals with jism-fingertips. I cursed ecstatically during the Liturgy of the Eucharist when the body of Christ touched my tongue, having in the past undergone a variety of diseases of that particular muscle, including glossitis caused by an off-brand toothpaste, chronic black hairy tongue, and the far more common thrush, most likely caused by my not rinsing thoroughly after using my asthma inhaler. I kicked the tuffet up, disrupting my row when they were absorbed in prayer. I stained the prie-dieu with the results of having consumed gone-over scallops. I added my own extemporaneous postscripts to the letters from Paul to the Corinthians. But what got me kicked out was taking notes. It's all just real estate, anyway." He laughs. It sounds like the call of the Atlantic Puffin.

He rises with a grunt and approaches the former priest, who flinches. He plunges his sharp fingernails into the man's forehead and pulls his hands apart, opening the head like a sideways valise. The letters of the alphabet are carved into the teeth. Wiegel pushes the teeth backward into the mouth, bending and splitting the gingiva horizontally. The skull splits horizontally, the back of it rising like a white flag. Wiegel types, his fingertips bouncing off the teeth; thin muscles acting as strikers slam bloody letters onto the flap of skull. He is teaching the defrocked priest how to write fiction. Mawkish sentiment. A main character whose appeal is such that you would marry him and thereupon cease to fuck him. A problem, like a peeping-tom paperboy or an impossible-to-kill cockroach infestation. A love interest, preferably an unattached florist who plays the glockenspiel or some such random disconnected combination of profession and skill. Romantic disappointment, the catastrophic failure of privileged expectation. An inciting incident like a massacre or the knifing of an altar boy or the downing of an aircraft with a phalanx of boy soldiers wielding slingshots. He writes his masterpiece until the ink runs out, and then he replaces it with his own. Ink soaks the carpet, red and shining. It squishes under the boots of the police when they arrive to worship. They doff their hats and recite their florid procedural prayers, nightsticks aloft.

Outside a stake-bound mutt unleashes a volley of barks like an auctioneer's spiel.

Head away from the cul-de-sac, take your first right, then your second right, take a left, drive about a half a mile, then take a right into the Queenan Park neighborhood. In the front yard of Marty Fenson's house, he, Fairweather Phil, Rick "Worst Case" Valerio, and Ghoulish Gould, ages ranging from 11 to 14, are trying to capture a snake, mostly white with oranges and browns and yellows, that is slithering into a hole in the earth between just under the low rock wall that borders the garden, when the neighborhood zombie lurches out from the woods, wet with brook water, algae draped like a stole over his shoulder. "Zombie Mike!" Phil shouts, and all at once the snake is forgotten.

Michael Aaron Ford was in a car accident one morning four months back. He lost control of his Ford Aspire on a rain-slicked 91 South exit ramp and hydroplaned into the guardrail, flipping the car, sending glass flying. The car burst into flames not long after he crawled out from under it. His injuries were surprisingly mild, and he was released from the hospital that night. The next morning his wife discovered the shower still running, blood swirling down the drain with the water, Michael nowhere to be found in the house nor on the grounds. His body was pulled from the woods that afternoon. Animals had been at it, chewed out the eyes, the entirety of the genitalia, one ear, most of the tongue, the webbing between the toes. Though the blanketed body was surrounded by state troopers, local police, a hastily assembled search party made up of people from that neighborhood and surrounding neighborhoods, dogs, and looky-loos, the body disappeared. Assuming an animal had somehow dragged it off, the crowd disbanded.

In the following weeks it had been spotted several times lurking in backyards, sprawling on the tennis court of the middle school, leaning unnaturally by the

Unitarian church, sitting dejectedly on a slowly swaying swing set seat, crouching in an unsecured shed during downpours, and, finally, shambling up and down the streets and the sidewalks, jerking, twitching, shivering, and muttering incomprehensibly or else bellowing. His widow, unnerved, cleared out as much as she could and bolted to parts unknown one day after she'd seen him stumbling into the woods behind their house.

Phil runs to the shed to get his aluminum bat. The other boys approach and surround the walking cadaver, which shudders to a halt and rocks back and forth on its feet, batting haplessly at the air with purple-black, swollen hands, its jaw hanging frighteningly low. Fenson steps on the back of its New Balance Casual Comfort Cross Trainer and puts the bottom of his own sneaker on the thing's upper back shin and pushes. The cadaver falls to the sidewalk, hands splayed, elbows bent. Gould stomps down hard between the cadaver's ass cheeks. It farts, a horrible, wet, rattling sound and the boys back away. They wave at the air, grimace, hold their noses. *Gah! Aw! What the fuck?!* Valerio projectile vomits. Phil approaches with the bat in two hands, stepping over the little brook of Cheeto-orange puke. He slams it down on the back of the cadaver's neck.

A shrill, cracked voice calls out. *"Boys, you boys stop that right this instant! Get away from him…get away!"*

From the yellow ranch across the street the source of the voice, a woman in a blue nightgown, is barreling down her front walk, the screen door behind her slapping the frame. Her heavy legs are white and profusely veined, and she waves her arms in the air, bingo-wings flapping. *"Gould! I grew up with your father! What would he think if he saw you now?"*

"Fuckin' Mrs. Tinker."

"Tinker the Stinker," says Phil, but he can never seem to make that one stick.

Fenson gets in one quick kick to the cadaver's stomach, the laces of his sneaker getting caught for a second under the xiphoid process. With a howl of rage he yanks it free and the boys scatter, laughing and screaming and calling out their ideas for places to rendezvous.

Rochelle Tinker, wife of forty years to Fred Tinker, a Claims Manager at Hartford Steamboiler, who died around the same time that Michael did, of complications connected to diabetes, kneels slowly and with some difficulty in the grass adjacent to the sidewalk. Grunting and wheezing, she grips the sleeve opposite and rolls the cadaver onto its back. Its empty sockets stare skyward.

"Tell me," she says in a conspiratorial whisper. "Do your digested eyes still see? Did your vision go kaleidoscopic when the coyotes ate them? Did you see the pink-red walls of their throats spinning, the light spiraling away?"

The cadaver opens its mouth, revealing grey, crumpled teeth, and says something akin to *aaarraaaaaaghyyyyooooooononononono*

Rochelle talks over him. "I want what you have. I don't want oblivion. Tell me – did you commune with witches? With devils? What secrets did they reveal? Who…or what…lies beyond the black gulfs? Did they not imbue you with the strength to fight back? I have so many questions, my love. I want to explore when I'm gone. I don't care how degraded or decrepit I get. What secrets did they tell you?

"Do they know my name?"

The cadaver says, "Listen."

Dear Gary,

They are keeping so many things from us, it's crazy. I know all about what you're going to say about conspiracy theories, but this isn't that. Here's one thing I'm talking about. An example. When I left your house the other evening, your clock, the one in the kitchen over the stove, its face grease-stained and smudged, read 7:55 pm. By the time the forty or so seconds it took me to get to the car had passed, the little clock in the hollow in the dashboard with the green square numbers read 7:54 pm. I arrived at the drive through at the Burger Purveyor at 8:11 pm, again according to the clock in my car. Through the window, past the workers, I saw that their clock, a wall clock similar to your kitchen clock but with bigger numbers and thicker arms that twirl around and all that, also said 8:11 pm. Everything lined up – the one minor variation between your house and my car can be chalked up to the little differences when clock-setting is left to humans and not to The Computer. But otherwise, everyone's on board with "the time." All people saying the same thing, over and over again, so certain, so sure. So deceived. This can't be right.

I happened to turn on the radio when I got home, my stomach full as a lord's, right when they were doing the station identification, and their time was the same as mine, the same as on my wall clock and my clock radio. I checked. I spun the dial down to around 88.5, looking for public radio, and a sinister voice told me that it's okay, it's correct, that's the time that is agreed upon for this particular time zone. Then I spun it up a little toward the middle of the dial, and a far more convincing voice asked me what they might gain from keeping from us the obvious glaring gulfs between the time they tell us it is and the time it actually is. Something must be done, the radio told me, and the radio's name today was "Blance Raftin." He is very wise and knows about many things, knows about how they control us, control our movements, restrict our freedom. He told me to watch—watch!—crowds. (A watch is a timepiece.) To listen to the specific ways I'm addressed. They never tell you the time in church, he said through the radio, nor in casinos, and these are holy places that know the truth about time, though when I went to try to verify this with a priest and with a croupier, neither would talk to me about it.

It's much bigger than I thought, if they can mess with time. Time! Think about it. Do your research. They can slip between those hours, the "official hour" and the real hour, and then they can do what they like with our bodies. With our minds. With our fluidity. We have to fight this. At first I thought the evil came from Sweden or Switzerland, where they make watches and clocks. That still might be true. But I'm not sure. Clocks are sold in so many places. I looked at clocks on Amazon. All the wall clocks said it was 10:10. The time on my home clocks was 12:03 pm. There was something about that time, I figured, that ten ten time. What did it mean? I scrolled down and was shocked. The digital clocks! The first I saw said 10:20 am. That's different from the wall clocks by TEN. Then another digital clock said 12:34 pm, the seeing of which threw me into a very confused depression.

Scrolling further there were discrepancies in even the wall clocks, but minor ones. 10:09. 10:12. Amazon is a computer, though, not a person, so clearly the website is mimicking the fallibility of human synchronization or, what do you call it when you…calibration. When I was done looking at Amazon, my clocks said 4:54 pm. Ron, I had not been on the internet for that long. But I was just as hungry as if I had.

Then the worst thing happened. I was out in the city picking up some things, and someone asked me the time. He had a half-smile, was wearing a t-shirt advertising a musician named R.E.M. His head was bald, but for a lick of hair from above his brow to the back of his neck indicating 12:30. He wore two watches. I could see plainly that they both also matched the time indicated by the makeshift clock on the dome of his head. Neither of these was anywhere near the supposed correct time. Saying nothing, I fled. Research taught me that R.E.M., he or her, had a record entitled OUT OF TIME.

So you see the breadth of the problem. All we need to do is figure out where to go. It might be someone named Big Ben, who I've learned lives in my apartment, his name is Benjamin Lebowitz and he must weigh just under 300 pounds. But I'm not sure if it's him. It's him, or it's Sweden or Switzerland. Or maybe it's downtown, where on the main corner two clocks, one on each corner of the Silverwater Bank, the one with the unblinking brass eyes above them, has lied about the time every instance I've seen it, matching itself with my watch and my phone, watching the pedestrians and the traffic.

Either way, I've armed myself. I asked the man at the gun shop to put the clock away before I would engage in commerce. He did so, with a smile that told me he knew, that we shared a secret. He also unclasped his watch and handed it to an underling, who brought it into the back room. You can see the church from the gun shop, by the way. I used some of my severance pay and some of my savings, and I purchased seven hand grenades, a Dickinson XXPA-12BS Hybrid Pump/Semi and a Black Diamond Specter XL Carbine, and the attendant ammunition. I also secured bulletproof vests, a flamethrower, and a set of war knives.

I need you to store these in your cellar for me. First you must remove all clocks from the house or at least disable them. Watches, wall clocks, microwave, stove, clock radio, laptop, television, DVD player, probably more that I haven't thought of.

My only worry is that these weapons won't work on the real culprit, the agents of the league of world governments. Not since I've seen the red men creeping between the seconds. These are new. They appear when you're close to knowing what is happening. When they appear it's just a flash, but with each flash they can remove words from the newspaper, words from the lips of the newscasters, words from books and instruction manuals. They're fast but they only get a few words at a time. But multiply that by however many seconds are in a day. It adds up.

Now that you know what I know, you will see them too. Here is how. Close your eyes when the second hand moves but open them before it settles. The red men will show a slice of themselves in the air in front of the clock. I don't know that conventional weaponry will work on them.

But if we send them a message by taking out people in full view of the Silverwater Bank eyes, and if we bring a clock with us to watch for the red men between seconds, we will kill as many as possible and then stop the clock between seconds, trapping the red men. Then we will hold them and question them. I'm sorry to have put them onto you, by the way, but I can't do this alone. My landlord is watching.

As the note on the envelope said, and as you saw, I heavily taped the letter all around with clear packaging tape. If you see any hint that it was removed, scars in the paper, a slice in the tape, place a hammer on the corner of Mudge and Topion Streets at the base of the street sign. Then await a reply.

Okay? Okay.

-Sagat

The Creeping Brain

One night, when I lay sleeping on my back, my brain broke loose from its moorings, and, alternating between flattening itself out and tightening itself into a long, maggot-like shape, it slithered down my throat and wound around my spinal column. From there it pushed its way between and around the organs of my torso, sniffing, tasting, learning, spreading its corruption. My heart struggled to beat without its usual signals. My blood flowed only because it was used to having done so. But my brain, sensing the trouble, sent its signals through my voice. *Beat,* my wife heard me say. *Now beat again. And beat.*

It told my voice to tell my wife to stay silent as to not impede its occult communications. She resisted, chatting aimlessly and merrily, so it had me…well…

The morning sun arose on a new widower, that is, me. Dirt lay under my fingernails like ten Amazon logos. I coughed dirt. Dirt filled my navel and my pores and stuck out like cinnamon sticks from my nostrils. I showered in very hot water. My brain had returned to its round room of bone from whence it sent comforting thoughts, and insisted I go about my normal life, which I did.

That night I lay on my stomach with one knee bent, like a swimmer. My brain stayed put. But the next night it left psychic notes for my various body parts and exited through my mouth to explore my house. My only sense of this happening was a mealy taste on my tongue. The young woman I'd taken home from the bar reports that I smacked my lips and made sounds like those of a man enjoying a rapturous meal after a period of starvation lasting just long enough to avoid causing permanent damage.

My brain propelled itself snake-like from room to room. It poked through my physical files and read the spines of my books. It startled the cat, who hissed at it, arched itself into an upside-down U, and bounced away like a furry rubber ball.

The next morning, I could not recall certain words. My pinky finger on my left hand stuck out rigid and unmovable. I could not imagine the taste of licorice, and I was frightened by some sort of L-shaped item with legs and cushions that sat in the corner opposite the television, and when I looked in the mirror, the short hairs above my eyes seemed wrong to me, intruders. I sliced them off with a knife I located in a box-shaped storage compartment that slid horizontally from under the counter below the microwave. This caused me to bleed.

The young woman from the bar sat me on a stool and daubed at my bleeding forehead with a bar towel, then another, then another, then a few more, and finally she gave me a hand mirror. The hairs had been replaced by blocky brown shapes, a development that pleased me.

She looked left and right and then shut down her phone. Once the screen was dark, she leaned forward and confided in me: "I believe that today my part is being played by a different actress."

"She's quite good," I replied. Then I yelled "CHAIR!" Feeling relief, I went straight to bed.

My brain squeezed itself from my ear and left the house by going under the door. It oozed down the road and found the cemetery. There it went from headstone to headstone to mortuary to monument to tree, searching, searching. An annoyed owl hooted. Bats fled in flapping clouds. The wrought iron fence spread its black ribs in an exhalation of graveyard breath.

It found what it wanted on an ancient stone whose carving read *I sentence you to be hanged by the neck until you are undead.*

You're never supposed to end a story with *it was all a dream.* That's a cheat. The work of something less than a hack, less than a piker, worse than an amateur. Having said that, the preceding was a daydream I dreamed in my grey office cubicle just before I died. When you die at your desk at Annelid Industries Incorporated (aka Annelid Industries International) they leave you there. Your coworkers are provided by management with Vapo-Rub to smear under their nostrils to prevent their inhaling the airborne particles from your rotting flesh. Though some opted to remove the filters from menthol cigarettes and plug their nostrils with those. Either way, the ventilation system in the office carries you away in nanoparticles. Recycles you. You are everywhere, inhaled and exhaled, consumed and shat out.

Your cubicle remains as a memorial. Your desk drawer, with its can of cashews, its empty supermarket bags, its clear packets of Chinese hot mustard and its white and red packets of Heinz ketchup, its curious coin with a symbol that looks something like a 4 and something like the letter A, the key to the secret door in the basement behind the moldering bankers boxes that were by law supposed to be disposed of in 1893, seven Bic pens, a spent lighter with the Blue Oyster Cult logo on it, the handwritten record of your supervisor's infidelity with a procession of scabby, messily painted-up prostitutes in Halloween "businesswoman" costumes, a snot-tissue wadded up like a dumpling, fourteen paperclips, two mouse turds, and a penny.

May your soul find its way to the wondrous place with massages and chocolate and mints and wine. May it leave this squalid place. May it forget conference calls. May it forget how your body jolted when the boss shrilly called your name; may it, in fact, forget your name as it approaches the bliss of sweet, unscented oblivion. Amen. Hallelujah. Fallujah. Now here's Mark "the Dark" Scarbourn with the Styx Fix.

Why You Are Evil

Your parents before they were your parents. Two people in the same section of the world. One just sixteen, the other two days from seventeen. A skinny dropout with buck teeth and a black sliver of a mustache. A knock-kneed girl with blonde pigtails of different lengths and eyes the color of topaz. In the Pioneer Valley. Not in Leeds but near enough to hear it, to feel its vibrations in their feet. Each could see the line of mountains from their respective houses.

They met by chance at the Three County Fair, in the line for fried dough. He spun around, sensing her eyes on him, and took her hand, never to give it back. Carla was a waitress, Patrick a druggist. They could barely hear each other over the roar of the demolition derby and the echoing voice of the announcer.

Had Carla published a personal advertisement entitled *Sick Fuck Seeks Same* she could not have found a better match, found herself the female half of a more darkly propitious union. The Folsom Wolf and his dark-eyed bride? Fred and Rosemary West? Doe-eye pikers.

Patrick and Carla were mutual hybristophiliacs. They killed, remained undetected, stingy with their DNA and castaway fragments even before DNA was an investigative tool. Shaved heads. Throwaway shoes. Bodies buried, sunk, crushed in compactors. Such an aphrodisiac. He humped her black and blue such that she had to recline on her sides, and she reamed him crossways, tore him bloody, with a garden claw.

Always people, never animals. The only rule.

How was the topic first broached? And who broached it? We'll never know. It was surely a function of the secret argot of insular couples, and none of our business. No, not even yours, one of several of the results of their coupling. Maybe it was a cautious confession. Maybe a secret blurted in the pink-red heat of violent union. Maybe a form of precognition. Maybe both opened their mouths to speak at the same time and word-for-word described the details of the ambition to foment an atrocity.

You? You were an experiment.

You were planned. And planned *for*. Schemed about. How they would treat you. The many things to which they would expose you. What they would do to and with you. Mentally only, of course, for physical is no fun. And too obvious. Overdone. Regarding family, anyway.

They wondered what glorious awfulness would eventually become of you, their damaged experiment. Would you be like them? Conversely, would you rebel and erase them from existence with a shotgun or, funnier, call the goddamned pigs on them, have them locked the fuck up? Or would you take FULL RESPONSIBILITY? Their laughter shook the shutters and startled the birds, raised goose pimples on the arms of the neighbors.

When her belly rode before her, preceding her by seconds into barrooms and boarding houses, she mimicked the joy of anticipation of motherhood she saw exhibited by other mothers-to-be. They told each other they glowed. They each felt the kicking feet of their babies-to-be. They squealed and chirped. She amused herself with the charade, told Patrick about it later as they splashed like hairy children in the bloody water of the clawfoot bathtub.

Oh, the music they played for you, the speakers held tight to her belly. WXXT's programming schedule was your pre-birth soundtrack, along with a special sampling of cassettes purchased from Fuzzbuzz Records & Tapes.

Worth it, she screamed through the pain of the miracle of birth. *Yes*, she cried when the doctor slapped your bottom. She laughed at your first tears, reveling in your reaction to expulsion from the warmth of the womb.

They got you home. It was just the three of you then. You had no agency, no recourse. To their credit, which of course I mete out grudgingly, you never felt unsafe. Never not provided for. Your education began on Day One, however. Once you grew, of course, you had a choice.

But you never had a choice.

Cassettes (Part 5)

The cover of the cassette is a folded snapshot of a small child in a field, wearing a peach-colored one-piece bathing suit. She has a fake white goatee glued around her mouth and a matching spiky white wig. Her arms are outstretched. A few grey goats stand on a wooden platform behind her, looking skyward.

The tape rolls.

A voice peals out a yodeling version of the Star Trek theme with a country-western twang. A noise creeps in, muffled friction, rough and uneven, like someone's wiping the microphone with a cloth. Far-off voices argue, the words lost to distance and foreground noise.

A creak like a loose floorboard, then a cheerful female voice:

<u>Luce:</u> Hello? Hell-o-ohh? Just kidding. You've reached Luce's voicemail. *She affects a Scottish burr:* I'm 'round the back, flingin' timbers. *Back to her usual American accent:* Leave a message after the bleep and I'll get back to you if I deem you worthy. Don't leave a goddamned novel.

<u>A deep voice:</u> Look, I woulda rather told you this in person, but whatever. When I was in the city, I went to get a massage. Yeah, one of those kinds. I don't think it's cheating, it's just hands, we can talk about it later if you're upset, but, you know, it's my feeling we had a kind of arrangement, a no-strings thing, even though we didn't actually (click)

A pause.

<u>Luce:</u> Hello? Hell-o-ohh? Just joking. You've reached Luce's voicemail. I'm out in the back, flingin' timbers. Leave a message after the bleep and I'll get back to you if I deem you worthy. Don't leave a novel.

Fax sounds. A distant voice, accented. *It was all rather...forensic. They say the priest had a tumor...that's why* (static) *the whole congregation* (static) *in the hymnals like bookmarks* (click)

A pause. Friction.

Luce: Hello? Hell-o-ohh? Just kidding. You've reached Luce's voicemail. I'm out back, flingin' timbers. Leave a message after the bleep and I'll get back to you if I deem you worthy. Don't leave a fucking novel.

The Deep Voice: …Christ, fuckin' answering machine. Cut me off, then I got a busy signal. I hate this shit. Pick up. No? Okay. So there's a hole in the table and you kind of put your face in it, so your neck's straight. I'm looking under the table and there's faint light. I can see the frame of the massage table. Not a lot to it, unfinished wood, splintery, with big bolts, the legs thick enough that there's no reinforcement, no need for it. There's carpeting under there. A matchbook. A penny. Dust bunnies like stringy clouds. The girl is massaging my head. I can see her feet in slippers, almost out of the range of my vision. I close my eyes a while and drift. The warm hands move down to my neck and shoulders.

I open my eyes again and this…person slides into view from under the foot of the table like he's a mechanic on a slider, but there's no noise, just the fuckin' Muzak. Dude is skinny AF, naked, with creepy huge eyes, no nose at all, and this wide mouth. I looked at his junk, some reason, don't even fuckin' ask. It looked like a goddamned deep-sea creature. I fuckin' flip out, I go to get up, to get the fuck outta there, and strong-ass hands grab my ankles and my wrists and hold me down. I didn't even hear the goddam door open. Meanwhile, the girl's whacking the sides of her hands on my back like everything's normal. The fuckin' guy under the table reaches up towards my face and he's got way too many fingers, all skinny, and his mouth is opening and (click)

Pause.

Luce: Hello? Hell-o-ohh? Just kidding. You've reached Luce's voicemail. I'm out in the back, flingin' timbers. Leave a message after the bleep and I'll get back to you if I deem you worthy. Don't leave a goddamned novel.

A child's voice, wavering, coming in and out of focus: …*capsules tumbling down my throat like bombs from a Douglas A-20 Havoc…* A woman's voice: *Come here. Get that out of there. Cough. COUGH, goddammit. Oh, shit Oh, shit.*

The Deep Voice: …so I'm driving home. It's late, but I can't tell how late. On my phone screen there's a blank spot where it used to show the time of day. The car clock is just blinking zeroes, and the radio is playing backwards pop and I can't make out the time when they announce it backwards. I get that it's "meh eep," and then "colck-o," then I'm lost. Sometimes *he's* sitting in the passenger seat. Sometimes *he's* not. I think it's whenever the light from a streetlamp gets in that he disappears. Honey, you wouldn't believe what he's telling me. Pack a bag. Pack a bag, Luce. I should be home soon. I'm going to try to get in before he does. To get to the door first. Unlock the door. Please unlock the...

Pause.

<u>Luce:</u> Hello? Hell-o-ohh? Just kidding. You've reached my voicemail. I'm out in the backyard, flingin' timbers. Leave a message after the beep and I'll get back to you if I deem you worthy. Don't leave an epic novel.

<u>The Deep Voice:</u> He made slices just below each shoulder and one at the top of each back of my thigh. He slid his arms into mine under the skin and his legs into mine. So when you see me, I'll be walking all awkwardly. There's a pistol in the nightstand. I know. But it was to protect you, baby, to protect us. If you can get in back of me, shoot me in the back. If you can't, shoot me in the fucking head. Right in the fucking head. I lov

Uncle Red Reads To-Day's News

The great angry orb of summer is the tip of a jaundiced, pointed finger that glows with radiation, hiding black cancers in the deceptive yellow cheer of its rays. O it causes me such discomfort. It turns my skin from white to red. It sears the dust on my eyeballs, compromising my vision. It swells my eyelids and irritates my glands. An unseemly stench emanates from the places where my skin folds. Nude and pale, before the dawn, anticipating the day, I seek out the basements of churches. There among moldering paintings; peeled wooden Jesuses; piled, moisture-swollen hymnals; fart-warped disused pews; and ancient records in rusted-out filing cabinets, I seek something resembling comfort. Being in darkness below ground among old things rejuvenates me. The absence of the Christ, more acute, more *pronounced*, here than it is upstairs, enlivens me. It gets the worms moving, so to speak, makes me feel alive. And it is from such a spot that I now provide for you, you lady and gentleman and child listeners of Leeds, reports of to-day's news.

The members of the Society for Detecting Unsavoury and Indecent Scoundrels, and likewise those who seek membership therein, are hereby notified that the torso of J. Warner Hoopenlapper, the founder and leader of said organization, has been found in the attic of his home, and the stripped limbs and appendages in the mailboxes of his various children, who live in far-flung regions of the Commonwealth. The head has not yet been located. The group shall meet again in secret to vote on a new leader. Details to arrive in an occulted fashion, free from the prying eyes of the so-called city leaders and the church.

An employee of the Boston & Maine Railroad claims to have seen an infant with one hand as hairy and as large as that of a full-grown man, on a disused section of track in the woods of Leeds. As the stricken man watched, the apparently feral creature snatched from the air and squeezed to death a hapless bluebird. It then regarded the man with eyes imbued with forbidden knowledge and said in a demoniac tone the mysterious words "the valley's home for the best commercial-free classic rock."

Governor Coolidge, who was expected to be present at the celebration of the Pilgrim tercentenary in the Academy of Music this Thursday evening, has sent word that he will be unable to attend due to the last-minute rescheduling of a meeting in Boston. However, several subscribers to, and an employee of, this very publication report having seen him at the edge of a marsh, engaged in animated and possibly contentious conversation with a very tall and very pale man with some sort of facial disfigurement, who wore a large hat and held aloft a red walking stick.

The Leeds Detective Part 2: The Tape Player

Detective Gregory Specter pulled his '51 Ford Country Squire into a space next to the Leeds Friendly's. The mostly empty parking lot sprawled between the restaurant, which had its own lot on the other side by its entrance, and an old factory building that housed a bank, a dental office, a whack-shack masquerading as a therapeutic massage establishment, and a variety of small offices. Behind the Friendly's, below a wooden walkway servicing a set of one-room low-income apartments, stood the glass-doored entrance to Fuzzbuzz Records and tapes.

Specter scooped up from in front of the passenger seat a handful of ketchup-splotched wax paper hamburger wrappers and cardboard fry containers, and gathered the straw papers scattered like flattened tapeworms. With a grunt of discomfort, he heaved himself out of the car. He dropped the trash in the city garbage can and headed over to the shop. The light was on in there. Decals on the narrow horizontal window next to the entryway advertised bands with names like Rancid, NOFX, Crispy Ambulance, and Half Man Half Biscuit.

Specter pushed the door open, an electronic ding heralding his arrival. No proprietor nor clerk was in evidence. No customers either. Reggae played over the sound system, incomprehensible, a lot of echo effects. He scanned the book rack. Future Shock by Alvin Toffler, The Red Notebook by Henry Miller, Violent Rigor by Philip Rippingcoat, titles by writers he'd never heard of, like Betty Rocksteady and Breece D'J Pancake, a book about parricide, and a slew of worn-spined true crime mass markets.

He sensed a presence, and turned see a man at the counter, appeared from as if out of nowhere. He peered. He knew this man.

The man gasped. "If it isn't Gregory Scanlon, as I fucking live and fucking breathe."

"Well, hello, Paul Winklepleck. Long time. I go by Specter now."

"And I go by Cooperford, not Winklepleck. Not anymore."

"Well, aren't we both a couple of mysterious characters," Specter said. "Assumed names. Aliases, one might say. Very shady."

"The past is the past," Cooperford said, shrugging.

"Indeed it is." He paused. A thoughtful look took over his face. "Though, as the man said, it's not even past."

"Fitzgerald, right?"

"Faulkner. I don't think you carry him."

"Guess not. Looking for anything in particular?"

Specter reached into his coat pocket and proffered his badge. Cooperford stiffened, which normally would have aroused Specter's suspicions. But Cooperford wasn't a suspect in anything, just paranoid. Exactly as he had been as a younger man, as a frontman. You'd make a suggestion to tweak a bass line, and he'd react as though you were trying to take over the direction of the band, as if it had any future whatsoever. "I'm here on official business, actually," Specter said.

"Crimes against music? If you want to confiscate the Maroon 5 records, I can show you the section."

"I don't know what any of what you just said means. I'm led to believe your establishment carries cassette players. Is that the case?"

"Not as a matter of course," Cooperford said. "But as a matter of fact, I do happen to have one available. It was one of the players customers could preview cassettes with. The mechanism's a little funky, and it might fuck up your tape if you're not careful, but you're welcome to it."

"What's the charge?"

"I was just going to toss it anyway. It's all yours."

Specter tilted his head. A noise, somewhere under the music. A voice calling, sustained. "Can you turn the music down?"

A cloud crossed Cooperford's face. Just for a second. What did it mean?

"I can't do that, man," he said.

"You...can't do that?"

Cooperford stuttered for a second, his eyes blinking rapidly, then he said, "No, sorry, I can do it. I just have to run downstairs where the volume controls are."

"No, don't bother, that's fine."

"Suit yourself. Tape player's behind the counter. I'll grab it for you."

Later, in his bed, Specter stared up at the ceiling. The fan beside his bed breathed loudly. Car lights painted strange shapes on his window-shades. Something had been suspicious there at the store. The source of the music seemed to be the stereo set behind the counter. Was there something in the basement? He knew the question had nagged him at the store, but he'd shut it off, insisting to himself that this wasn't even a questioning nor an official visit. He'd even explained away what he'd heard as part of the song that was playing. Stupid. Stupid.

Goddammit, he should have checked. He was losing it. He'd make it a point to drop back in. After he listened to the tape they'd found in the mouth of the dead girl.

Uncle Red Reads To-Day's News

It was a night of high windes and badde dreams in the darkly beautiful city of Leeds, my friends, my followers, my faithful. The starts swung on strings of light and the clouds shimmied and shook and changed direction like capricious cats or squirrels on a busy roadway, all looked over by the shadow-stricken horror-face of the moon.

There is much news to report.

Professor Charles Chalkflinger reports a calumnious conspiracy by a cabal of pupils claiming he berates, cajoles, and denigrates them, when in fact all he does is provide his carefully wrought lessons on which he works "until the late hours every blessed day on the calendar." Further, Dr. Chalkflinger asserts that the source of the invective described by the students is in fact one or more of those self-same students using misdirection and voice-throwing and other secrets of ventriloquism, and that the voice or voices issue not only vituperation but also grotesqueries, dark insinuations, and utterings of a sexually vile nature directed not at the students, but at the venerable professor himself, as well as at the fine institution at which he plies his trade. The professor is on involuntary sabbatical pending an investigation.

Police apprehended a man sleeping on the cold marble floor of the Leeds Columbarium overnight. The man could not be woken, so he was transported to Cooley Dickinson hospital, where doctors concluded the man was not comatose, a theory proffered by Officer Gould Queenan, but in fact was in a state of torpor similar to that of bears. Horrified witnesses at the columbarium report that upon the removal of the unnamed man, the vessels containing the ashes of the dead shook and trembled and finally cracked, releasing dusty wraiths that danced and threw themselves about with loathsome wails and,

127

achieving forms and shapes presumably approximating their former corporeal bodies, engaged in acts of fornication in a variety of bizarre, contorted formations and positions unattainable to the living, whose bodies are governed by regretful limitations. The moans and groans of the convulsing, copulating dead were extremely disturbing to the occupants of the neighborhood adjacent to the institution, and police, acting upon a hunch, returned the slumbering man to his spot on the floor. This, thankfully, caused the dead to gather themselves and return to their urns, though it is feared that the ashes may have mixed and combined. Officials from the FBI in concert with the Federal Communications Commission are in the process of contacting and informing the relatives of the affected deceased.

Died, on the 10th inst. of a bilious fever, Mr. Louis "Quarter horse" Mitcham, the third son of Mr. Daniel Mitcham, aged 41 years. An artist, his unlocked cabin-studio in the woods of Leeds is unofficially accessible for those with an interest in occult paintings of a disquieting nature and portraits of notorious local figures, in watercolor on ivory. He has left a widow to bemoan his untimely fate whilst wishing the public to know that she will be auditioning robust and worthy suitors after a respectable yet brief interval, and a son intoxicated by the profitable possibilities opened up by the loss.

A school is commended in the rooms over the store of Messrs. Pimple & Rascall & Rottene, where will be taught hermeticism, techgnosticism, meat science, scatatheosophy, cryptodemonology, radio propagation, and paraphiliasophy, together with other sciences and disciplines commonly attended to in the finest European schools.

Leonard Sincage of Goat Meadow Road offers for sale one of the most profitable farms of its size in the town of Leeds. It comprises an impressive proportion of tillage, pasturage, meadow, and woodland. Several gable-fronted barns, a disused charnel house, and an antiquated altar festooned with bibelots, baubles, and curious gewgaws may be found on the farther reaches of the property.

A black and brown catte of unknown provenance has been making its way into the houses of the New City neighborhood in Leeds at nighttime and frightening residents with hisses, growls, caterwauling, chattering, chirping, singing, dancing curious dances on its hind legs, bathing with avidity its swollen hind parts, spraying, befouling family bibles, playing discordant pieces on pianos, and using typewriters to compose foul paeans and poems and think pieces and prayers and exhortations to obscenity.

In an alluvial waterway behind the Leeds Sanitarium was found a severed human hand of gargantuan proportions, as that of a giant. The hand spanned six foot across and eight- and one-half foot in length. Under the large, longish fingernails were found pebbles, grass, and mud; and a tattoo of an occult symbol was emblazoned upon the back of the hand, the main feature of the design a pattern of lines mirroring those of the dorsal veinous network beneath the skin. A bone like the stripped trunk of a dead tree jutted from the ragged remains of the wrist, and feasting upon the flesh there were maggots, also of alarming size, and the odour was said by the authorities to be unendurable. No body nor giant person has been located, nor do any footprints indicate the presence of a person of that size.

The Library Patron

1

The Montague Wright Public Library is situated comfortably back from the sidewalk that borders the curved easternmost section of Forbes Street close to where it intersects with Main, just west of downtown Leeds, across from the gates of the women's college. Constructed in the waning years of the 19th century, the Richardsonian Romanesque structure is considered by historians to be one of Leeds's more picturesque buildings. It is composed of rusticated granite and sandstone, and features round-headed towers and a recessed entrance under a vaulted Guastavino arch. The upper windows are of stained glass. The walkway that surrounds the building weaves its way around ancient stones and modest gardens that have graced the spot since before the time of its former notorious occupant.

The library building was built on the foundation upon which previously had stood the mansion of notable Leeds occultist and poet Skelton Tornweather, after the edifice was set afire by affronted townsfolk in 1862. The arson came not long after the publication of a slim chapbook of Tornweather's poetry entitled The Cambion Cantos IV-XI, *several verses of which the city blamed for the corruption of some of its children, though there has been no concrete connection established.*

In the years intervening between the fire and the library's construction, the land was shielded by black tarpaulins and anointed with holy water. Priests from neighboring parishes were brought in to cleanse of sin the land and the air and what remained of the cellar and the labyrinths beneath, the latter of which stonemasons from the nearby city of Springfield subsequently walled off.

You may request access to the Rare Book & Special Collections Room, which, as its name suggests, contains rare and antique books as well as historical documents, at the front desk just beyond the entrance, between the Reading Room and the Reference Hall. Two library employees, a research assistant and a security guard, will accompany you. Both are equipped with body cameras. Unless you are disabled, you will ascend via the east stairway. If you are disabled, know that the elevator has four cameras whose monitors are manned, and which record, 24 hours a day, 7 days a week. The computers to which they record are equipped with state-of-the-art facial recognition software, and can identify patrons, even if the lower half of their face is masked and they are wearing sunglasses or even makeup.

At the top of the third-floor stairs, or from the adjacent elevator, you will head right past several reading rooms and vaults to a glass door with a button adjacent to it that will activate a buzzer inside.

Rare Books & Special Collections staff will unlock the door when the buzzer is activated. In the small anteroom, you will be searched. Items that are verboten: suitcases, valises, briefcases, backpacks, duffel bags, cameras, mobile phones, paper including sticky notes, writing implements, knives, liquids of any kind including water. Your valuables and license (or other identification) will be confiscated and returned to you upon your departure.

Only then will you be permitted into the Rare Book & Special Collections room.

To your left you will find the desk behind which the Rare Book & Special Collections Clerk will be available to assist you. To your right are four rows comprising two tables apiece, each with a brass banker lamp with a glass red shade, and a magnifier. Straight ahead, running the length of the far wall, perpendicular to the tables, stand the stacks of locked glass-fronted cases in which our books reside, most of their spines legible through the glass. You may browse (visually) or consult a bound catalog which also separately lists volumes whose spines are too thin or too worn to read through the glass. Several extremely rare items are kept in a locked safe in the office located adjacent to the desk. These may not be brought to your table but can be viewed at the desk in the attendance of the Rare Book & Special Collections Clerk. Inform the clerk as to which volumes you wish to see, using the alphanumeric code to the left of the title. There is a log which you must sign and in which you must indicate the titles and codes for each book you wish to see. Since some volumes require the reader to don gloves to protect the integrity of the paper, six pairs will be handed to you, not to be disposed of until all books are returned to their homes. You may bring to a study table no more than two books at a time.

You may access no more than six books in one day.

The man sat at the table with two books spaced evenly before him, a large, foxed volume with a leather cover and delicate pages sepia with age; and a slim booklet, stained and worn, bound with thread. He pulled apart the white curtains of his hair and tied it all behind his head with a violet elastic. He adjusted his spectacles. His distorted reflection in the highly polished wood gazed blurrily up past the books back at him. With a large, flat, pale hand he slid the larger of the two volumes over to cover that blasted reflection. It appeared to gasp as it was obscured, though he'd been sure to keep his own expression neutral.

He took a deep breath and whipped open the larger book to its center pages as though tearing a bandage from tender flesh. He beheld what was written there. Then he opened the smaller book with some difficulty, given the loss of tactile sensation caused by the rubber gloves. He put his hand on the edge of the chair as if to rise and was startled to sense a man seated at his right-hand side.

He turned and gasped, for indeed a man was there, a man…or a cadaver. For the skin and muscle of its face was gone, torn away from the top of the forehead just below the hairline to the ears to the chin, revealing much of the bone of the skull. The tattered skin that framed the abomination was a painful-looking bronze color with white stipples of peeling, as though over-tanned under UV light. A healthy tongue, pinkish-red and speckled with papillae, rested behind a full complement of teeth framed with the black scraps of whatever damaged gingiva remained. He wore a pressed black suit over a black shirt with long, pointed collars tipped with silver and a red-corded bolo tie with sharp, shining aiguillettes and a complex and inscrutable emblem on its clasp.

The man looked at the eyes of this apparition. The surface was murky glass smudged with fingerprints. A red triangle floated forward from the depths of each eye. On the left one were raised white letters, blurred but getting clearer as it approached. It read "Outlook Dire." On the right was etched a stylized tooth with fang-like roots. Slowly that icosahedron spun, the tooth turning away, to show another face. This one read, "Try again."

Something loosened in the man's mouth. He moved his tongue around his top teeth until he felt movement. Something landed on his tongue. Knowing what it was before he saw it, he pushed the tooth out of his mouth and onto his palm. It lay there, small and bereft, like something dead washed up on a crenellated shore of skin.

The skull-faced man chuckled.

Shhhh, the clerk said from his desk, his sibilant admonition bubbly with spittle.

The man looked to the desk, where the clerk glared. "I'm sorry," he whispered. "But it wasn't me, it was…"

He looked back. The skull-faced man was no longer in the chair next to him. The clerk shook his head, glared for a moment, and then went back to whatever it was he'd been doing.

The skull-faced man now stood in the shadows between the stacks at the far end. With a long, blue-gloved finger he beckoned the man.

3

At the group table just by the stacks of magazines sat the man, a newspaper in front of him, open, atop which sat a mass market paperback, closed.

He wore a grey pinstriped Salvation Army suit (with the tag still stapled onto the collar with one of those tiny staples) over a white t-shirt with a stretched-out neck. He was somewhere between 55 and elderly, with grey, wavy hair combed down and maybe three days' worth of grey stubble to match.

The only sounds were breathing, the clicks and clacks of fingers depressing buttons on keyboards, and the occasional sigh or snicker as people consulted publications of various sizes and shapes and on many different matters and topics.

All the windows shattered, the glass falling inward. The crowd gasped as one, then, shrieking and chattering, moved toward the center of each room, shielding their heads from the raining shards.

The man stood. "The stomach begs for the blade!" he cried in a thick Central Massachusetts accent. "The cluster of intestines wants like all of us to be free, to be strung, uncoiled, laid out straight, glimmering juicy in the fire light, a jump-rope for countless daemonic imps!"

The crowd shifted away from him, other patrons rising and kicking back their chairs and backing away, hands out in case the man was armed. The library staff adjusted their glasses and shushed the man, taut fingers lain across red-painted lips, bisecting them.

"The wormy goat approaches," he added. "along with His beneficent patriarchate. May his mad bleat enlighten us all!"

He reached into his coat and pulled out a ceremonial athame with a goat-head pommel and a brass worm cluster screwed into the hilt. From the stacks and onto the balcony above shimmed thirteen nude women, pale and shapely and redheaded, whipping their hips and tracing their throats with long black nails.

The library patron rose and dragged away the table with the help of library staff, whose eyes had gone white. Drool swayed in mucousy strings from their lips. In the cleared-away space the dancers gathered, and the man stripped off his clothing, flinging everything to the walls. Then he broke into a funky, naked, head-jutting, junk-thrusting strut, waving the knife about madly, the dancers mirroring his steps, howling.

Behind this, the elevator doors slid open and black hardbound books like bats swarmed out, covers flapping, dropping invective like ordnance, the words landing in little plops on the carpet. All I wanted was to see the title of the paperback the man had been reading. But in the frenzy of the moment, I could not locate it. I batted away books, crawled under disused library card catalog cabinets. It was nowhere. Two pale hands grabbed my ankles and pulled me to the center of the dancefloor. I could smell sulfur. I could smell sweet perfume like the juice of booze and berries. I could smell the sex of the women, earthy, healthy, life-affirming. I could smell worms and goat cheese and the nose-stinging demon smells of the red pimpled rolls of caps I would hit with a hammer in my youth.

I took the hands of the library patron and we swung in a circle, everything around us spinning in the opposite direction, white flesh, pink nipples, all blurring into a wall like the inside of a sex cyclone. In the distance military drums beat. Helicopters shouted their pulsing approach from the south.

He comes! shouted the man.

Sure of hoof and sharp of horn! the ladies sang.

High in a corner office in a skyrise in Washington D.C. a grey-haired man in a blue suit watched the celebration on his monitor. A crease of a frown looked permanently stamped upon his stern, stone-like face. "It's happening," he said to the people whose heads sat in square sections on the adjacent monitor. His voice was grim and thin, his tone solemn. "Assemble the squad."

Tzjub

Tzjub lived in offal, dwelt in carrion, within walls composed of piled cadavers, hollowed husks that had bled into one another and then stiffened and coagulated. Intestines coiled like garden hoses cradling rotting hearts at their centers, more intestines hanging in loose coils from the rafters, split horizontally, dried turds lined up like abandoned subway cars within. Fat lungs and flat livers draped over piles of powdered bone. Maggots and flies, the circle of life. Sloping drifts of shed fingernails and toenails like the discarded scales of some clickety-clackety snake. The buzzy hum, the clicks of heating pipes and the creaks of the house settling.

Every so often Master would pour more down the chute, tumbling organs rolling over each other, landing in the slop, or whole bodies sliding down like the grotesque patrons of some deranged waterpark. Tzjub glistened and gleamed, sharpened its arms on its legs, sharpened its hands on its chin. It chopped and sliced and slit. It clothed itself in stains, knowing it must never be naked, for to be naked was to be dead. Oh, the surge of joy it felt as it tore and ripped and cut, sluicing gore through its chambers. If Tzjub only had lips to lick and a tongue with which to lick them.

Master invented Tzjub two years ago today, happy birthday, Tzjub, steel in steel, solder and fasten, hone and hew. Master cut himself often over the course of the endeavor, cackling, holding open the window of his skin and looking in, ripping the wound open with his fingers, snaking the tip of his tongue in, tasting, savoring. When the mechanical work was complete, he opened the Great Book, read aloud a passage, the long-neglected nail of his index finger underlining as he read. He baptized Tzjub in urine, flicked graveyard dirt mixed with powders whose source one must not reveal, no, never. Tzjub, born screaming, edge sliding against edge. Master plucked a fat infant from a metal bucket. Its fists grasped at the air, fat little pink fingers. He flung it at Tzjub and Tzjub caught it in his blades. He washed himself in its blood and juices. Before long, Tzjub began to scream again. Master threw in three more infants, these babbling and spittle-slopping, and then left in a hurry, stabbing arms into coat sleeves, stomping into waiting boots.

And thusly they lived, Master upstairs in his inscrutable world, Tzjub downstairs in a revelry of carnage and putrefaction, closed off by a plastic-lined door and gazed upon by windows cemented shut. Until the day that Master himself slid down the chute, green and gangrenous, naked, balls and pecker flopping, distended ass-hole hanging out like a tapered purple tail, toes and fingers akimbo, mouth agape, his final gift to Tzjub, which Tzjub destroyed with singular, hungry zeal and gratitude.

The chute remained empty after that, dried up like a parched throat, and everything began to dry up, to go to dust. The stains on Tzjub began to fade. He screeched in rage, metal scraping on metal, screeched himself dull until he had to sharpen himself again. He sensed the door above him. With great pain and with many false starts and clanking tumbles, he climbed the dusty stairs and went to work on the plastic-lined door. A world of flesh awaited, lusting for laceration.

Untitled Part 2 – by Pixie Pottle

"He's with me."

At this the man in the suit with the faded pink shirt stared stupidly at me, his eyes unfocused, his mouth reeking of drink, his slack, drooping bottom lip revealing dark red gums under chipped teeth. I took him by the hand—a warm, feverish hand at that—and led him up onto the stage. When I let go, he trip-stumbled over to the piano, pulled out the bench with a loud screeching sound, and after a series of mishaps managed to sit on it. He commenced to wobble.

"Play," I commanded, and he lifted the slide whistle, a look of reverence taking over his face as though he was holding aloft some ancient relic of profound religious significance.

"The piano, you fool."

He placed the slide whistle gingerly at his side on the bench, then tapped a low note with the middle finger of his left hand. He tapped it again. Then again, and more, until he had a kind of a beat going, steadier than I would have thought possible. Soon he brought his right hand into play, its fingers dancing over the high notes, producing a sound that reminded me of reflected lights twinkling in a tar-black river.

I took the microphone from the stand and held it tightly, lovingly in my sweating fist. I spoke over the music, letting the beat guide my delivery:

I will follow thee
Into record shops where you flip through the selections
Into restaurants where you sip at tepid tea
And frown at the daily paper
Into laundromats where your clothes spin and your sad blue
Plastic

Basket
sits bereft
Into hotels where you meet with clients in darkened rooms
To transact secret business
Into three-story malls where you lean on the railing and stare at the tops of
heads
Into tenements where you get your toxic fixes
Into graveyards where you commune with the dry and muddy dead

The suit man's hands stopped on the piano. The audience, not knowing whether to applaud, stood silent. I opened my mouth as though to continue. The silence was gorgeous. It was decadent. I gulped it like it was sweet whiskey with hints of pear and mint and stomach acid.

The Fourteenth Floor

On the first day of the summer of his twenty-seventh year, a lesser[1] Leeds occultist by the name of Philip Rippingcoat sat in a guest chair in the oak-paneled office of Marcus Leadermeyer, the owner and manager of the Gowdy Lodge, the twenty-story hotel acquired by the Hilton Hotels corporation in June of 1925 and then hastily sold back to its original owners for a dollar four months later in a secret deal that had investors scratching their heads.

Rippingcoat was slender and slightly bowlegged, with a small potbelly. He was clad in a ceremonial red robe with draping sleeves and a cowl over tights. His feet were encased in tight, shining boots that reached halfway to the knee. He sat with one leg crossed over the other and laconically stroked his wisp of a beard with the long, black-hued fingernail of his *digitus minimus manus*. His demand hung in the room like a singularly unpleasant fetor. Leadermeyer, who looked rather like a swollen, nauseous, toothless version of Buster Keaton, banished from his face his initial aghast expression, trading it for a narrow-eyed stare of suspicion. In point of fact, he had every reason to be suspicious. The Rippingcoat and Leadermeyer families had been at loggerheads since their great-grandfathers' days. The exact nature of the initial disagreement is lost to time, but the animus remained no less intractable, and was, in fact, exacerbated by the latter's conversion in the 1970s to a mystic form of Christianity.

"You want to what?" Leadermeyer said, his voice a pipe-seared rasp.

"I should like to…what's the word…*book* the fourteenth floor in its entirety."

---

[1] Though he might object to that designation

Leadermeyer tried and failed to keep the outrage out of his voice. "All twelve rooms and both suites?"

"Indeed. And the hallways. Starting this very night."

"Impossible. The rooms are engaged. All of them. Many of the guests are part of a block of rooms for the Poetry Convoca..."[2]

"Throw them out," Rippingcoat said. "Also, I shan't want the elevator stopping on my floor, and I'd like 'No Trespassing" or somesuch signs placed on the doors leading there."

"*Your* floor?! If you want this accommodation so badly, *you* tell the guests."

"Trust me, they will much prefer it if *you* inform them. If I do it, I will have little choice but to engage my votary. Blood will be spilt. And you have the loveliest carpets. I'd hate to see them ruined."

When it was done, Leadermeyer retreated to his suite on the first floor, the sole set of rooms on that level not designed for meetings nor events. The echoes of meticulously rendered insults in iambic pentameter and plausible rhyming threats and well-phrased accusations rattled around his poor brain. He'd had to offer compensation to all but one of the guests, and vouchers to that one. All of them decided to try to bargain. He'd capitulated every time, to the tune of, well, *too much money*. He was too exhausted to be angry. He splashed an audacious amount of sherry into a pink, tulip-shaped glass and also onto his desk and lastly onto some important papers, the latter of which he yanked away, cursing, and flung to the floor out of the various paths of the spreading liquid. After wiping up the mess and retrieving and reorganizing his documents whilst moaning and groaning with gusto, he disrobed and lowered himself into the bath, placing his glass gingerly on the tub's ledge. The bubbles blanketed him in warmth and aromas of jasmine and clary sage.

Slowly, silence supplanted the echoes of the evening's vicious voices. There would be time to grapple with this incursion, to form his defense when the hostile opinion pieces were published, as they would inevitably be, and to decide what to do regarding the hostile takeover of Floor 14. Tonight was for him, for peace, for relaxation, for the comfort and consolation and contemplation of

[2]The fifth iteration of The Poeticon, a notorious drunken revelry disguised as a poetry convocation, drawing middling-to-great poets from around the world, including Robert Batshifter, whose *Notes from a Leaning Outhouse* electrified and radicalized a generation; and Walter Bellbeery, a notorious whiskey-hound and author of a much-derided epic poem, rhyming, untitled, spanning thirteen volumes.

God's many-headed love, His loving emerald eyes, His long, many-jointed fingers, and the swing through consecrated air of His holy ax. The radiator sighed. A drop from the faucet hit the surface of the tub water with a plopping sound. *Welcome aboard, sploop of water,* thought Leadermeyer. *Make yourself at home.*

He was just drifting off the sleep when the noise started. Cheers and raucous laughter. An ecstatic holler of slurred words he couldn't make out, but that he knew were mostly obscene. Glass shattering. Something hitting the ground outside with a massive thud, actually agitating the water, making it slosh against the opposite ends of the tub, making the empty clothes hangers jingle like slender gymnasts colliding on their horizontal bar.

He leapt to his feet, a bulbous tower of bubbles like a ghost on the boil, but with a half-turgid purplish pecker head jutting from the foam.

Up on the fourteenth floor, WXXT played from every room., even from the speakers in the ceilings. *The Satanic Hip Hop Hour with MC Beezle and DJ Loose* was on, as it always was this day at this time, blasting out from the open doorways, the bass shaking the framed pictures on the walls. One radio receiver was getting the signal just a tick late, which led to an echo effect that increased in volume the closer one got to the defective device. Frenetic jazz with a hip-hop beat blasted from all corners, someone babbling over it, jumping topics from art forgery to hidden meanings in children's literature to boar taint to the unreleased Satanic songs of Sammy Davis Jr. which the babbler claimed in rhythmic rhyme to be in negotiations to acquire from a reluctant seller.

Philip Rippingcoat, clad only in palm-tree flip flops and a long, open kimono depicting swamps and gnarled trees and lightning-swaddled tall gothic houses on rolling hills, strutted down the hall, his hips thrust forward, nodding his head to the beat, knees bent, hands palm-up, fingers curling and uncurling as though accepting gaudy baubles from invisible admirers.

A few yards in front of him, a naked woman, zaftig, pale, and pig-tailed, ran across the hall, from room 1402 to room 1403, tittering with frantic joy, her pink-blotched flesh bouncing and jiggling. From 1403 came a thrilled whoop and the fanfare of kazoos. Something like lava or syrup, black with sparks and streaks of red and orange, oozed slowly from the doorway of 1402 after the woman, causing the carpet underneath it to emit blue smoke. Rippingcoat leapt spryly over the oozing stuff without missing a beat.

He turned the next corner, leaning most groovily and at an impressively acute angle to the floor without falling over, then straightening out again, snapping his fingers and beatboxing, his chest waving side to side like a metronome. A hillock of grey and white goat fur adorned the floor before him. He circumvented it and then saw the apparently recently shorn goat walking on its hind legs. Patches of fur remained on its knobby joints. Piebald, nicked, and somewhat unsteady, it took a staggering left into a snack machine alcove, and moments later a male and female voice from somewhere back there shouted in unison[3] *Spiffy! Just marvelously spiffy!*

Rippingcoat was grooving now. He wet his finger, stuck it into the shallow pocket of the kimono, and drew it back, pushing whatever was in there up high into each nostril, sniffing hungrily.

He pivoted into the next open door on the right, where on a king-sized bed a giant purple leech lay, contracting and lengthening in time with the breathing of the thin, nude, elderly man, chafed and chapped and scarred, who clung to the thing's ridged purple side and was biting into and slurping at the segment nearest its anterior sucker. The man said something[4] to him through a mouthful of blood, but Rippingcoat couldn't make it out. "What?" he said mockingly as he backed away and out of the room and continued on his merry journey without waiting for the reprise.

He took the corner hopping on one leg, and the hallway that stretched before him was full of yellow-feathered birds flapping madly from the open window at one end to the open window at the other. Rippingcoat flattened himself against the wall. Instead of bird-faces and beaks, these creatures had the swollen, pinched features of newborn infant humans, and they were all made up, painted and adorned with foundation, mascara, eyeshadow, and eyelash extensions, as though it had been applied by a beautician in some tony salon. They squealed and chirped and shrieked as Rippingcoat crossed his forearms over his face to protect his eyes.

When the noise started to abate, he looked at the last of them as they exited the window into the starlit night. Under their tail feathers were tiny white human-like buttocks. One of the birds squeezed out a stream of white and cherry shit when it bumped the molding. It ran like melted ice cream down the wall.

From around the corner then strode Anne, long of neck, smooth of skin, elegant in a white dress that flattered her figure, her face bare of makeup, which never failed to excite him; it seemed naked in a way that he instinctively felt should be forbidden. She may as well have been entirely undressed. She glanced

---

[3] and in a thick Boston accent

[4] "Thank you for inviting her, she's truly beautiful, my love, my life, my provider, my mate and my midnight meal, my darling dear."

at him coolly and turned to behold the decampment of the strange birds, her head tilted.

He reached her side and put his arm around her lower back. He pulled her to his hip.

"My dear, my darling," he said to her, unconsciously echoing the ardent leech-lover from the previous page. She turned to face him and reached down low, turning her palm upwards, and she stroked him roughly but lovingly from perineum to lower abdomen, squeezing him as she went. He said, his voice breaking only once, at the point of the squeeze, "As near in the past as 1899, one could *not SEE from* this vantage point without the ability to levitate?"

"One could have sat atop a tree."

"There was nary a tree here!" he shouted, and then caught himself, lowered his voice. "My point is that have a spectacular vantage point here. This high up, the rules of physics and metaphysics and matter are malleable. And we have room service."

"The FCC is coming, aren't they?" she said. She sounded sad. Despairing.

"Them and others," he said. "But we will sit this one out here as observers. No FCC. No cops. No right-wing radio hosts brandishing the guns of God. And when the fight is nearly won, by our side, of course, you and I and my votary shall, like the magnificent cowards we are, swoop down and join in the glory and devour and imbibe the spoils."

The door to the stairwell burst open then, and a swarm of policemen with riot shields and guns filled the end of the hall, bellowing about their strong desire to see hands and the advisability of dropping immediately to the floor. They lobbed smoke bombs into the air, which burst with ear-assailing explosions, sending out spiraling smoky coils of pink and purple that filled the hall with fog. Anne shrieked and dropped, raising her hands. Rippingcoat laughed as the cops flung their shields to the side and began kick-dancing all out of sync like unpracticed Rockettes. "A delightful prank perpetrated by these pranksters, my dear," he said, "and nothing more."

He knew better, of course. These would-be warriors were not perpetrators of a prank; they were victims of one. They had no agency, no control over their own bodies, hadn't since that morning, the brainless martinets. Fringe dangled from the arms and legs of their uniforms. Under their transparent face-shields they wore identical white kewpie doll masks with red ovals for cheeks linked by an upturned black line of a mouth, a nub of a nose, and eyes that looked ever rightward, topped with vertical lines denoting eyelashes. They turned away and swung their buttocks from side to side as Philip pulled from his kimono pockets two small pistols, cute little things that looked like kids' toys, his lady pistols, he

143

called them, and he blew those dancing dodo birds full of small holes. Anne rose and stood next to him. He handed her one of the pistols and she went among them, finishing off any that moved. Pop, and spray of blood. Pop, and hiss of defeat. Pop, and a death rattle. Pop, pop, pop, pop, pop.

The party had only just begun.

Gary

David Wilcox walked in the front door, removed his shoes, and fished his phone from his pocket as he walked through the kitchen to his living room, where a stranger was sitting in the easy chair, smoking a long cigarette. David jumped, dropped his phone, made a noise like BUH.

"Gary," the stranger said, by way of introduction, as if by doing so he was no longer a stranger. Gary was tall, with a blonde buzz-cut. For a split second it seemed that the man had too many limbs, somehow, arms like a bug's limbs, a jumble of overlapping arms and a pile of legs crossed over one another, the cigarette jutting from a tangle of fingers. David blinked, and Gary was just a man, tall and long-limbed, clad in tan khakis and a grey sweatshirt. He was barefoot. Something about the arrangement of his bland features repelled David, and even though he now had the acceptable number of limbs, there still was a hard-to-quantify *wrongness* in the way the man was … arranged.

"What are you doing in my house?"

Gary laughed as though he'd just heard a terribly funny joke. He slapped his knee with a broad hand. He had no fingernails. No toenails either.

"What's for dinner tonight, David? Maybe let's thaw out that meatloaf in the microwave."

David dipped down, snatched up his phone, and walked briskly to the bathroom. He closed and locked the door. He dialed 911.

*

He waited in the bathroom, listening for the police car to pull into the driveway. He figured that if Gary got to the door first, he'd surely claim this was *his* apartment and that *David* was the intruder. That was the way these things worked. *What things?* No time to go down that road, not now. Where had he

145

put the rental agreement? Was it in his files, or piled with other assorted paperwork—tax returns, instruction manuals, food delivery menus—in his catchall drawer? Surely he had mail around somewhere with his name above the address…or did he?

When the knock on the door came, David fumbled with the doorknob, tripped over the jamb, scrambled into the kitchen. Two policemen stood on the porch with their arms crossed. One was overweight with a mustache and an unshaven double chin, the other frightfully thin, with ears that stuck out like opened car doors. "You called 911?" the skinny one said, sounding irritated and impatient.

***

When they entered the living room, Gary stood, untangling his limbs and briefly exposing a small round belly with pale and pink striations. "Gentlemen!" Gary said.

"Gary!" the officers shouted in unison. They sounded delighted. Wide grins creased their faces. "You didn't tell us it was *Gary*," the overweight officer said, narrowing his eyes at David, who could only stare back, mouth hanging open.

"Officers," Gary said. "It's lovely to see you. I arrived here just this afternoon, and, I have to say, this man has—and I am trying to be respectful here—not been very hospitable."

David sputtered. "Hospitable? *Hospitable?*"

"I'm sure he's sorry," the skinny officer said. David saw with astonishment that his hand moved just slightly back toward the gun in his holster. "Are you sorry?"

"I'm…sorry," David said.

"Will you try to be more hospitable?"

"I will."

"Promise?"

"Oh, come on."

Now the officer rested his hand on the heel of the gun. "Do. You. Promise?"

"I promise," David said through gritted teeth.

"You promise what?"

***

When the police left, David excused himself with a forced tone of politeness, which Gary ignored completely, and closed himself in the bedroom. He sat on the edge of the bed, trying to regulate his breathing. Rosa would be back from her work conference in Pittsburgh in three days. Should he call her now? Try to get rid of the problem first?

How, though? David was not a fighter. A half a flight of stairs winded him. He couldn't throw a baseball to save his life, never mind a punch.

He wondered inanely if the police had a complaint line.

Okay. He'd call her. She had always been the level-headed one, had less of a propensity to let emotion get in the way of logic. She could talk him through this.

***

"Hey, honey."

He tried to regulate his voice, to sound calm. "How's it going with the conference?"

She sighed. "Oh, you know. We have to do group exercises and they kind of goad you into participating. It's exhausting. I just want to sit and take my notes and not be part of some *performance*. I'm chugging really bad coffee, still fighting to keep my eyelids open. How about you? Keeping yourself occupied?"

"Rosa, something weird is going on. There's a guy who got into our house and he won't leave."

Her voice went up an octave. "A *guy*? What? An intruder? A burglar? Did you call the police? Where is he now? Where are you?"

"The police seemed to know him. They told me not to be rude to him."

There was a period of silence. David could practically hear her thinking.

"What's his name?" she asked.

***

David tried several times to call Rosa back, but it went to voicemail. Probably bad hotel Wi-Fi. She'd call him, he figured. He kept his phone in his hand. The more time went by without a call, the more dread threatened to overtake him. Finally, he rang her back. It rang and rang. It didn't go to voicemail. David dropped onto the bed, reclined, and closed his eyes. Not long after, he fell into a deep sleep.

***

When he woke, it was well past midnight. His stomach ached with hunger.

147

The situation with the stranger seeped back into his mind, its temporary sleep-banishment over with. He grabbed his phone and saw with dismay bordering on panic that Rosa hadn't tried to call him back. Groaning, he rose from the bed, and an unexpected jolt of hope hit him. Maybe Gary had let himself out, having had his fun. Maybe he was on to the next person. Maybe it was over.

From the kitchen, he could see that the living room light was still on. He stood very still and listened. Gary was talking in there. Talking to himself? Or was he on the phone? To whom? He crept toward the doorway as quietly as possible, until he could a sliver of the room.

The voice stopped as soon as David saw Gary's feet, which were on the ottoman. They were vibrating, a blur. There were six feet, eight feet, four, seven. His face was in repose, though, his eyes blank, dead, staring into the middle distance. That face. The eyes, one slightly higher than the other. The nose, almost feminine. The cheekbones, fairly prominent. The mouth, small and pale-lipped. The curved chin. Was it a familiar face? The more David looked at it, the more it prodded his memory. Did he just look like someone David knew? Or some person of middling fame, like a character actor?

Gary's arms were missing. Fleshy knobs rotated slowly in their place, like nubs of bone just under the skin. David took a tentative step forward, and the floor creaked. Gary's arms reappeared as though they'd been in some kind of invisible fog. They were red. His hands and fingers were swollen, his thumbs almost purple. A growl came from somewhere within Gary's body, and that was when David remembered Gary from his dreams.

Dark. Stormy.

It was a dark and stormy night. Well, it fucking *was*. It was as though someone had pinched out each and every star between spit-moistened index finger and thumb. As though black-clad thieves with black-stockinged faces had thrown a black velvet bag over the moon and driven it away in a black hearse with blacked-out windows.

And the wind. How it cried of loss. How it evoked the howl of the wrenched-open mausoleum door, of the yawning grave hungry for its cadaver, for its dark due.

Even lightning was estranged from its brother thunder, and truanted their appointment. Sister rain came, though, late as always, but with fierce and strident complaints about that which delayed her, and beating her many fists into the mud and concrete.

Below, the streetlights stood dark, busted, like thin men bereft of arms. The windows of the houses were eyes long ago closed by the fingers of some glum coroner. The grid was down.

And yet dissonant, sibilant, slinky music played from…somewhere. From more than one place, in fact. From a battery-powered radio in every house in Leeds? Yes, that must be it.

Kazum

Greg Van Der Schloss sat in his car in the line at the drive-thru, tapping the steering wheel with his index fingers, the menu and microphone in his view, so close, as the saying goes, but yet so far. In front of him, a maroon minivan with a COEXIST bumper sticker sat interminably at the speaker stand, the driver engaging in what could at this point only be casual conversation with the cashier.

"Come on," Greg muttered. Time, as displayed on his dashboard in green was, to his dismay, marching inexorably forward, the start of the workday getting ever-mcloser. A pungent, mechanical odor drifted to his nostrils, intruding on the aroma of frying oil, and he hoped fervently that the source was someone else's car. Finally, the placatory-stickered minivan rolled forth to the restaurant window and Greg was able to pilot his car forward to take its place at the speaker.

"Just a moment," a faraway, disinterested voice muttered through a sprinkling of static.

"Sure," Greg said. "Of course."

Ahead, a hand sheathed in a clear vinyl glove emerged from the window, a cup and a straw in its grasp. A fat, bare pink hand slid slowly and mechanically from the minivan and plucked away the straw. Time continued to pass. Too much time. If not for the fact that cars were streaming by in either direction on the road beyond the restaurant, Greg might've thought time had frozen. If it had, he mused, he'd pull down someone's pants for fun.

What the hell was going on? He was maybe a half a minute from giving up on this whole venture and going to work hungry and uncaffeinated and goddamn pissed the fuck off.

Eventually the plump hand slid out again from the car window, stroked the cup gently, as one would the cheek of a child, and then grabbed it and yanked it into the car. Before the transition was fully complete, the minivan lurched forward, rocked and bounced its way over the curb, crushing a few of the landscaped bushes and flowers, and screeched out onto the road spraying wood chips, going the wrong way, a cacophony of horns expressing their extreme outrage in its wake. *What was that all about? Also… that's all the guy was getting after all that rigamarole? A drink?*

"…getcha?" a static-shrouded voice spat from the speaker.

Greg ordered, though there was no indication that anyone was listening. The speaker squawked out what he hoped was an invitation to pull up. He pulled his facemask from the rearview mirror and fitted the straps around his ears, then drove to the pass-thru window and glanced in. The lights were off inside. Somewhere back in a haze of steam, figures hulked and hunched. Weird music leaked out from the window. It sounded like Muzak played backward, sinuous and strange.

A kid with a mop of jet-black hair and a wisp of a mustache, unmasked, wearing a black t-shirt, appeared at the window clutching a grease-stained paper bag in a ketchup-stained fist. Greg handed over his debit card. The kid snatched it away and flung it back into the darkness. Then he grinned vacuously, showing his teeth.

"Hey, what the *fuck*…" Greg began, and the kid hurled the bag of food overhand into the car – it flew over Greg's lap, hit the passenger-side door, and landed on the passenger seat – and the bi-parting drive-thru windows slammed shut. A fist swam briefly into view, its middle finger extended upward, and then disappeared, like the thing in a Magic 8-Ball. There was a *glug glug glug* sound, and steaming hot coffee began to spill out onto the seat. Greg swept the whole mess to the floor with a growl of frustration and rage.

Too much time had gone by now, no time to deal with this nonsense, and there was a meeting at which his presence was mandatory. Fifteen minutes to make a twenty-four-minute commute. He hesitated, then said *fuck it*, and sped off. On the way, he called his bank to cancel the card. The line rang and rang. Then the call connected. A burst of static, and then what sounded like the same weird backward Muzak from the restaurant. At long last an electronic voice, female, slowly and methodically listed the directory extensions with the perennial warning that the numbers had recently changed. Maybe it was because he was running late, and was annoyed as hell, but the recording sounded slowed down. Maddening.

He clicked 4, the selection for canceling his card. Without a pause, a different computerized voice bleated, "We are unable to cancel or make any changes to your card at this time. Please call ba…" and the call was cut off.

***

The lot was mostly filled up, so Greg had to park at the outer edge by the woods. He walked-jogged to the door, phone in hand, trying repeatedly and without success to access his bank app. He was *sure* he had the password right. The wind kicked up, and a whiff of the oncoming winter was detectable in the air. A troupe of dead, dried leaves skittered across his path as though also late for something.

Glancing up, he noticed that one of the second-floor windows was cracked, a spider-web of crooked lines radiating out from a small hole. In the adjacent window, someone he didn't recognize had pressed his or her face against the glass, smushing the features, rendering them grotesque. He waved instinctively. The figure did not wave back.

Greg badged his way into reception, but the desk was unmanned, the reception area itself dark, the chair sitting untenanted in the shifting, pulsing glow of the computer monitor's screensaver. He needed someone to buzz him through the interior door. He put his hands to the glass and peered. Dark too. No one in sight. He closed the bank app and dialed Ronny's number. "Yo."

"Hey, it's Greg."

"Hey, Schlosser-man, where are you?"

"Downstairs. Listen, I…"

"I said where *were* you?"

"You said…never mind, listen, I'm not *that* late, it's only…"

"Yeah, meeting's canceled, bro."

"Great. Glad I broke my ass to get here. How come it's cancelled? We closed or something?"

"Closed? Nah. Ha. Not *closed*, exactly. You should come in."

"Yeah,   sure   …   uh,   what   …   what   is   that   music?"

"Oh, they're piping something in now. It's new. Make the place homier, they said, now we're not working from home anymore. Probably got some subliminal motivational shit in it. It even plays in the bathrooms. You should come in."

"Pat's not out here, I need someone to buzz me in."

A long sigh. "Alright, buddy. You stay right where you are, 'kay? You. Should. Come in. So I'll buzz you in. Hey?"

"Yeah? Uh…Ronny?"

"Have you ever heard the saddest song you've ever heard?"

"Have I…?" and the line disconnected.

Something's wrong. Really wrong. I should get the hell out.

But this was his job. His livelihood. He'd wait for Ronny and if anything looked goofy, he'd leg it back to the car and figure the rest out later. Thus resolved, he peered through the glass down the long, dark center hall and waited for Ronny to appear. Just shadows, unmoving. Stillness. Like a photograph.

His phone notification sounded, an echoing low note. He glanced down. A personal email notification sat across the top of the lock screen. *Account Alert. Transaction.* Okay, probably just the breakfast. Still, he had to get that card cancelled.

It sounded again. *Account alert. Transaction.* A second notification. The sound. A third. Another. Another. They spilled down his screen like closing credits.

Something moved deep in the shadows at the far end of the hall. Ronny's face emerged from the darkness, upside down and low to the ground, swinging back and forth, up and down, like a pendulum; behind it undulated an upsetting and intricate formation of knotted limbs. Then it sprang at Greg. It was fast. Frightfully fast.

Unnaturally fast.

If You Ever Want to Know What It's Like to Take Apart a Human Body I Can Tell You

Genghis Kent and Toxoplasma Gandhi were not twins, not even kin, but they looked very much alike. Medium-length black hair combed down, pugnacious features. Long necks. Fat eyes. Thin, pale lips closer to the nose than to the chin. Dangling arms.

Kent was tall and Toxy was short. That was how one could tell them apart, unless one viewed them from the chest up on a television screen, which was a very unlikely scenario indeed.

The titular offer was made by Toxy to Kent on a morose, muddy Monday, and the reception was as enthusiastic as the latter could muster. So Toxy G. beckoned Kent follow.

Over hill they went and down dale. Through tangles and brambles and pecker-bushes. Alongside rushing waters and down darksome paths that repelled light and burnished dread. At long last they came to a whispering field of dead grasses and disturbed dirt, in the center of which lay a concrete hole from which the curved top legs of a ladder jutted.

The ladder led down to the darkness of the sewer. Toxy lit a torch made from the thick end of a branch from the maple tree adjacent to the abandoned hamburger cart; seven pairs of white Hanes briefs with flex-waistbands, size XL; and a length of twine. Kent carried an ancient, rusty Maxwell House can filled three-quarters of the way with kerosene for replenishment as needed. And down they went, Toxy first, Kent next.

"Hey," said Kent, nearly dropping the can. "It's Ms. Margaret Ashton Whibley. Except dead!"

And indeed it was. Ms. Whibley lay face-up, one hand lain primly over the other at her midsection. She was clad in a long blue dress and matching flats with brass buckles. A string of pearls encircled her neck. Her mouth hung

154

crookedly open. A line of dried blood stretched between her nose and her upper lip. One of her eyes had sunken into the skull; the other was absent. A squarish indentation the rough size of a sledgehammer's end marred her upper forehead. Her white hair was in disarray.

"Shhh," said Toxy. "The echoes are bugfuck down here. People might hear you in their kitchen sinks."

"Or their toilets!" Kent snickered.

"Quieter."

"*Or their toilets. How did Ms. Whibley get here?*" Kent, who was unable to whisper for reasons which he was unable to articulate, said in a very low tone.

"She, um…well, she died."

"*How did she die?*"

Toxy considered what a suitable answer might be.

Kent waited, then said, "*Ms. Whibley is protected.*"

"Protected?" Toxy looked nervous now.

The flame on the torch flickered noisily (*flappa flappa flappa*) and then extinguished, sending up a plume of grey smoke and leaving only glowing red specks in the blackened fabric. Kent held out the Maxwell House can of kerosene, and Toxy dipped the torch in it.

Kent screeched and threw the hot can upward. Flames leapt from the aperture, spilling a fiery ring around the circumference of the sewer pipe, between the two men. Intense heat and light, sudden and disorienting. The can rolled, still spilling fire. Toxy, who was on the side closer to the ladder, retreated backward, holding out his hands, leaving Kent with both the body of Ms. Whibley and the flames between him and freedom. Behind him, the sewer tunnel was all darkness, its direction, its terminus, a mystery.

And then Toxy was scrambling up the ladder and gone. Kent jogged spasmodically in place for a few moments, considering running through the fire to freedom. Instead he began to blow on the flames as hard as he could, producing a wavering, high pitched wheeze and very little in the way of air.

A splash of water sounded, and Kent turned. An older man in a white suit stood a few yards down the tunnel, the darkness looming behind him. He had a wide, friendly grin bracketed by *greater than* and *less than* furrows. His eyes twinkled. A hat sat at a jaunty angle on his head. His hands were clasped at his back. He winked at Kent, and then pursed his lips and blew. His breath, which reeked of tobacco and skunk-spray, had considerably more efficacy than Kent's had. The flame went out all at once. Darkness claimed the sewer pipe.

Above, a mass of black clouds had settled over the field, having brought with it an early twilight. A gust of wind caused the treetops to whisper loudly and tousled the dry grass. Next to the opening of the sewer hole stood the man in the white suit and hat, sawing a bow across the neck of a red-veined, white violin. The stick of the bow was a human fibula; the hair that ran frog-to-tip had been yanked without consent from the head of a folksinger. The music was mournful without being morose, slightly dissonant, but still pretty. A disinterested witness, were there one, would think the scene expertly scored by a despondent composer given to suicidal fancies.

Toxoplasma Gandhi stood as if transfixed at the edge of the field by the pothole-dimpled road. The contents of his skull boiled in their bony vessel, producing a sound much like that of backed-up water breaking through a wad of soap-caked hair in the drain of a bathtub. Blood poured freely from both nostrils, followed by a deluge of chunks of bloodied tissue.

At the sewer opening, Kent's hands appeared, grasping the top rung of the latter. He hoisted himself upward, his visage pale and devoid of expression. And then he tumbled out, revealing that his body below the waist was sheared away, an eely profusion of unstrung intestines tangling below. He pulled himself along the ground for as long as he could, toward Toxy who, though surely dead or mostly so, still stood.

Now the field is overgrown and all but abandoned, the road that led to it having fallen into disuse. Toxy still stands there, skeletal, clothing long worn away, shielded from apprehension by a nigh-impenetrable tangle of brambles. Kent was, per his written wishes, cremated and his ashes built into an hourglass, that he might live and die repeatedly at the whim of his keeper, who still often plays the violin in the man's memory. Ms. Whitby is in the care of a minatory confederacy of physicians, practitioners of a particular occult discipline, that her protection might stand even despite the recent affront.

Pets or Meat

"Did you know," Jason said, "that there are two kinds of clowns?"

I had arrived that afternoon at Jason's Bluestem, Washington home, tired and sore from having flown in directly from Bradley Airport, a little bit south of Leeds, Massachusetts, where we had been classmates. I had undergone a series of personal and professional failures that ended with me restrained at Cooley Dick with deep cuts in my wrists and the strong desire to either die or restart everything.

I had only my wallet with a little cash and a debit card and license, and three days' worth of clothing in a duffel bag. I'd put my library into storage and abandoned the rest. Jason was kind enough to call and invite me into his home and his life, an act of generosity I could never have foreseen when I knew him three decades earlier.

He'd been a quiet, angry boy. He wore all black, shielded his face with dyed-black hair. He listened to angry music and read books the stores kept behind the counters for fear of theft. Now that kind of thing is accepted. Then it was not.

I was more acquaintance than friend. I was wary of his brooding silence, of a coiled violence I detected in him. But I protected him from the bullies who kicked the backs of his heels, yanked his backpack 'til he fell, and defaced or befouled his locker. I was suspended for giving one of them, a sneering jock with a greasy mullet and fat white arms, a well-deserved fat lip.

Jason was called into the office when some of a notebook snatched from his locker prompted the faculty to think him capable of shooting up the school. This was before school shootings were even a phenomenon. Shootings were then associated mainly with the postal service. I don't know what came of it. He didn't get in trouble that I saw.

A cab dropped me off at the junction of Route 2 and a root-strewn dirt road—Jason's driveway—that stretched about a mile through tall trees. I walked to his house from there, grateful to be shielded from the heat of summer by a canopy of trees. Birdsong and rustling foliage soundtracked the long, pleasant walk; a breeze laden with natural scents buoyed my spirits.

The house was a yellow and white two-story clapboard affair with a yard that stretched off eastward and was bordered by thick forest. A grey barn with no doors stood behind the house—in his call Jason had told me a family of wary and wild-eyed stray cats and kittens lived in there. You couldn't get near them, he said, but he left food for them twice a day, which they ate gratefully but watchfully, ready to retreat into the shadows at the merest provocation.

At the far end of the yard stood a fenced-in wood and wire enclosure mimicking the structure and colors of the house, but with ramps and broad balconies on its exterior. I recognized it from a video he'd sent me in which a couple of hardy-looking goats munched brainlessly on feed from a rusted-out trough by the fence. Now large, brightly colored flowers of some kind filled the trough, leading me to believe it was now untenanted.

Jason now wore the outfit of a farmer, his hair back to its natural brown, with a prodigious grey insurgency surrounding a bald spot. His grin was wide, generous, genuine. He wore dirt and grass-stained denim overalls, wheat-colored work boots, and a plaid flannel shirt of black, blue, and brown. He was taller than I remembered, or at least not as stooped as he used to be. He was recognizable only by his nose, which had a lump on the bridge, and his eyes, which though no longer bordered with smudgy make-up, were still strikingly blue.

Within minutes of my arrival, we sprawled in lawn chairs with cupholders in the arms, drinking beer and eating, not coincidentally, goat jerky.

"Clowns?"

"Two kinds. Well…maybe there are subgroups or small enclaves…but there are generally just the two. Birthday clowns and circus clowns. There's a rivalry. They don't like one another."

"So…"

"I prefer circus clowns. They're more athletic."

"Prefer for what?"

"Come on," he said, and pushed himself with some effort from his chair. I followed him to the house. A cloud of mosquitos floated by the stone fountain. A flock of geese in V-formation flew far above us, honking excitedly amongst themselves.

I sat at the table in Jason's kitchen, which, despite a newish stainless-steel refrigerator and a gas range of contemporary design, was largely unchanged from when the house had been built, nearly a century earlier. Lots of well-worn wood. Ancient crisscrossing beams at the peaked ceiling. Wall cabinetry with cast-iron hinges. Dim light from brass and glass wall sconces, and a sepia chandelier suspended from the ceiling with chains. A dry sink and hutch stood across from the cast iron sink and drainboard at the double window. Makeshift shelves along the west wall teemed with dusty jars and old-style tin containers with labels indicating contents of oatmeal, farina, Cream of Wheat, along with a vast variety of soups and spices.

Jason pulled from the stuffed-full refrigerator a foam tray wrapped in cellophane. He lit the stove burner under a carbon steel skillet, and freed from the tray a couple of thick, greyish cutlets with some kind of bright white rind. I assumed they'd been patted, or rather caked, with flour. He frisbeed them one after the other onto the skillet, which hissed and smoked. Jason lifted the window and unscrewed the fire alarm from the ceiling, putting it on top of a cracker tin on one of the shelves.

The smell was sort of like that of steak or bison with a curious almost soapy undercurrent. After having had only peanuts and beer over the duration of the day, it nonetheless made my mouth water.

After a few minutes he flipped them with a metal spatula, waited a few moments, and slid them onto a platter. I wondered what any of this had to do with clowns. He hadn't brought up the topic. Neither had I. It didn't interest me.

We went back outside. Jason started a bonfire. We ate the steaks. They were good. Rich and juicy and flavorful. We drank. A lot.

It was twilight. I'd dozed off. Jason had passed out and was face-up on the lawn, legs akimbo, arms at his sides. With some effort I managed to flip him over onto his stomach. Then I stumbled into the house, pulled myself by the railing up the stairs, zig-zagged down the hall, and hit the guest bed hard.

I woke up to the sound of the door creaking open, heavy breathing, rustling. A snort. "Jason?" I muttered.

In reply came a hoarse baritone cackle. I bolted upright and hit the light. A small brown and grey goat stood in the doorway, regarding me with a serene smile and wise, curious eyes.

I got up out of bed, my heart thumping. I approached the animal, hands in the air like an innocent in a disreputable alley trying to calm an agitated cop.

When I got up to it without incident, I reached one hand forward slowly and rubbed my index finger on its knobby little head just above the eyes. It regarded me, then strode over to the bed, jumped up, and folded its legs beneath it. It nodded.

Another laugh, this one from the yard, high and wild but decidedly human, definitely not Jason. The goat popped its head up, alarmed.

I looked out the window. Jason still lay sprawled on the lawn. For a fearful moment I thought he might be dead, but then he scratched his neck and rolled onto his side and curled up. There was movement out by the goat enclosure.

I went downstairs. From the back door I could see that the enclosure was lit from inside, wavering light, as from an array of candles. I walked in that direction, full, buzzing, dizzy with the changes in my life, with how far I'd come from everything familiar, and how little time it had taken.

A clown bounded down the ramp on white-gloved hands and knees. I stopped in my tracks, a few yards away. He wore a puffy aquamarine jumpsuit with oversized fuzzy pink buttons, an oversized fluorescent blue bowtie, and large pink shoes fringed with grass stains. A red outline of a cathedral bordered each eye and the same color traced his nasolabial folds. His movement was fluid and somehow wrong, as though his spine were jointed like an arm. He made his jouncing, jolting way over to the trough and I could see now in his eyes a feral, unthinking wildness. What I had earlier assumed to be flowers I now saw was cotton candy. The clown ate noisily, slavering, jaw opening widely and sliding side-to-side, pink and blue drool oozing down his chin.

A second clown cantered into view from behind the enclosure. This one wore a tweed waistcoat and linen knickerbockers. Its makeup was minimal, just a wide red mouth in the shape of a frown; painted eyes; and a round, red nose. Its hair was stringy and wet and brown.

Seeing its brother, it started. It growled and then charged, kicking up dirt, rearing back, encircling with both arms the upper thighs of the first one and biting him hard on the buttock. Hissing, the first turned. The second stood tall and put up white fists which he rotated menacingly in the air and I felt something whistle past my ear, singeing the lobe. White light flashed. Rushing in my ears like water.

I crouched, holding my ear. The second clown's head blew apart like one of Gallagher's watermelons. Its wig flew high into the sky like an ejector seat from a damaged aircraft. The first clown scrambled over and began to gather the pieces of greasepaint-flesh and clumps of bloodied brains and skull fragments, piling them next to a bucket that towered with grass-strewn circus peanuts. Its single-minded, non-frantic movements reminded me of a chimpanzee.

Through damaged ears I heard the muted tooting of many plastic horns, and through tear-blurred eyes I saw more clowns exiting the pen, some warped and deformed, some missing limbs, some tiny, like spider monkeys. A few of them were women, bare greasepainted breasts dangling and swaying. They jostled and elbowed each other and tittered and squeaked and squealed.

Jason was next to me then, laying down his rifle, easing me to the ground, inspecting my ear. The sting of pain when he touched it was secondary to the shock of what I'd seen. What was this? Jason was speaking to me, but I couldn't hear him.

Then he was rubbing his hands, full of white glop, all over my face. I tried pulling away, but he grabbed a hardful of my hair. He pushed something onto my nose. Then he was stripping me down. Sounds rushed back into my ear as though I'd surfaced from underwater. Jason's rough breathing. A cacophony of plastic horns. Overhead somewhere, an airplane.

A filthy clown suit polka-dotted like a Twister mat dangled from the back pocket of Jason's overalls. His voice came to me now. "Which kind?" he demanded, grasping my chin and lifting my face to his. His spittle landed on my eyes, my tongue. "*Which kind?*"

The red wig landed on the ground between us.

I'm Gonna Knock That Halo Right Off Your Head, Mister

What the…not even a blessed live human being… (pause) *Okay, look. Listen. My name is Robert Brocken and I'm calling to report a violation.* Several *violations. Obscenities, really. The station is around or about 87.1. FM. I'm calling from Williamsburg, a little bit north of Leeds. I can't even repeat most of what these people were saying. I'm a Christian. A decent man. I have young daughters. To think they might stumble onto… This is beyond outrageous. A clear and present danger to the community.*

I tried to reach the station myself. One of their public service announcements gave a number for their suicide helpline. A man answered. Sirs, this was anything but a suicide helpline. They tried to persuade me to kill myself! This is what I mean by a danger.

All I get when I call the local police is a busy signal. The state cops just laughed at me. So I expect a call back today. *I want to know precisely what you're going to do to shut this outfit down. And I want a timeline. I'm prepared to fill in a report, to meet with someone, whatever I need to do to stop this filth.*

Call me back. My number is ____-____-_____. I eagerly await your call.

The man stood uncertainly in the darkened motel room, a black travel bag at his feet. The clock ticked too fast and too loud. The man's foot tapped softly along on the carpeted floor. His eyes were closed.

After a time, he opened his eyes and lifted the bag onto a small, cheap table that abutted an uncomfortable looking chair. He dug through the bag's contents and lifted out a camera—the old kind, the kind with film. He stepped out into the newly arrived spring air. He strode along the balcony and descended the stairs.

The cemetery lay across the parking lot from the motel. He crossed the lot, put his back against the fence, facing the motel, and snapped a picture of the door and window of his room. Then he crossed the lot, climbed the stairs to the first landing, paused, considering, and turned to take a picture of the cemetery.

He stopped. Someone was standing there. At the far end of the cemetery under a tree. Looking directly at him. Stout, in pale clothing, white-bearded. The features were blurry. A sliver of pain pierced his temple and below his left eye. He took the picture and hurried back along the balcony.

Back in the room, he took a picture of his reflection in the mirror, the flash's reflection leaving purple blots floating in his vision. He walked to the window and separated the vertical blinds with his thumb and index finger. The figure in the cemetery was gone.

Off to the west, the occasional car whooshed by on North Pleasant Street, and a few pedestrians walked around, headed to an early breakfast, maybe, or to sit and watch the town come to life. A young couple walked through the cemetery, toting identical coffee cups. A large black bird stared from atop a tombstone, its head flipping from position to position like a series of slides.

No one appeared to be looking up at the motel. When the man had called the FCC, he had told very little, had left out a lot. Most importantly, he'd omitted the fact that the voice on the radio addressed him directly... by name. He had left out the vile threats to him and to his family.

Now the man sat heavily on the edge of the bed and turned on the television. He flipped through channels, not really registering what they were showing him. His eyes shut, but the sudden vibration of his cell phone lifted him right off the bed. *Jesus*, he thought, putting a hand to his chest. A blasphemy. These people had him using Christ's name in vain.

The display read *UNKNOWN CALLER*. He pressed the green talk button and held the phone to his ear. "Mr Brocken?"

"Who's asking?"

"Mr. Brocken, this is Agent Theodore Ashton from the Federal Communication Commission. We received your message this morning..."

"I'm not at my home," Brocken said. Details he omitted before he also did not offer now. He did not tell the agent what had happened after he had hung up after leaving his message. The phone calls and hang-ups. The tapping on the glass. The bending of the trees. The rippling of the living room floor.

Ashton asked for his location and he gave an address across the street from the motel, a laundromat he could see from the balcony.

"I'm sending two agents out," Ashton said. "They'll have some questions for you."

"I should hope so. I have answers for them. You know, Sir, in my business, we return calls right away. That way..."

The agent disconnected.

When are they coming? And...Federal Communication Commission? Wasn't it Federal Communications Commission?

He called the number he'd first used to call in the complaint. It rang and rang. Then it connected. Through static he heard a woman's voice call "Henry? Oh, Henry?"

"This is Robert. Robert Brockton. I just spoke to..."

"With what shall I fix it?" the voice whispered, wavering in tone and pitch.

The man hung up and went to the balcony. A black SUV was parallel parking in front of the laundromat. The door of the laundromat opened. The stout man with the white beard and the light-colored clothing came out and joined two men in grey suits who'd exited the SUV. The three men looked up at him. All their features were blurred as by a cloud of haze.

The three smiled as one.

The Social Media Friend

James Warzaw's social media profile went dark last Thursday with frustrating finality. In various threads we—a geographically far-flung community of visual artists—recounted the last weeks of his online existence as we saw it, filtered as it was through the various unknowable   algorithms and happenstance regarding who was logged in at what time, as James Warzaw would, we surmised, delete many of his posts within an hour of posting them. We were able to put together a fractured, most certainly flawed narrative, and this got us no closer to any kind of clarity nor explanation.

At first there was no hint of trouble. His posts consisted largely of brief movie reviews, pictures of himself—pudgy-faced; unshaven; thick, unkempt brows— wincing into sunlight, backed by cityscapes or pine-lined parks dotted with pergolas and public art (his expression indicated a genuinely vacuous, generalized joy, like that on the face of a dog being embraced by its human), complaints about his job, not enough to do making the days seem endless and yet stressful, and requests for advice regarding meal planning. He was inoffensive enough to remain on our friends list but not memorable enough to invade our thoughts in any meaningful way outside our illuminated screens.

How did we become friends with him? The topic came up and we simply do not know. He was not himself a visual artist, nor did he belong to any creative communities that neighbored or overlapped with ours. No one claimed him as a gateway friend, definitely not offline, and not online; yet at some point we must all have either requested his virtual friendship or accepted his request for the same.

Often he'd shared self-taken pictures with his mother, who wore her silver and black hair long and had a natural beauty, enhanced by eyes that smiled but carried a hint of having seen more trouble than their share. Their house, what we could see of it in the background, was decorated in a gauche, countrified style, with sprays of tied hay and red-checkered wainscoting, patchwork quilts, overalls-clad dolls with bean-black eyes and bright red yarn for hair.

The first sign of something being off was in one of these pictures. Some of us saved it to our phones. In it, he grins at the camera, his eyes unfocused. One of his teeth is conspicuously missing. Some kind of orange crust limns his left nostril. His mother, next to him, looks off to the right, beyond where we can see. Her eyes, as always, smile, but her mouth is curled in disgust. The upper right of the frame is slightly warped and discolored, a disquieting brownish-blue speckled with burn marks.

I hear scratching from the inside of my skull, he posted on Sunday late in the evening. His first comment said, "I can feel it now." His next post, thirty minutes later, was a video. He held his head to the camera lens until it was just a blur of acne-strewn forehead. "Turn the volume up," he said, and indeed, once we did so, we could hear a faint scratching.

We searched for the symptom online and found nothing. We urged him to go to the Emergency room, sent him money electronically to pay his way. An hour later he posted a blurry picture of the waiting room, crying, red faced children in their parents' laps; couples, bleary-eyed, leaning on one another, the blue blur of a news channel on the wall-mounted flat screen television, all reflected in a large picture window.

In the morning he posted only "that didn't help-the nurses passed." We asked—begged—for clarification, but he posted nothing further on the topic. He did post a link to cartoon television show from decades ago with LOL as his caption. An online news search turned up the lockdown of a hospital geographically near to his professed hometown. It was scanty as to details but was accompanied by a picture of a building surrounded by police SUVs and men in riot gear.

The next morning Warzaw posted a shot of the brick and glass front of a convenience store, taken from behind the dusty dashboard of a car. "Mmm, coffee," the caption read.

His feed went silent. Other matters occupied our attention. Illness. The loss of a beloved pet. Matters of politics, social calamities, personal controversies, depression. One of us was in a motorcycle wreck and was partially paralyzed. One of us lost her mother to bone cancer.

The next time we heard from Warzaw was the pop-up notification that he had gone live.

Hands

Officer Dale O'Donoghue said, "That what I thought it was?"

"Dunno, wa'n't lookin'," said Bret Thompson, his partner, absorbed by the hangnail at which he was picking, still not looking up.

It was October, a little past one a.m., chilly, the city deserted except for a small crowd leaving the lit-up music venue down one of the side streets, dispersing quietly, most with hands in pockets, plumes of breath trailing them like thought balloons.

"Failure to signal." O'Donoghue called in the stop, then hit the lights and let the siren whoop just once. The blinker came on but the car, a late-model Cadillac, kept going, speeding up just slightly.

"Fuck's he doing?"

Now Thompson looked up. "Nothing yet."

Soon they were beyond the city lights, on a quiet road, the few houses up long driveways through woods. The brake lights flashed as the car pulled over onto the shoulder in a dark patch between two non-working streetlamps. The officers glanced at one another, then at the car. As the cruiser rolled to a stop, both men saw the shadow in the front seat lower its shoulder, pause, and then straighten.

"Ha. Floor," Thompson said.

"Yup."

"Passengers?"

O'Donoghue peered at the darkened car. There was movement in the back and passenger seat, but it was odd, fluid, like rolling water. He couldn't tell if the source was human or animal. He got on the radio to the dispatcher, who sounded vaguely annoyed. "Backup there in five," the pissy voice crackled in the speaker.

"Gonna light 'im up," O'Donoghue said, and trained the spotlight on the car. The driver's head lowered out of view.

To Thompson: "Here wo go."

On speaker: "Driver! Sit up! Now! Hands out the driver's side window, slow!"
Nothing.

"Let me see those hands. This is for my safety and yours! Hands!"
Again, nothing.

Thompson said, "Fuck this" and unholstered his weapon. He stepped out of the car. O'Donoghue followed suit. As Thompson approached the passenger side, a pair of pale, slender hands stuck themselves out the driver's side window. The fingers, encircled with many rings of ornate design, wriggled. Then a third hand emerged, similarly decorated, and a fourth. Then more, filling the whole of the open window, fingers all swaying like underwater coral.

A bouquet of hands slithered from the passenger side window at the end of long white arms. Thompson stopped. He aimed his weapon at the car and began to back up.

O'Donoghue watched in frozen horror as one of the arms stretched long and noodle-like from the passenger side window and the long-fingered hand grabbed his partner by the throat and squeezed. Thompson's face went purple-black. His eyes bulged. His tongue popped out from his mouth. Then with a hideous wet sound his head came clean off. The head hit the ground and then rolled alongside the curb in the dirt and the gravel and the discarded cigarette butts. Thompson's body stumbled after it, firing its weapon wildly. More arms came out the window, slender hands grabbing Thompson's collar and sleeve and pant leg and raising his headless body into the air. One of the hands snatched his revolver, another his shoe.

O'Donoghue backed up and got back in the car, backed up, spraying gravel, and sped away, saying *No, no, nosir, nuh-uh, negative, negatory* even as flexing, clutching hands approached and loomed in the rearview and side mirrors, lit red by the rear lights.

He sped down the road, farther from the city center. The hands grew smaller and smaller in the rearview, and then they were gone. What was that? What *was* that? *What was that?!*

Twin dots of headlights crested the hill behind him, then lit up everything around him like a UFO abduction-in-progress. The treeline and the road swam with the undulating shadows of slender arms and hands.

The car pulled back, then stopped short. O'Donoghue was propelled forward. The last thing he saw was the airbags blossoming like fast-motion flowers, springing forth to meet him, but the impact was far from the last thing he felt.

WXXT Listener Testimonial #6: Walter Nonelan

The first time I heard WXXT, the radio man told me that Carol Channing was hiding in my closet. I rose from my bed. The floor was cold. I didn't look in the closet, didn't even touch the door to determine whether it was warm. I considered barricading it, but I was somewhat skeptical (though not enough to make me look) so instead I lined shoes and sneakers along the bottom of the doorframe. When I woke up, the footwear was at an acute angle away from the door, which was still closed…or, rather, closed again. In one of the Nikes sat a bluish egg. It was cold to the touch and I sensed things tumbling and writhing within. I put the egg gingerly into the front pocket of my backpack and emptied it into the dumpster on my way to school.

The next time I heard WXXT I was in my thirties, living alone, having been dumped by my libertine girlfriend, who was then sleeping loudly with my across-the-hall neighbor, the one who washed his clothing with disinfectant spray bottles, and I saw she had her eye on my next-door neighbor, who I think played baseball for a living, somehow, though I have no concrete reason to think that.

Carol's here, a voice said, and I saw the dark rectangle of my open closet in the murk of midnight. A warm body slithered up my leg, straddled my thigh. Her slack lips dragged on my collarbone. "I don't find this erotic," I said.

She murmured her reply in a haggard voice: *I don't want you to find this erotic*, and as she said it warm liquid poured out onto my leg and her tongue flew around my ear like a frantic wet moth at a lit bulb.

She pulled away. *I feel foolish*, she said.

"You're all right," I replied, and she embraced me tightly, her wiry arms encircling my chest, her wet weeping face pressed into my neck. A felt something push up into my underwear, and then into me. Sharp. It hurt. I felt her grinning against my face, and then a cold sensation turning corners in my guts, poking, tickling. The radio played a laconic waltz. Eggs spilled out onto the bed, eggs or bubbles, I couldn't quite see.

I lay in a daze. I heard the eggs hatching. I felt them too. The ones against the warmth of my body. Something blurry walked by my face with an arrogant stride. It smelled vinegary and perfumy and like unwashed crotch and like spiced pork and like bubblegum all at once. It was all lips, eyes, and legs, pink and purple, from what I could see. It made up lyrics to the waltz that came from the radio and the other hatchlings joined in, singing raucously. I couldn't tell whether it was English or not. I suppose it was.

One of them pinched my penis with its wee fingernails. When I look at it now, lifting my belly with one hand and pulling taut the foreskin with the other, I can still see the pair of purple-black bruises, looking like the way people draw the nose holes on a skeleton.

I grabbed one and ate it, a voice dropping from the mad chorus. It tasted just like it smelled. My body tried to revolt, to vomit, but I clasped my hands over my mouth and nose until I felt movement in my ears.

So anyway, now I'm a fan, a listener. I survive by eating hatchlings, and they are also fine company. I think we're going to start a band. The lineup will require a lot of revising. I envision being played on the air, poisoning the Pioneer Valley with my slick viscous fluids. I see us touring under the WXXT banner, in a white van going from place to place. My bandmates will be my snacks. We'll bring cassettes to sell. It'll be fucking awesome. We just need a name.

Untitled Part 1 by Pixie Pottle

A man in a grey suit over a faded pink shirt stumbles weeping along the sidewalk. He staggers forward and uses a telephone pole (pimpled with staples from long-gone fliers) to steady himself, pushes himself off and stumbles across the walk to lean on the white brick of the Apple store. He has a pinkish aura of romantic disappointment about him.

He pulls a slide whistle from the torn lining of his jacket and holds the mouthpiece to his lips. He pulls and retracts the handle of the plunger. The instrument does not have the comically fatuous quality of its brethren; it sounds reverent, mournful, even profound.

Someone above pries open a window and a brown egg flies out, hitting the man in the neck, the clear white of the egg oozing down his back, the yolk cradling comfortably like a cat between the man's shirt collar and unshaven neck. From another window across the way a voice cries out in a hysteric tone: "Much of what you say has the ring of truth to it!"

"Boooo," called someone else.

Behind him I crept, the tape rolling, the cassette recording. He walked into the former Elks hall with its new sign which read "House of the Rising Stepson."

I waited a few beats and I knocked on the door. "BRING OUT YOUR DAD," I called.

That, of course, is the passphrase. I was perplexed and titillated by the fact that they bypassed this formality to admit the man in the suit with the slide-whistle with its mournful tone and the egg yolk still intact in his collar and the staggering gait and the unshaven neck and the faded pink shirt.

The door opened, revealing the dark pine of the hallway and the smell of ale and burnt-in tobacco and the flyers tacked up in an unreadable profusion on the bulletin board and the Budweiser sign that lit everything in red. I walked past the old man bar on the left and the ghoul bar on the right to the main bar, where the man with the slide whistle kept trying to force his way onstage with a band that was setting up. A vinyl banner told me the band's name was The Ligature Marksmen. A roadie in a denim vest and a red Speedo kept pushing him back down off the riser, his pale, hairy arms jiggling with the effort.

I hit the bar and ordered a White Russian, which the bartender brought to me with alacrity. I did not have to pay extra for the alacrity. You see, they know me here.

They allowed me, as they always do, to hook up my recording device to the sound system. I took the glass in my hand and threaded my way through the thickening crowd to the stage. "He's with me," I said.

Cul-de-Sacrilege

1. I remember church as an endless series of incantations and contextless speeches, punctuated by the affectless chanting of obsequious inanities. Call-and-response. Listen and repeat. Stand. Sit. Kneel. Grab your toes. Clasp the sweaty hands of your neighbor and wipe their germs on your lips. Issue unalloyed praise to an imaginary madman, to his affected son, and for a ghost, that is, the restless spirit of a dead person, who are all one and the same. There is the consumption of flesh. The imbibing of blood. Parishioners with their breasts pushed up and together, the grey vertical line of cleavage spattered with glitter. Boys in miniature suits kneeling on padded tuffets. Stained glass men in purple robes, their white beards dancing at angles, cavorting in a violent dumbshow on windows that admit little in the way of natural light. And it all culminates in a cute, heartwarming little speech about the humor of the business of living. And the flock walks out blinking into the searing rays of sunlight.

2. In the balcony pew, priests rub hosts like slivers of soap into their armpits and groins. They snicker and grin, pull the kinked hairs from the wafers and fling them at one another. Then they reflatten and smooth out the wafers and slide them into the no-contact dispenser, where they will be ejected by the pull of a golden trigger from an opaque vertical tube onto the jutting wet waiting tongues of the faithful. The dispensers were, incidentally, purchased from a Church Supplies website. The product page says without explanation "not for Catholic use." The Baptist church is not Catholic, though they flout many of the rules of Baptist Churches, seeing them as simply guidelines.

3. In the private garden out back, the Facilities Manager swings naked on a cotton rope hammock, his body as white as the clouds that sail above in the blue ocean of sky, but for his face and his groin, equally red, and his grin, ink-black teeth. Calamity in his midsection. Caterpillars flee on many legs and spiders climb their webs in disgusted haste. Even the flies flee to spread their filth elsewhere. He is spiritual, he tells his wife's friends, who crowd him with their tongues, yet not religious.

4. The Calvary Baptist Church spells its own name incorrectly on the local advertisement placemats at the Bluebonnet. So bespattered with the fake maple syrup is the "Cavalry" Baptist Church. "Pray For America," the sign outside reads when a Democrat is elected President. It reads "Hallelujah" for Republicans.

5. Stuart Hess, the owner of Hessian Landscaping ("BECAUSE YOUR LAWN, THAT'S WHY") on a Sunday morning walked down the steps of the church and into the parking lot. Nearly being creamed by a Honda Civic whose driver, another parishioner, called out a word decidedly Unchristian, he passed his work truck and walked halfway down the lawn toward the road. He pushed his hands together as though in prayer and looked heavenward. And there he froze. His wife Margo, who'd stopped to compliment the priest on an electrifying sermon, spotted him and wondered what on earth he was doing. When she got up to him, he did not respond to her questions. He didn't move at all. He stood, his face devoid of expression. She shook him by the shoulders. She checked his pulse, which seemed slow. She wasn't sure, though. A concerned crowd gathered. The Executive Pastor called 911 on his smartphone upon which he had an app that masquerades as a calculator but when a code is entered it opens up pictures of an unsavory nature. Police, Fire, and Ambulance arrived. An EMT took Stuart's pulse. "He's gone," the EMT said. His wife fell to her knees and wept.

6. Yet no one could budge his body. He could not be lifted. He could not be toppled. He could not be slid. Two officers pulled on one leg. Officer O'Neil suffered a bilateral hernia for his trouble. Due to an unexpected issue with the anesthesia, he would die during surgery without having left a living will. The police dispersed the crowd so that certain less picturesque methods could be employed.

7. Shovels did not work.

8. A crane did not work.

9. A steamroller did not work.

10. A backhoe did not work.

11. Axes, employed at night, did not cut into the flesh and left many policemen with numbed arms and hands.

12. Before the light of dawn shone, The Whittier Construction Company erected fencing and privacy screens. Still the body stood.

13. Fire was employed to no effect.

14. A week after the death of Stuart Hess, his jaw dropped to the ground and out crawled a 13-inch-long phasmid in the shape of a cross. Its many legs were too slender to see. More crawled out, and then they poured as the man's clothing and flesh twitched and jumped. Some carried brain matter in tiny claws. They dispersed toting flesh and fabric. The skeleton of Stuart Hess went chalky and the wind carried it away in swirling clouds and little joyous twisters. Hallelujah. Because your lawn, that's why. Pray for America. He's gone.

15. Amen.

My Own Rotten Leg

She was bowlegged and had vitiligo. I had halitosis and grey-leg. We tugged our masks down to make out. Airborne buboes fluttered around the car windows seeking entry. On the radio, the morning men, still on the air even though it was night, in hoarse and worn voices mocked the victims' pictures as they leafed through the morning Gazette. *Old blue neck is back*, Jerry "Rude" Waters said, and snickered. The Dean of Dust replied *He's in possession of swollen property.*
Off-road blood bog tickets are half off like that guy's arm.
I've never seen a man throw up his own balls before.
None of it lessened the mood. We washed down her pro-psychosis meds with sweet Riesling. She reached down and tied the strings of my mask around the base. I puffed her inhaler three times into the Dark Doorway and four into the Pink Pavilion. She gasped and slathered me with sanitizer. We coughed into each other, trading teeth.
She was a cat sniffing a dandelion. I was a deranged spelunker in a cave of marrow.
After, we reclined in the back seat, staring up at the oblong moon of the dome light. "The books are in the trunk," I said.
"So that's what the scratching's all about."
"There are bugs that eat books," I said. "But I think these are safe."
"How do we get to them if we can't go outside?"
"We'll have to bore through," I said. "Bore through or chew," though we both

knew that wasn't going to happen.

And when black-robed death, tall and gaunt and red, squatted on the hood, splay-toed and gore-eyed, oh, how we laughed.

The morning men directed our deaths like conductors with microphones for batons. I could smell the rot of my leg and the hell of my breath and the strawberry shake going to liquid in the cup holder. I could hear the harsh percussion of her femurs snapping.

Oh how Sadie and the Slurpers sang:

Cap-and-saddle
Roar and rattle
And the dreamer is killed in his dream.

Map and tattle
Flesh and paddle
And the screamer is killed by her scream.

WXXT, the morning men said in unison, *where the Earworm is a Real Worm.*

The Leeds Detective Part 3: I Must Not Rock

Specter pulled into his spot at the station house. This was probably the closest he'd gotten to actually getting his car in between the lines. The interior of the car reeked of the coffee that had spilled when he'd stopped short to avoid hitting a sick, apparently disoriented raccoon that was walking backward across the street on its hind legs, its front legs doing strange things in the air, thrusting and pointing as though it was making an impassioned argument. The cupholder had jounced, knocking the lid askew and tilting the cup, causing a light brown waterfall.

How, he thought, *can coffee smell so good in the cup and so bad on car seats?*

Thankfully, he still had half a cup left. But it was lukewarm now, and the station house microwave made everything taste like charred tomato sauce, since no one ever saw fit to clean the fucking thing—the interior was stained and crusted, none of its former white visible at all.

Still, his buoyant mood was unshakeable. The cassette had been taken to the evidence room, and now he had a player. A cassette taken from the mouth of a cadaver. How lucky can one detective get? What secrets would it yield? Down what strange paths might it lead him? Maybe he'd end up the subject of an HBO miniseries. Who would play him? Tom Noonan! Or maybe…Michael Smiley, if he could do an American accent.

Musing thusly, he slung his guitar case over his shoulder and carried his cooling coffee and the cassette player into the station and dropped them onto the scattered papers that covered every part of the desk except the small square where the lamentably out-of-date monitor sat. He signed in at the evidence room, ignoring the clerk's stuttering and waving, using the usual wavy scribble that he used in place of an actual signature.

He hit the light switch and gasped. It took a lot to make Gregory Specter gasp. In this case, possibly the fourth gasp in his life, what caused him to gasp was the fact that the banker's box for the Impaled on the Tree Girl sat on the floor in the center of the room, its top next to it. Still there were the crime scene photographs; his copious notes, including potential new song lyrics; leaves and branches; and a handkerchief. Missing was the cassette.

Chewing the inside of his cheek, he went back to the evidence room window. "I tried to tell you," the clerk said.

"Who?"

"Fearn."

"Why?"

"He didn't say. But he left the interview room to sign out the tape."

"Who'd he have in there?"

"Jeremy Scheer."

'Fuck." Scheer had been one of the kids who disappeared and then shown up again a bunch of years later in a deteriorated state. His mind was broken and his memory shattered from whatever had happened to him; his parents had both since died, his sister fled the town and had left nothing in the way of a forwarding address. Now he haunted the shelters and the homeless tent cities, occasionally emerging to get kicked out of Thorne's and Bruegger's onto the sidewalk where he'd hassle townsfolk and tourists alike with strange, off-color comments, non-sequiturs, bizarre accusations, and unsettling physical tics and dances.

Which always led to him being hauled back to the station. Which always led to another frustrating, fruitless interrogation to try to spark something in his corrupted grey meat to find out what the hell was going on in Leeds, what was going on in the woods, in the abandoned houses, what the hell was going on with the goddamned radio.

Specter and Fearn were both relatively new to the department, and their work with Scheer drew a lot of baleful eyes from the other cops, for no reason anyone told him, and he got the idea it was best not to ask. Weird city, man. But Specter liked shit weird.

"Any C.I.s got eyes on Scheer?"

"Finn Groomer, I think."

"Got his number?"

Nurse Veskor

Cosmo Malis exhaled a lungful of pipe smoke before continuing: "...the dog eventually recovered, at least physically—he still to this day evinces a terror of long-fingered women—but Dichelet would never again be the adventurer or, indeed, the man he once was."

The crowd exhaled as one, and Malis allowed himself an enigmatic smile timed just as the smoke cloud dissipated like a ghost summoned back to the other side.

The setting was a manor house sat at the base of the mountain range that bordered Leeds at the north, a well-appointed great hall lit only by the raging flames in four capacious fireplaces, the walls lined with oak barrister bookcases crowded with pristine and lovingly cared-for volumes of old. Between cases hung colorful tapestries depicting a rolling, forest-lined field populated with mustachioed and bearded rifle-toting men in Victorian finery. Under burgeoning black clouds, the men were cornering, tussling with, or else running from curiously elongated dogs with hand-like paws and snouts curled into vicious snarls. There was an aura of hysteria about the pieces; more than one attendee would be troubled by nightmares directly related to the art.

The guests, elegant and sophisticated and seething with a variety of repressed lusts, sat in velvet armchairs situated around antique chests with buckles and brass clasps. Many sipped brandy or wine. Malis himself drank from a glass of warm water into which three drops each of lemon juice and lime juice had been squeezed. For him the imbibing would come later, in the hours when consciousness teased and tortured and tormented him, holding sleep in a thrice-locked cell without windows.

A cultured but hoarse voice from the seated crowd called out: "Another one!"

The crowd hooted their enthused concurrence. Malis adjusted his monocle and glanced at the grandfather clock, but its arms had long ago been broken off and employed in a violent assault against a server by a guest who'd had an intemperate reaction to a hallucinogen of unknown but exotic provenance.

"Another story I can tell, but 'twill be brief and there shall be no more after."

Sounds of muted disappointment. Murmurs and whispers. Restlessness and sighs. Hushing and shushing. Malis sat back, crossed one leg over the other, and swept his steely gaze back and forth across the assembled party until the hint was taken by all and all went silent.

A knot in the fireplace popped, causing several men to exclaim loudly, one to curse. Malis chuckled.

In the hospital now known as Cooley Dickinson, he said, *a new nurse arrived by motorcar one unseasonably warm October evening. It so happened that one of the other nurses had failed to appear for her two most recent shifts, and neither she nor her husband could be reached—they had, it was discovered, abandoned their house, leaving their horses and vehicles behind, for parts unknown.*

The new nurse offered her services and provided credentials and certificates which looked to all involved to be genuine. Her authoritative yet warm manner and her powerful, piercing gaze dissuaded verification, brooked no dispute, repulsed the merest thought of contradiction. But more than this, she answered questions, even pointed ones, with forbearance and genial humor. Confidence and charisma were but two of her strong suits; the third was her ability to command and direct a conversation.

Before we continue, I must note that the new nurse, who called herself Dr. Antonia Veskor, wore a black surgical mask which no one saw her remove, nor even adjust. Though this did strike the doctors, nurses, and staff as exceedingly strange, no one asked about it and it was clear that in any event no explanation would have been forthcoming. Best let it lie.

Four days after the arrival of Nurse Veskor, a distraught and disoriented woman arrived on foot at the hospital on the verge of labor. It was a day of unsettled weather, of shifting clouds and sun showers and stutters of far-off thunder. The woman was soaked, her brown hair covering her face. She had curious marks upon the backs of her hands, scars in complex swirls and crosshatches traced over with bluish ink. Her belly stood out round and taut.

The nurses hastened to wash her and dry her and apply bichloride solution, to shave away the hair and grease her pubis with lard to ease the passage of the oncoming neonate. They gave her Somnoform in part to quell her agonies, but also so that her shrieking might abate.

When she was in the stirrups and the crown of the child pushed itself outward, blue and lined with dark black hair, the new nurse proffered a requested scalpel and instead of handing it to the doctor, plunged it into the doctor's breastbone, switched it to the other hand, and cut the throat of the other nurse. She flung away the weapon and slipped the strap of the mask from behind her ear, revealing a wide, hideous mouth, rows and rows of pointed teeth all the way down the palate, and from the center of the throat wriggled a loathsome nest of black tentacular tongues, slender, each with a tiny fang-filled mouth.

The screams brought the administrators running. The doors burst open and they froze at the hideous sight of the nurse wrenching apart the thighs of the patient with such force that the cracking of femur and pubis could be heard even over their shocked screams. The nurse then formed a seal between her hideous mouth and the blossoming aperture of the patient, such that the baby saw not the merest flash of light between the birth canal and the throat of the ungodly creature down which it was pulled.

The latter then whipped around, the umbilical cord dangling like a spurting hose from her jaw. She leapt to the ceiling, her head rotating so that her chin jutted out over the bones of her back, and scuttled along the ceiling, down the transom, and out of the room.

The new would-have-been mother's hair had gone bone white. The ministrations of the doctors, affected as they were by the preceding events, could not save her life. She had lost too much blood, or else the shock had killed her. Either way, she ended up a torn and wretched thing, legs askew, bones jutting, the look of horror on her face a horror in itself.

One wonders, does one not, about the early days of childbirth, when it was but a midwife and an expectant mother. Could one trust the midwife? Would not in those long lost times midwifery be the simplest path for an cannibalistic creature who wants the freshest food possible?

Lastly, imagine the short life of this new being, pulled from the comfort of the womb not into the welcoming arms of its mother, but down the spiked maw of a monster, those tentacles encircling it, squeezing it, nipping its extremities.

But, and I shall leave you with this, what if cannibalism, consumption of the fetus is not the end for that tiny fragile soul? What if the victims walk among us yet today, any chance for a normal existence snatched from them before they could cry?

Malis had held his eyes closed at this post-denouement musing, as though he was musing upon the possible fate of the accursed neonate, as if he did not know exactly what transpired, as if was not intimately familiar with the misapprehensions of the witnesses to this grotesque event, as if he did not mourn every day the loss of his real mother. When he opened them, it was his turn to gasp. The fires were no longer raging; in the red glow of the remaining embers, the crowd stood facing him.

Their silence lasted some time, but then…just two or three at first, then more, then yet more…they began to launch curious syllables into the air, one after the other, going around the room, until everyone spoke and the syllables joined together as words that informed Malis clearly and explicitly of what would come next for him in his accursed existence.

Matthew Works in Microabrasives

I do not like the town. I do not like how far back the houses sit from the road. And I do not like the spaces between the houses. They're too small to allow for privacy, but too large to accommodate the light from the houses that border them, and therefore too dark at night. Anything could hide there. This is by design.

There is much to dislike.

How the phone wires jump-rope between the light poles. The menace in the curves where the side streets bend out of view from the main thoroughfare, the hints of what may dwell there. How in the pale penumbras in the outer reaches of the safety lights the shadows congregate and co-mingle, the *sacra privata* in the silent parking lots while the darkened superstores stare.

How the cemeteries seem active at night though on the surface they are still, silent, empty. How the sickly but seductive sirens of the waste treatment sluiceway bare their deflated breasts at me as I pass, in defiance of my lusts. How each window above the shuttered shops of downtown frames a looming silhouette.

The small patch of grass that moves in the wrong direction in defiance of the wind. The bright colorful lights in the starless sky, the ones that stream toward one another, shorten, and at a central point collect themselves in thin paper tubes with turgid wicks, tubes that then fall silently down to the ground. I try not to step on them in the parks, I avoid them on the sidewalks, on the catwalk that repeatedly bends back on itself over the train tracks, trying to escape the dark, eschatological graffiti scrawled on its slats and railings.

The office chair moored like an orphaned animal in the high weeds at the edge of the wetlands.

How the radio changes at night, all the stations going dark, save one. The things I hear. Orchestras beaten and bloodied and killed even as the remaining members continue to play, not a note out of place, not a cymbal crash too short or too long in its resonance. A 3 a.m. two-act one-man show with the performer suiciding in the intermission. Infanticide disco. Coprophagic polka. Dacryphilic Jazz. Formicophilia Choirs. Sacrilegious spirituals and demoniac gospels.

It isn't until I say it out loud that I realize how bad it actually is. This is what I told the FCC man on the phone.

And he told me I'm not the only one who's called. Said to get out of the area. That I might be in danger.

And I might be. But at least I have some hope now. They might come and clean up the city. I can't afford to move. I can't afford to stay. Death and madness peer in my windows and crouch outside my doors. They lurk in the vents and slither through the pipes in the walls. Invisible, they tincture the very air. Breathing is dangerous. Phones are tapped. The heat is oppressive.

I can drive around a while, sleep in it in lay-bys and parking lots.

I almost don't care what happens to me.

They're coming, the FCC, with a team of shamans and exorcists and exterminators, to rid this town of its troubles. Hallelujah and a-mother fuggin' men.

Here Comes Heather with a Baby Carriage

Here she comes now, bopping along Dryads Green adjacent to the quadrangle, hips swinging back & forth like the pendulum of a grandfather clock. She's chewing gum, got them horse teeth, got a tongue freeze-pop red. Square sunglasses with yellow frames, big shining rings, fake green-blonde. Fluorescent pink ear buds blasting the Flat Rat Steamin' Semen Hour on WXXT, just a buzz to others, but a world inside Heather's head, a world populated by spleen-demons twirling lassos of clogged intestine and filtering onto the airwaves forbidden rhymes in coded cadences.

A prick (my lord) in a flatbed Ford slows down so its driver can bellow something incomprehensible, a come-on, obscene invective, maybe both. Her hands jump from the handle and as the stroller jounces under its own power down the incline her two ring-encircled middle fingers unspool, her yellow nails like the extracted fangs of some cartoon werewolf.

The truck farts a black cloud like a burnt comic strip thoughtcloud as it peels out.

The stroller is luxurious. Top of the line. High quality, anti-rust aluminum alloy. Lemonade pink eco-friendly fabric. Ergonomic. Adjustable high-view pram. A cup-holder with a stabilizer. A basket underneath for supplies. All terrain: got those anti-shock springs for the potholes and ruptures and fissures and craters that plague the walks and parks and trails of Leeds.

And approaching her from Paradise Road is Michael, who works in microplastics. He's got on crocs and a shirt that reads Leeds Rocks, and that's pebbles and boulders and backpack straps on his shoulders. His nails are unclipped and he's drumming in the air; he's got black PX7s shrieking the WXXT Flat Rat Steamin' Semen Hour into his earholes, dissolving the wax, eroding the eardrums, burning away the thin wicks of hair deep down in there, sending curdled blood surging to his extremities.

What's that smell? thought Michael, and it got thicker as he thinks it, the smell of spoilage, the reek of rot, like ammonia, fumes surging through his mucous membranes, playing hell with his gorge, spilling bile into his gut, and then around the corner bopped Heather with the swinging hips, and the carriage dripping something red-black, no, not dripping, the rotting gore sloshed up the sides and splashed down, and he could *see* the fumes rising from it, distorting the background scenery, and reaching from the basin was a small purple arm, a rigor-frozen hand bedecked with horseflies.

And the two met and faced each other, neither ceding the right of way. Michael retched.

"Would you like to feed him?" Heather asked with her sweetest, candiest voice, and she pulled from her purse a bottle of milk that looked like bleached brains. Michael, entranced, bewitched, just a little bit turned on, took the bottle and unscrewed the cap. A head popped up from the surface of liquid gore, sodden, squashed like a stepped-on tomato, flattened features, flatworm lips, deflated cheeks, slitted bulges for eyes.

And the music roared in the earbuds and in the headphones and the thing in the human muck sloshed about, mouth gaping, neck bending and folding, as though dragged from beneath by some wretched fanged abomination. And the ground went to liquid and swallowed the houses and then fell away, taking with it the roads and the lawns and the fields, sediment raining down into eternity, leaving the sidewalk alone, suspended over infinity, and upon it unspeakable atrocities and rituals commenced.

The Leeds Detective Part 4

"Well, shit," Dana Sheridan said, looking out her apartment window just as the rain intensified. She snatched her phone from the arm of the couch, nearly knocking over her whiskey glass, and opened the radar app. A massive splotch of dark green like an amorphous airborne alien zygote crept over the waving lines repping the mountain range, heading right for Leeds. She'd been hoping the heavy stuff would hold off until after dinner. Kathryn and Lucinda were taking her out to celebrate her having broken up with Darren. Lucinda was hoping to catch Dana on the rebound, Dana knew, but though she wasn't into it, a little harmless flirtation might be a bit of a lark. Get the boys looking their...*her* way. The three had reservations at The Garden Table, an upscale place in downtown, five long blocks from the parking garage, and parking was at a premium now that the students had returned to the city. There'd be a lot of walking to get there, and the rain would be seething, bouncing off the sidewalks, forming deep puddles and small rivers in the streets and sidewalks and lots they'd have to traverse.

Dana hailed from Hideout, Utah. The women's college drew her to Leeds. She studied social anthropology and blackout drinking. Two months into her second semester, she managed to get a sweet apartment through off-campus housing services after her roommate Trish, a dour, diffident theater major who favored black eyeliner and pencil-heels with straps that wound around her calves like ligature, leaving red stripes on her pale flesh, had killed herself in their dormitory room. Dana hadn't been the one to find the body—she'd been out to dinner with Darren and saw the lights of the emergency vehicles on the quad when he'd dropped her off. Something's up, she'd thought, not imagining it'd have anything to do with her. It was a big dorm housing hundreds of students —192 double units plus a computer lab and laundry, with a cafeteria-style dining hall in the basement.

But then she encountered the crowd of EMTs and cops and firemen moving around busily on her floor, and then she saw the door to her room open, two frowning men wheeling out the body, draped in a stained white sheet, on an x-legged stretcher with shopping-cart wheels.

Trish's loss, her gain.

She looked at the wall clock. The girls were going to be here any minute, and even her umbrella wouldn't keep the rain from ruining the suede shoes she'd intended to wear. What else would go with her blouse, she wondered. She glanced back out the window and started. What the hell was this? She put her hands to the glass, cupped like fleshy binoculars, and looked through them.

A young man in a hooded sweatshirt was walking down by the railroad tracks, and next to him loped something impossibly tall and misshapen, horns jutting from its snouted head. Her first thought was *moose*, but those weren't the seashell-like antlers that adorned moose-heads; they were thin, long, and pointed; adorned with sharp, curved thorns. Not to mention it walked on two legs. The thing was leaning leeringly near the man's head as though goading him. The pair passed behind a thick tree, and then just the man emerged from the other side, alone, as the rain picked up again.

Dana looked at her whisky with her head tilted. Looking for what? Sediment from Rohypnol or ketamine? A sunken acid tab? Ridiculous. She'd opened the bottle herself just tonight, and it hadn't been out of her sight. Her drink hadn't been spiked. Maybe she had a tumor.

The doorbell rang and she jumped. Best not tell the girls about this one.

***

Finn Groomer walked along the railroad tracks under the pedestrian bridge, sweatshirt hood pulled tight around his thin face; stained, torn jeans sagging; boots splooshing in the black mud. A filter from a mostly-smoked Marlboro stuck to his bottom lip like a bee seeking pollen from the remains of a depleted flower. All was muted greys and browns, rust-tinged rain dripping from drain spouts and overhangs, a fine mist fogging the air. To his right a grid of apartment windows flickered with lights from candles and televisions. Before him the piers of the highway bridge rose into humming fog.

At the base of one pier, facing away from Finn, a dead raccoon sat splayed, chin on the cement foundation, tail raised and fluttering in the wind. The voice in his head, blessedly dormant for over a week, now spoke up. *You're gonna wanna fuck that racoon, buddy.*

Finn scoffed. But his heart started fluttering in its bony cage.

188

It's so soft in there, so hot and moist, and the maggots, they'll tickle...

Shut the fuck up," Finn Groomer said aloud through clenched teeth. "Shut the fuck *up*."

The raccoon began to hum, a high, lovely voice, soothing and sweet and undeniably sexual. Finn felt an unwelcome stirring below.

Then the mist before him lit up yellow, and a Crown Victoria rolled into view, splashing muddy water in fan-shaped waves. The hum stopped. Finn's phone buzzed in his sweatshirt pocket and he shook off the trance into which he'd been sinking and silenced the phone with a thin, dirt-caked fingernail. He approached the car. The rain-bubbled side window cranked downward hitchingly, and Finn crouched to look in.

"Fuckin' Specter," he said.

"Nice to see you too, handsome. You don't answer your phone these days?" The detective squinted, looked closer. "Jesus *Fuck*, man, what happened since I last saw you? Someone put you through the wringer."

Finn shrugged. "I give a fuck?"

The rain started up again, arrhythmic percussion slapping the roof and windshield. The downpours promised by the dour local weatherman were clearly imminent. Broken clocks and all that. Specter pushed the door open and sat back in his seat, eyebrows raised, finger tapping the steering wheel with impatience. Finn hesitated and then shrugged. He slid into the passenger seat, closed the door. Christ, the kid brought the chill right in with him. Specter turned the heat up a notch. "What you got for me?"

"Put the radio on."

"Finn…"

"Put the radio on and I'll tell you where Scheer is. That's what you want to know, right? That's all you fuckin' pigs ever want to know."

"Important this time."

Pointing a finger: "Radio."

Specter reached out and turned the knob, scanned down to the lower numbers. Turned the knob back and forth, slowly. Nothing but static. A few seconds of some blustery right-wing crank pontificating brainlessly. Then more static. Specter raised an eyebrow at Finn.

"Just checking," Finn said in a low, cracked voice. He looked like he desperately wanted to burst into tears, but would die before he'd let himself do so.

"So. Scheer?"

"Another one of you cops grabbed him off Gothic Street. Headed to the con."

"…the convict?"

"Convention."
"Where?"

***

Finn watched as the taillights receded into the rainy evening, blurring, fading to ghosts, and then disappearing. The lights of the apartment building dimmed, as did the streetlights. Darkness now. The odor of ammonia, blood, and burnt wood assaulted his nostrils. *About that raccoon,* whispered the voice, now dripping with malevolence. A spotlight shot past Finn's head and lit up the raccoon's rump in a shimmering yellow circle. Gems sparkled in its fur. A frilly lace strap, hot pink, encircled the tip of its tail. Sultry music played from the sewers and drainpipes. Finn sighed with despair and involuntary yet undeniable desire, stronger than any actual hunger he'd ever felt. He walked over to it, unzipping his pants, his expression as blank as that of a shrouded skull.

***

Detective Specter pulled up to the hotel in the pounding rain. Blue and red lights spun around the white wall and the floor-to-ceiling windows and doors between the entrance and the overhang. Emergency vehicles with **LEEDS** on the doors amassed on the lot and the walk under the portico. He parked nearby. A thunderclap slammed down hard like a celestial bulkhead, making the car tremble on its tires. He pulled the cassette player from the back seat and slid it into the pocket of his overcoat, and exited the car.

A couple of uniforms, one tall, one plump, approached him with defiance as he trotted over, and he lifted his hood and nodded at them. "Ah, Detective Specter. Come on through," the plump one said.

"Got a problem with one of our own," said the tall one.

And on a stretcher, being hauled to the open doors of an ambulance by a couple of grim-faced EMTs, lay Fearn. His wrists were clasped in flex cuffs. His hair had gone bright white—a phenomenon about which Specter had heard, but hadn't believed was real—and his lips and lower face were smeared with blood. He opened his mouth in a ghastly grin and Specter saw with alarm that all his teeth were gone, and the tip of his tongue was chewed to pulp. "EVERYTHING," Fearn shouted. "EVERYTHING EVERYTHING EVERYTHING EVERY…" and one of the EMTs emptied a syringe into his shoulder, causing him to trail off, mumbling, groaning, fading to grey. Drool pooled in his mouth and oozed down his cheeks, drawing streaks in the bloodstains. A fecal stench permeated the air. The EMTs hustled him into the ambulance, slammed the doors, and sped off.

Specter said, "He shat his pants?"

The tall cop scoffed and said, "What do *you* think?"

Specter turned toward the hotel. "The heck's going on in there?"

The plump cop and the tall cop looked at each other, then at Specter. They looked haunted. The plump one said, "Erm…" and two other cops (both of medium height) tumbled through the glass doors, shattering the glass and shredding their pant legs, tripping over one another, shrieking in falsetto that would under other circumstances have been hilarious, and ran wordlessly into the night. A few moments later the screeching of tires and the blasting of car horns sounded, then thudding impacts and glass breaking. The plump one and the tall one ran toward the chaos.

Specter shrugged. He entered the hotel.

They Must Rock

Doug Danelet and Will Brutealange sat at the table they paid $500.00 total for. Behind them hung a banner with their names on it in a spooky font; that one ran them $50.00. Each had copies of his books on a series of artlessly placed acrylic easels. The show had started at 10:00 am and exactly one person had bought Doug's "Service With A Scythe," a pity purchase to be sure, a creepy-skinny bearded guy in a Poe t-shirt who wandered over, frowning, and didn't even listen to the spiel before laying a sweaty ten-spot on the table. Doug didn't realize 'til after the guy left that he could have offered to sign it. No one had bought Will's "The Zombie Serial Killer," which means that no one there that day would ever be subjected to the opening paragraph, which had two typos and a misplaced apostrophe and exposition that would fail to hook even the most forgiving reader, all this only a fraction of what was to come.

To be fair, their customer service skills were worse than the items they had on offer. Doug and Will barely looked up from the books they were reading (the latest King, and some old Koontz, respectively) to acknowledge passers-by.

Adrienne Barbeau, who had been sitting across from them for most of the day, had split early after a busy day of signing 8x10s and DVDs, so they didn't even have her chest to look at anymore.

Finally, bored, having eaten three donuts, and glanced at the clock countless times, Doug said, "I have a weed story for ya."

Will perked up. "Oh yeah?"

"Yeah. So this guy from work, right, he tells me he got this like, government grade weed. No paranoia, he said. He, like, emphasized that because I'd told him a thousand times weed makes me paranoid, I don't have any fun, I'd rather drink thirteen beers."

"You're crazy."

"So I drive out to his place and he's telling me he got the weed from a guy who works in a lab and it's pure and not cut with any bullshit and he's emphasizing the no-paranoia deal. He hasn't tried it, but the dude swears it's the best high, whatever. He busts out the one-hitter. He lights it up, we pass it back n' forth. I got the light-headedness going on, the giggles, whatever, pretty good so far. So we decide to go get fuckin' burgers and fries and shakes at Raphael's. We'll each take our own car, each head home from there. He's giggling all the way out to his car, I get in mine. I find a spot downtown and see him ambling up the ramp to get in line. Then it hits me, hard. There's no way I can face another human being, never mind tell them to get me food. I'm fucked up beyond the ability to even be part of society. I'm parked there, freaking the fuck out, like saying aloud, I can't, I can't, I can't."

"So wha'd you do?"

"I drove home."

"You didn't call him?"

"This was pre-cell phone, dude."

"You drove home wasted."

"*So* wasted, though. Like I kept not knowing where I was, then at the last second before I'm about to panic, I see a familiar house, whatever. Somehow I get home. My roommate and his girlfriend are watching Barfly. I didn't even say a word to them, just barrel of the stairs to my room and close the door. I spend the next two hours terrified of the titles of my own books, thinking they're sending me threatening messages. Finally, I go downstairs and order a pizza. Ate the whole goddamned thing and then I slept for ten hours straight."

"So, what happened with your co-worker?"

"He gets seated at a corner table, orders a drink, keeps going to the door to look for me. He gets, like, totally convinced that I'm a secret FBI agent or DEA guy or whatever, and that he's going to get arrested. The waitress is in on it too; she hasn't been back since he ordered his drink. So he sneaks out, walks home rather than getting in his car, and then he's up all night waiting for the knock on the door."

"No paranoia."

"Government grade."

A hand landed on the table in front of them. A rubber hand. Doug and Will looked up into the fractured face of a child plastered onto the head of a tall, bent-up man. The man-child drew in air, all the air in the room, all the air in the world. All the banners and flags and ribbons in the room were drawn toward him. And then he let the air out in a shriek that stopped everyone cold, stopped everyone in their tracks. He began digging at his chest, still screaming. As the flesh fell away in dried-blood strips like overtaxed bandages, revealed in the hollow of his chest was a tangle of wires and a cluster of small black stereo speakers like mesh-covered eggs. Over their surface, strange, slick, segmented creatures crawled on thick, bent legs, translucent, yellow-veined wings plastered to their blood-soaked backs.

The man-child reached a hand into the mass and pulled out a small black speaker plug at the end of a coarse black wire. The tiny, metal-ringed aperture slurped at the air, palpitating grotesquely. "It's hungry," said Jeremy Scheer in the hoarse, exhausted voice of a child. "I'm hungry too," he added. "I've been so hungry for such a long time."

***

"What the fuck is that?" shouted Dean Rouche, his hands over his ears. "What human being can scream like that?"

"Never mind that," Emily said. Her hands were clamped over her ears too, and she spoke loudly to be heard over the screaming. "What the fuck is *that*?"

She pointed to the table, where the cassette whose label read *Michael Death Incantations* trembled and jumped, clattered and spun. It landed on its side and the case opened like a door. The two spools inside began spinning, faster and faster, sending black smoke spiraling ceilingward until finally one of the spools ejected itself, cassette ribbon taut behind it, zipping to a corner of the ceiling, bouncing, criss-crossing, a great black web weaving itself into being, accompanied by a screeching, high-pitched, wavering babble-and-whine of audio playing at an impossibly high speed. A kid carrying a bag of merchandise stumbled into a stray strand and fell dead. When his head hit the concrete floor, it cracked open like a Pac-Man head, and teeth spilled from it, a mass of them, different sizes, different forms, fangs, molars, the tiny teeth of cats, the tinier teeth of fish, the large, yellow-stained teeth of horses and cows and goats. A strand of tape landed on the shoulder of a young woman selling magnets, and it lashed her diagonally into two. One of her legs, a triangular sheared part-body still attached to it, stepped, hopped, and collapsed. The other bent at the knee and dropped straight down. Orange blood pooled under her halves, slick and malodorous, and people slid and fell as it spread, their own heads cracking open. From one head radio dials spilled. From another, a slew of soaked, swollen mass market books with lurid but unreadable covers. From another, tiny, rolling black discs that grew until they were the size of record albums, slicing through the feet and calves of the crowds trying to flee. From all of the bodies of the fallen and the slain, pink bolts shot up into the ever-expanding cassette tape web, adding yet more high-pitched voices to the babbling cacophony.

And then everything stopped.

With screeching, lisping backward babbles, the tape retreated from all its angles back into the cassette, its great web shrinking, dissipating, and finally the spool itself slid back into the cassette and wound itself tight. The cassette shut, hopped a few times with a loud clatter, and was still.

As Dean Rouche and Emily stared, dumbfounded, a man in an overcoat strode from the crowd, snatched the cassette off the table, and strode away.

***

And moments later, Detective Specter stood over the body of Jeremy Scheer, which still held up its torso with bent, atrophied elbows. Specter placed the tape player on the table next to the unsold books of Doug Danelet and Will Brutealange, who sat dead in their chairs, heads split open down the center, both Y-shaped, wide-eyed heads overstuffed with a mass of wet October leaves. He slid the cassette in and hit play.

Nothing.

He found the volume dial on the side and spun it to MAX. But over the sighs and groans of the remaining survivors, he could barely hear a thing.

Then Doug Danelet's dead body jumped and bounced in its chair, spilling wet leaves down his chest, into his lap, and onto the floor. The cloud of brown and orange and red and yellow leaves in his split-open noggin shook and twitched. Somewhere in there, twigs snapped. Detective Specter pulled his weapon from his holster and aimed. A snake shot out...but no. Specter pointed his weapon at the floor. It wasn't a snake. It was a *cord*. It landed at Specter's feet. He bent and picked it up. One end fit neatly into a small slot next to the volume button on the tape player. The other he jammed into the plug jutting from the wrenched-open chest of Jeremy Scheer. A whine of feedback shot through the hall. Then *Michael's Death Incantations* played for the crowd. They ate it up.

Cassettes (Part 6: The Landau Bars)

Paul Cooperford, formerly, a long time ago, Paul Winklepleck, and still a proud bearer of that name, even if it had to go underground from time to time, he was still and always a Winklepleck, gunned the fucking engine and the retrofitted and augmented Federal Coach Cadillac XT5 Renaissance hearse shot black fire from its polished chrome exhaust ports and ground pavement into hamburger meat under its spiked tires. The S-shaped scrolls on the rear quarter panel spun like roulette wheels, slicing wind to invisible ribbons. Before him the open road transformed and changed; he drove through the rings of a rollicking circus, great elephants rearing back as he passed through their ranks, clowns somersaulting over the hood and splitting open like sacks of flour on the reinforced windshield, many-colored lights blinked and crowds roared and waved and hooted and winged tigers dropped flaming hoops that bounced on the road and pulled in alongside the hearse on both sides; he drove down the dirt and stone avenues of ancient Leeds, sending horses and carriages tumbling end over end and crows sailing in great undulating clouds overhead and woman lifting their breasts in randy salutes out of hotel windows above apothecaries and haberdashers and public houses; he drove through the thick, dense woods of who-knows-when, ancient and venerable, winding around huge trees and sending up algae-streaked waves as he powered through brooks and streams and tributaries, and owls turned their heads in outrage at the power chords blasting like serrated thunder from the speakers in quadrophonic sound; he drove down a bright, blinding chicory-bordered highway, the sun racing toward him, promising head-on collision, defenestration, decapitation, incineration, delivering on none of it. He hit a switch and the windshield slid into the ceiling and the whole top accordioned and folded and slid into a slot behind the back seat. The wind set about its task of drying the blood on his face and in his lashes and his nostrils and on his lips. He scraped at it with his fingernails and bit it

196

from them with sharp teeth and all was perfect and right with the world and then Stockton was standing in front of the car and he jammed both boots on the brake and the 18' wheels with pearl nickel finish dug great grooves into the highway and in a blink he was standing aside the car, leaning an elbow on the top of the door, lighting a black cigarette with a red filter. Stockton, tall, flaring nostrils, was just a flickering apparition, changing form and features like someone churning through cable channels, like the scenery through which Winklepleck had passed; he was man and goat and stallion and snake and it made Paul a little dizzy looking at him, to tell you the truth. He jammed the cigarette into the side of his mouth and walked back to the mood-lit casket compartment, where a black duffel teemed with cassettes, Maxell, BASF, Memorex, and Fuji, the labels scrawled with titles like *Lungz-a-Poppin'*, *Ping Pong Machete Massacre 1989, Evisceration Dirges, Death Rattle Mambo, Michael's Death Incantations,* and *Backwards Infant Babble Reveals Truths*. He hoisted the duffel, threw a strap over his shoulder, and limped it over to Stockton. He laid his burden on the ground and knelt, touching his forehead to the hot pavement until it sizzled. He knew his cassettes were worthy of airplay, but every time he wondered if they'd truly find favor. He tried to act as though his life didn't depend on it. Content. Always provide content. Content or death. Would that his sounds would please the dark fathers of Leeds.

When he raised up his head, Stockton was gone. In his place was a shrink-wrapped tower of brand new, virgin cassettes in five-packs and two-fer flat packs and singles, 30-minutes, 60-minutes, 90-minutes. He admired them for a while, then he hopped back in the hearse, executed a K-turn, and backed up to the pile. As the sun seethed above him, he loaded them into the back of the hearse, all of them save one. That one he unwrapped, peeled the static-clingy wrapper from his hand with some difficulty and a few retries, and eased into the cassette player of the hearse. He filled its empty hiss with his own dark songs as the blood yet dried on his face.

Uncle Red Reads To-Day's News

Mrs. Herbert Wilhelmina Walloughby of 88 Tremens Terrace reported Sunday that the inner doorways of her home have become mouths. She first noticed the irregular phenomenon upon slipping whilst attempting entrance to her pantry and for purchase grabbing onto the molding, which proved atypically moist and yielding. Upon retreating to the center of her kitchen, she saw with growing horror that large teeth had sprouted down from the reddening head jamb and up from between threshold and sill, and that an unseemly throbbing tongue probed from the very aether, near the top center of the passageway. Similarly affected were the other doorways that led, respectively, to the living room, dining room, and enclosed porch, trapping her in the kitchen. Her shrill hysteria caused significant difficulty for officials to parse; the best interpretation is that the mouths were attempting to masticate, causing structural damage to the stately Victorian home, which was erected in 1897 and is listed in the historical registry of houses. Police and EMTs were advised to occult the house behind hermetically sealed black tarpaulins and introduce nickel tetracarbonyl into the atmosphere via insulated piping. An alternate solution, proposed during a debrief on live television, would have been to extricate Mrs. Walloughby via one of the two windows, which appeared to be immune to the transformation. This was emphasized in the minutes should the event recur. As for the house and the late Mrs. Walloughby (may she delight in eternal repose at the right hand of our lord and savior), both now remain in a newly constructed impenetrable enclosure of brick, but sounds and tremors and departing and returning shadows suggest the house is now otherwise tenanted.

Cassettes

Cassettes

ABOUT THE AUTHOR

Matthew M. Bartlett was born in 1970 in Hartford, Connecticut. Much has happened since then.

Made in the USA
Middletown, DE
24 January 2026

27536130R00119